LEFT FOR
DEAD

By Paul Engleman:

The Mark Renzler books:

Dead in Center Field
Catch a Fallen Angel
Murder-In-Law
Who Shot Longshot Sam?
Left for Dead

The Phil Moony books:

The Man with My Name
*The Man with My Cat

*forthcoming

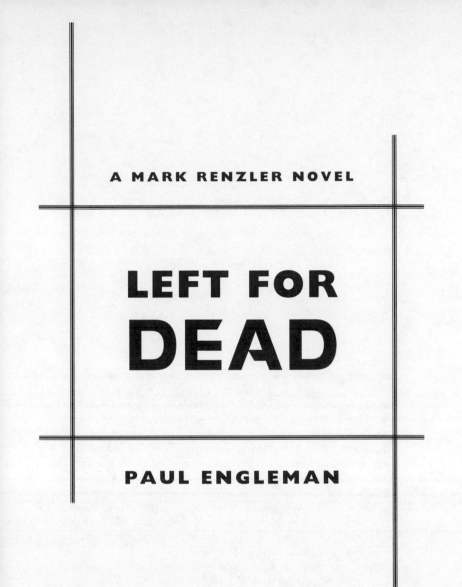

A MARK RENZLER NOVEL

LEFT FOR
DEAD

PAUL ENGLEMAN

St. Martin's Press ⚞ New York

This is for Chris, still the world's best nephew

Some of the people, places, and events mentioned in this book are real. For example, Fred Hampton was shot twice in the head from close range while asleep in his bed by a Chicago police officer during a pre-dawn raid conducted with a spurious search warrant. But the characters and plot are products of the author's imagination, and any inference of similarity to actual living persons is the result of paranoia or wishful thinking on the part of the reader.

ISBN 0-312-13534-3

First Edition: February 1996

10 9 8 7 6 5 4 3 2 1

Acknowledgments

Thanks to Flint Taylor of the People's Law Office for providing volumes of information and being willing to spend hours answering my questions over the last twenty years. Thanks also to Jeff Haas, Akua Njeri, Tom Young, and the following people who have provided information or shared their thoughts, even if reluctantly, about Fred Hampton, the Black Panther Party, the Chicago police, and the FBI: Bob Blau, Jim Collins, John Conroy, William J. Cooley, Barbara D'Amato, Joan and Ted Elbert, Jim Grogan, Hugh Holton, John Jemillo, Chaka Khan, Peter Kuttner, Jerris Leonard, Roy Martin Mitchell, James Montgomery, Debbie Nelson, Lu Palmer, Judge Ellis Reid, Mike Royko, Congressman Bobby Rush, Jack Ryan, Loretta Smith, Rev. Tom Strieter, Thomas Sullivan, Craig Tobin, Camillo Volini, Jim Warren, Dr. Quentin Young, and Michael Zielenziger. And thanks, as usual, to Barb Carney, Tony Judge, Keith Kahla, Tom Ravfiel, and Jim Trupin.

"*If you're asked to make a commitment at the age of twenty, and you say I don't want to make no commitment only because of the simple reason that I'm too young to die, I want to live a little longer, what you did is . . . you're dead already.*"

—**Fred Hampton**

ONE

The last time I saw Harmony Rollins, she was spread-eagled across my kitchen table. In staccato bursts between short, guttural breaths, she invoked God the father, son and Holy Ghost not to stop. The muscles in her thighs stretched tighter than telephone wires, and tiny beads of sweat shimmered all the way to the top of her bell-bottom jeans, which were pulled to her knees. Her back was arched in a perfect parabola of lust, a vision marred only by the vinyl Christmas tablecloth my mother had given me—the one with Santa's grinning mug in the center—riding upward with each torrid heave-ho.

If I live to be a hundred, I'll never forget the sweltering summer afternoon in 1968 when Harmony Rollins taught me what really great sex was. Unfortunately, I wasn't a participant in the historic event. Merely an observer, and an unobserved one at that. But to this day, I still stir involuntarily at the sight of denim bell-bottoms, a surefire memory trigger of the best sex I never had.

It so happened that the lucky guy was my best friend and sometimes partner Nate Moore. If I wasn't the one partaking of Harmony's charms, Nate would be my next choice. But if his ticker had given out and Harmony had asked me to pick up where he left off, I wouldn't have stopped to check his vital signs.

I'd be lying if I said I wasn't tempted to stick around and watch Harmony turn the world on its ass that day. But I caught a glimpse of Nate's sweaty face, contorted in the agony

1

of someone passing a kidney stone, and that detracted from the overall pleasure of the experience. I decided I better get the hell out of there or I'd never be able to sit at that table with him again.

You may wonder why I wasn't miffed at their carrying on with such abandon in my apartment. Nate's place was being painted that weekend, and my wife and I were heading upstate. Since he had a friend visiting, I had forked over the keys to my kingdom. Although our agreement didn't expressly prohibit desecration of my mother's tablecloth, good sense dictated choosing a safer location for wild copulation. Nate goes 260 pounds when he's not sweating, and Harmony was a big girl herself. Plus the table had been on its last legs for the last ten years. But in the heat of battle, some people are willing to take risks. Making beautiful music with Harmony was one I would have taken myself.

I had stumbled in on them unannounced, returning a day earlier than expected and hoping they might cheer me up. My weekend had been a disaster. Katie, my wife, had been staying out in Jersey with her parents for the last month, and this was supposed to be make-it-or-break-it time for us, a last-ditch effort to see if we could keep the wedding party going longer than three years. We had pretty much reached an answer before we reached the New York Thruway, but we pushed on to Monticello, where I managed to lose my shirt at the track and my temper at the Holiday Inn. We drove back to Jersey in silence, not even a perfunctory good-bye when I dropped her off at Mom and Dad's.

After finding Nate and Harmony locked in lust, I slipped out to my local for a drink or ten. When I got back around midnight, my pal was sitting at the table in his underwear, eating a peanut butter sandwich and drinking a beer.

"Damn, it's too bad you didn't get home sooner," he said. "Harmony left half an hour ago. You just missed seeing her."

I didn't let on that I had missed less than he could have imagined.

"Well, at least you got a chance to meet her before you left," Nate said. "She's a sweet kid, isn't she?"

I nodded. "Very sweet. And just how old a kid is she?"

"Oh, I'd say about twenty-two now."

"And just how is it that you know her?"

"I've known her since she was this big." Nate held his hand level with the table. "I was friends with her mom back in Holyoke, Mass. Liza. Now there's one great lady. She had an art gallery. That was the first place I showed my work."

Although Nate is built like a linebacker, he's a painter. When he tells people what he does for a living, they assume he's talking about houses. But he does his stuff on canvas, and of late has gotten very successful at it.

He chuckled. "Liza always called me Nathan. And Harmony—she used to call me *Uncle* Nathan. That used to get a laugh when I'd take her to Nick's Nest for a hot dog. Got a lot of dirty looks too."

"I'll bet." I knew from Nate that his hometown had been the first planned industrial city in the country. But black people weren't something the founding fathers had planned on.

"My niece." Nate shook his head and sighed. "What a sweet kid. Sweet and *smart*."

"And beautiful."

"Yeah, that too."

"Seems like an odd departure time," I said. "I figured she'd be staying overnight."

"Yeah, that was the plan. But the people she was going with decided to leave early." Harmony was on her way to Chicago to attend the Democratic convention. She wasn't a delegate, but she was planning to take part in some extracurricular activities that had been planned. In the few minutes we'd talked, I'd found out she was active in SDS, the Students for a De-

3

mocratic Society. Or, as one New York radio host liked to call it, Students for Destroying Society.

Harmony sent me a thank-you card for my hospitality, proving that not all hippies and yippies were ungrateful brats. She also enclosed two hits of blotter acid. At least that's what Nate said it was when I described the tiny cardboard squares I had found in the envelope.

"What did you do with them?" he demanded.

"I threw them out—"

"You did *what?*" He bolted to the trash can. I let him start digging under two days' worth of coffee grounds and cigarette butts before finishing my sentence.

"—three days ago. If you want to find them, you'll have to go through Streets and San."

"I don't believe it."

"Hey, how was I supposed to know what it was?"

Nate stared at me incredulously and shook his head.

"And besides, what do *you* want with it?" I said. "I keep telling you: You're too old for this hippie shit."

"Age has nothing to do with it. State of mind and condition of soul are what matters. And yours, Renzler, are in thoroughly rotten shape."

I kept up on Harmony's doings through Nate, who received intermittent reports over the next few years. At the convention, she got her head bashed in by a cop named O'Leary and patched up by a doctor named O'Boyle. She got arrested and thrown in jail, then had her case thrown out by a judge named O'Reilly, largely through the efforts of a lawyer named O'-Malley. She decided she liked Chicago and opted to stay there instead of returning east for her senior year of college. I think the decision had something to do with Dr. O'Boyle, but it might have been Esq. O'Malley that she had taken a shine to.

At one point, Nate told me Harmony had gotten involved

4

with the Black Panthers and was working in some program serving food to ghetto kids. A couple of years later, 'round about 1970, he got a postcard with Mayor Daley's grinning mug on the front and a note on the back: *Very windy here, and duh shit has hit duh fan.* Harmony was headed to San Francisco, maybe with some flowers in her hair.

The next update came from L.A., where she was trying to launch a singing career in some dive of a nightclub. I know it was a dive because I tried to look her up when I was out there. But she was gone, long gone, I was told, pursuing a movie career, and hadn't left a forwarding address. Sure enough, a few months later, she dropped Nate a line saying she'd soon be on the wide screen, or at least the drive-in screen, in a movie called *Sweet Sweetback's Baadasssss Song.*

I was out of town the week it played at my local theater, but Nate made the Times Square premiere and reported that Harmony had turned in a major-league performance in a minor role. Next came word that she had landed a small part in *Shaft.* I also managed to miss that, even though it had wider distribution and longer staying power, thanks to an interminable but immensely popular soundtrack song that blasted out of every Orange Julius in the city every day for what seemed like a year.

Last year, Nate got the big news. Harmony would soon be starring in her own film, *Sister Shamus,* in which she played a female private eye. Now that one I definitely wanted to see, but it never got close to my neighborhood theater. I'm not sure it even made it to the Bronx, although I'd been faithfully checking the listings in the *Post* for six months.

Now, as I sat in my living room, which doubles as my office, and looked across the coffee table, which doubles as my desk, at the star of the movie, I was doing a double take. No woman of passing acquaintance had ever held so much interest for me. Seeing her again for the first time in too long, sitting on my couch, legs crossed, in a snug red wool dress and black boots, the only thing I could think about was that incredible day four years ago with the bell-bottoms on the kitchen table that was now being held up on one side with a stack of old magazines and racing programs.

It was a nice thought, but it also made me feel like something of a heel. I knew damn well Harmony Rollins wasn't there to wish me a merry Chistmas, even though the season for cheer was upon us. Nate hadn't given me the details of why Harmony wanted to see me—he hadn't really gotten any details when she had phoned him the day before. He just told me that she sounded troubled and was coming to talk business.

In my business, that usually means trouble.

T W O

I poured Harmony a drink in the good glass and probably poured it on too thick about what a pleasure it was to see her again.

She flashed me a smile that some guys would pay to see— satin-soft lips framed by dimples that expanded to a double set when it spread to a full-tilt grin. "I wasn't sure you'd remember me, sugar, being we only met for a few minutes that one time." She had a voice some guys would pay to hear—contralto smothered with whipped cream.

"I never forget a beautiful face."

"Shee-it." Harmony took a long drag of a long cigarette and

grinned at Nate, who was sitting beside her. "This guy talks the same sweet jive you do, Nathan."

"Oh, yeah, he's a real jive turkey," Nate said through the cloud of smoke she exhaled in his direction.

Harmony fixed her smile on me while nodding at Nate. "How long have *you* been friends with this guy?" She rolled her big brown eyes in mock contempt, and as she did so, I saw that her right one sat still in the socket. I hadn't noticed that when we had met, so it must have happened since. I would have taken note of a detail like that, because I've got a dead eye myself.

"Going on fifteen years now," I said.

"Hell, that's nothing. I've been putting up with his smart-assin' for—what is it, Nathan, twenty-five years now?"

"Yeah, give or take a quarter of a century."

"Did he tell you I used to call him Uncle?" Harmony let out a laugh that started out throaty but turned a little shrill, with a tremolo at the end.

I nodded and smiled, and my eye caught her attention.

"My, my, you've got one, too." She grinned and tapped her finger high up on her cheek. As I looked closer, I could see a thin scar that started above her brow and ran down to her eye-lld.

"Indeed I do." I took a slug of bourbon and savored the warm feeling that comes with finding an instant soul mate.

"How'd you get yours?"

"Playing baseball. I got hit with a pitch."

"He used to play professionally," Nate said.

"No shit."

"Just minor-league ball. That was a long time ago."

"I got mine when this pig O'Leary clubbed me at the sixty-eight convention." There was more pride than anger in her tone. "My battle scar from the movement. It's a bitch, ain't it?"

"Yeah, but it gives us character."

She leaned forward and clinked my glass—of bourbon, that is. "Right on, sugar."

"Was that cop any relation to Mrs. O'Leary?" Nate asked.

"Who's Mrs. O'Leary?"

"It was her cow that started the Chicago Fire."

"I doubt it." Harmony crushed out her butt in my New York Rangers ashtray. "But he might've been related to the cow."

"Nate tells me your movie career's going really well."

"Oh, yeah, it's rolling along." Harmony crossed two slender fingers, one of which had a sapphire the size of a golf ball. "Let's just hope it keeps up."

"You didn't hear the latest. Harmony won a BLOSCAR."

"No. I didn't win. I just got nominated. Pam Grier—she was the winner, hands down."

I lit a cigarette. "BLOS—?"

"BLOSCARS. The black Oscars. It's like the Academy Awards, only just for us folks."

"I see." I toasted with my drink. "Congratulations."

Her smile turned sheepish. "It's not that big a deal. They held it in Gary, Indiana. Wasn't even televised." She sighed, and the brightness drained from her face. "Well, I guess I better explain what it is I need to see you about."

I nodded. "The sooner you do, the sooner I can help."

"It's my little brother. I'm afraid something's happened to him." She reached into a soft red leather bag the size that Santa might carry and pulled out a yellowed newspaper clipping. "This is the only picture I've got."

It was a good one. I think my bad eye might have moved when I took a look. Even without the machine gun and the black leather jacket zipped open to reveal his naked chest, Harmony's little brother was one of the scariest-looking dudes I'd

8

ever seen. A line under the photo identified him as Henry "Harpo" Rollins.

"Your brother looks like he can take care of himself."

"Looks can be deceiving. He's really just a sweet kid."

If Henry Rollins was a sweet kid, looks had to be very deceiving. "Why is he called Harpo?"

"That's his movement name. People called him that because he played harmonica."

"His *movement* name?"

"That's right."

"Is Harmony a movement name?"

"No. That was my daddy's idea." She let out a short laugh. "One of the few good ones he ever had. He was kind of a rolling stone—you know, like the Temptations song?"

I didn't. She hummed a few bars and I still didn't.

Nate sighed heavily. "Renzler, when's the last time you passed the Orange Julius at Seventy-second and Amsterdam?"

"Oh sure, now I know it." It was the song that had replaced the theme song to *Shaft*.

"Anyway," Harmony said, "Harpo is what he started calling himself when he got involved with the Panthers."

"That would be the Black Panthers, I assume."

"That's right. Of course he's changed his name since he went underground. You've got to when the FBI's looking for you."

"The FBI's looking for him?"

"Oh, yeah. They've practically had a nationwide manhunt for over a year now. That picture there is from *The New York Times*."

I've always been a *New York Post/Daily News* kind of guy. Even with those I usually skip right to the sports section.

"He's wanted for the burglary of that FBI office in Media, Pennsylvania, last year. You heard about that, didn't you?"

I began to read the clipping. "Was this the one with the priests?"

"You mean the Berrigan brothers? No. They were with the Harrisburg 10. They got indicted on a bogus charge of conspiracy to kidnap Henry Kissinger. This one was done by a group called the Citizens Commission to Investigate the FBI. They stole a bunch of documents and leaked them to the press and exposed the FBI for spying on people. There was tons of stuff in the papers. I'm sure you read about it."

I nodded, not sure if this was important. Evidently, I didn't nod confidently enough.

Harmony shook her head. "Nathan, I can see this boy needs an education."

"Yeah, that's what I told you."

"You told her that? What does that mean?"

"It means you got some things to learn about politics."

Nate says I'm a libertarian, which is fine with me. It sounds much better than ignoramus. But if pressed about where I stand, I usually say I'm apolitical. I didn't think it was a good idea to mention that to Harmony Rollins.

"Why don't we leave the politics out for a minute," I said. "Just tell me what happened recently that makes you think your brother's in danger."

She raised a finger to hold me off. "I'm getting to that. First you got to understand a few things. Four years ago, J. Edgar Hoover called the Black Panther Party the greatest threat to the nation's security. Since then it's been coming out in the media that the FBI was infiltrating black organizations, and the reason it came out was because of the Pennsylvania break-in. That started the ball rolling. You see—"

"You don't need to convince me Hoover wasn't Cinderella," I said. "And I don't need *The New York Times* to figure out the FBI has informants in extremist groups."

"Not just extremist groups!" Harmony wagged her finger

at me. "You got to be careful throwing around words like that. They were keeping files on Coretta Scott King, Ralph Abernathy, Joe Namath . . ."

"Joe Namath?" Come to think of it, I had read about that one in the sports pages of the *Daily News.*

"Yeah, that's right, sugar. A football player. And what about Martin Luther King? He wasn't extremist, but they spied all over his ass. The FBI has been spying on law-abiding citizens for years. Even this new guy, the one that replaced Hoover last May—" Harmony snapped her fingers to trigger a recollection.

"L. Patrick Gray," Nate prompted.

"Yeah, that's right, Gray. He even admitted they were keeping files on congressmen since 1950. You understand what I'm saying?"

I shrugged. "I don't understand why you equate congressmen with law-abiding citizens."

She stared at me a moment, then broke into her double-dimpled grin. "You got me there."

"Let's get me to your brother. *Was* he involved in the break-in?"

"Not exactly."

I raised my eyebrows.

"I know, it sounds confusing. Harpo didn't have anything to do with the one in Pennsylvania. But it gave him the idea to break into another FBI office—in Beloit, Wisconsin."

"Let me get this straight. He was charged for one break-in, but he was really involved in another?"

"Exactly."

"How did that come about?"

"Obviously, someone gave them a tip and they ran with it."

I nodded, though I didn't see anything obvious about it.

"Harpo, he got some *incredible* stuff. The Pennsylvania memos, they were just the tip of the iceberg compared to the documents he got ahold of. He had evidence the FBI has a whole clandestine program to infiltrate and destroy political groups. It's called COINTELPRO."

I glanced at Nate for confirmation, but even he looked a little skeptical about that one.

"They infiltrated the civil-rights movement, antiwar groups, the Panthers. And they weren't just spying. They had these agents who were provocateurs, trying to get these groups to do illegal stuff so the FBI could bust them."

"This has all been in the newspapers?" I asked.

"No. It was in the documents Harpo stole. But the most important thing he discovered was that the FBI was involved in the murder of Fred Hampton. You know who Fred Hampton was, don't you?"

I did, though I didn't know why. "Was he the Black Panther killed in a shoot-out with the Chicago police a few years ago?"

"Shoot-out! There wasn't no shoot-out! Fred was murdered in his sleep. It was so blatant, they even had this pig Hanrahan, the state's attorney out there, up on charges. But he just got off last month. Total whitewash. There wasn't one mention about the FBI calling the shots during the entire trial." Harmony clenched her teeth. "I want to kill somebody every time I think about it." She closed her eyes for a moment. "I'm sorry, I know I'm getting off the track."

"There's nothing here about any Wisconsin break-in," I said.

"I know. It never came out."

"Why not?"

"Because the FBI doesn't like to *announce* that people are able to break into their offices, that's why."

Now I was totally confused. If Harmony wasn't a friend, I would have shown her the door. "This doesn't make sense. The FBI doesn't *have* to announce it. If Harpo had hot information, why didn't *he* take the stuff to the press? Wasn't that the idea? To expose the FBI?"

12

"I know, I hear you." Harmony pulled out another cigarette. Nate lit it for her. "Harpo had a partner, see, and the partner was holding the documents while Harpo was talking to a reporter at the *Chicago Daily News*. But she disappeared."

"Disappeared?"

"Yeah, that's right. Then, a couple days later, Harpo got named as a suspect in the Pennsylvania break-in. That's when he decided to go deep underground. He had plastic surgery, the whole bit. The next time I heard from him was three months ago when he called to wish me happy birthday. He was living in Paterson, New Jersey. That's why I decided to talk to you. I remember Nathan saying you grew up near there."

I nodded. She had a good memory. "Do you know the name of his partner?"

"No, just that it was a woman."

"What was he doing in Paterson? Is he still with the Black Panthers?"

"No. The Panthers are dead, sugar. Destroyed with your tax dollars. They were finished the moment Fred Hampton got murdered. Harpo joined a group called the People's Revolutionary Front. I don't know much about them. Just that they're a Marxist group that splintered from the SWP."

"SWP?"

"Socialist Workers Party."

I must have rolled my eyes, because Harmony jumped to her brother's defense. "Hey, I know what you're thinking. Maybe it sounds silly to you. I was in the movement, but I sold out. At least Harpo's still working at it."

I wasn't sure exactly what Harpo was working at, but I didn't dispute the point. "When did this break-in happen?" I asked, glancing at the news clip.

"The Pennsylvania burglary took place in March of seventy-one. The one in Wisconsin, that was four months later, in July."

"So that's like—"

"Seventeen months." Harmony had the edge on me in math.

"How many times have you heard from him since?"

"Just twice. The FBI's got me under surveillance. Once a month some creep shows up at my door asking if I've heard from him. They hassle my mother, too. The one time Harpo called, he phoned this woman we know in Chicago. She phoned me, then I went to a phone booth and called him. I'm sure they've got my line tapped."

I nodded. Just because you're paranoid doesn't mean they're not out to get you. "If Harpo's been able to elude the feds for this long—"

"I know what you're going to say. Why worry now? You see, the next time he called was ten days ago. He phoned me direct. He said he was in trouble and had to split fast. He sounded scared. I've never heard him sound so scared. He needed money, so I wired five hundred dollars to Western Union in Paterson. I made him promise to call in a couple of days. When I didn't hear back from him, I got worried and called Western Union. He never picked up the money."

"No chance he got some from someone else?"

"I doubt it. I phoned the number I had from that time he called. He told me never to call, but I did anyway. I spoke to his girlfriend, Sheila. She said he went out one morning and didn't come back. She's worried about him too."

"You think the FBI was closing in on him?"

"That's what I'm afraid of, yeah."

"Did his girlfriend know where he was headed that day?"

"She wouldn't talk over the phone, and I don't blame her. The only reason she spoke to me at all is because Harpo told her about me. I think maybe she'd tell me more in person."

I lit a cigarette and took a long drag. "I hope she can tell us a lot."

"Hey, I know it won't be easy. But I've got to at least try and find him. Mama's been real sick lately. After Harpo called that time, I was hoping things had settled down enough so we'd be able to figure out a way to see each other for Christmas." Tears were forming at the corners of her eyes, but she forced a smile. "Doesn't that sound bourgeois?"

"You're asking the wrong guy," I said. "The only word I associate with 'holiday plans' is 'suicidal.' "

She chuckled. "I guess we've got different tendencies."

I took a deep breath. "If the FBI can't find your brother, chances are we won't be able to either. He's probably changed his name again, and we don't even know what he looks like."

"The last name he was using was James Brown."

"He picked a common one. That was a smart idea."

"He called himself that after the singer."

I guess my expression made it clear that I didn't know who that was. Harmony gave Nate a puzzled look.

"Sweetheart," he said, "you're talking to the only man in America who's never heard 'Papa's Got a Brand New Bag.' "

Harmony looked at me and shook her head sadly. I guess I was more in need of an education than she thought.

THREE

Harmony disappeared into her bag and emerged holding a file folder that was bulging with news clippings. "I wasn't sure I'd remember all that needed to be covered, so I brought along a few things for you to read."

That was the understatement of the year. Nate smiled sympathetically. "A guy's lips get tired just *thinking* about it, don't they?"

I ignored him and watched her take another dip into the bag. This time she came up holding a stack of bills.

"I can pay you anything you need," she said.

I shook my head. "Not necessary."

"I insist. I'm making lots of bread these days." She peeled off four crisp fifties. "I like spreading it around."

I pushed her hand away. "I make it a policy not to charge my friends. That would be kind of *bourgeois,* don't you think?"

Harmony shot a grin at Nate. "My, my, he's learning fast."

Nate shrugged. "I've been working on him for years."

"Why don't you work on making us another drink."

Harmony slid the bills under the Mickey Mantle glass that holds my pens and paper clips. My apartment is a museum of cheap sports souvenirs. "Hold on to this anyway," she said. "Let's just call it petty bourgeois cash."

I called Ma Bell and traced the phone number Harmony had for Harpo to Sheila Love on Jasper Street in Paterson. I don't usually take clients along on an investigation, but I made an exception for Harmony. I figured Sheila would be more willing to talk to a forty-year-old white guy if Harpo's sister was on hand, but mostly I liked the idea of having Harmony for company.

"Does anyone feel like taking a spin?" I said.

"Right now?" Nate is one of those New Yorkers for whom a trip outside the city requires a few days of mental preparation. He also hates my car, a 1962 Corvair.

"After you've finished your drink."

"All the way to Jersey?"

"It's only across the river."

"Isn't it rush hour or something?"

"It's always rush hour."

"You got a problem here, Nathan?"

"Suburbaphobia," I explained.

"Fear has nothing to do with it. It's a matter of loathing. I've got to make a call." Nate picked up the phone and began dialing. A few months earlier he had taken up with a young artist named Constance. She had moved in with him three weeks before, and since then had proved to be more or less a constant pain in the neck. At the tender age of forty-eight, Nate was getting his first taste of married life. They hadn't formally tied the knot, but the noose was tightening quickly.

I could tell when Constance answered, because he lowered his usually booming voice to a lovey-dovey whisper. I asked Harmony if she was staying at his place.

"Just for tonight." She nodded toward Nate. "I think it would work out better if I got a hotel room."

"You're more than welcome to stay here."

"Oh, no, you're already doing enough. I couldn't put you to any more trouble."

"No trouble at all. Matter of fact, it would be a pleasure. It's been a while since this place had a woman to class it up."

"That's right. You were married the last time I saw you."

"When you last saw me, that was about the last ten minutes of my marriage."

"Well, if you really don't mind, it would only be a couple of days. I'm going to Holyoke to see Mama for Christmas."

"Great. You can stay here tonight. You like cats?"

"Hate 'em. You got one?" She gazed around the apartment.

"He only shows his ugly face when he gets hungry."

"That sounds like the last guy I was living with." She looked at Nate, who was shaking his head as he put down the phone. "Nathan, I'm going to stay here tonight."

Nate wagged a finger at me. "Watch it, pal. You're moving in awful fast on my only niece."

"I thought it might be a little crowded over at the Uncle Inn."

He shrugged. "Period of adjustment, that's all. After two marriages, surely you know about that."

"Sure do. I'm the most well-adjusted guy in Manhattan. I'm glad to see you getting a turn."

"Do you mind if I don't go along?"

"What's the matter, sugar? You picking out wallpaper tonight?"

Nate glowered. "I hope you enjoy the comforts of his car."

"Couldn't be worse than that cab you got us at the airport."

Nate shot me a knowing grin. I kept my mouth shut, figuring it would be better to let Harmony get the bad news for herself. But she took it in graceful stride as she settled into the bucket seat and curled her long sleek legs to compensate for the lack of space. "Hey, this little thing's pretty funky."

"Wait till we get moving."

I headed up Riverside Drive and crossed over at the George Washington Bridge. It had gotten chilly in the last couple of days, and as we passed the sign welcoming us to the Garden State, a northwest wind was swirling snow flurries into the winter mix.

"I haven't seen snow since I moved to L.A," Harmony said. "Maybe we'll have a white Christmas."

"It's still four days away. In New York, the stuff turns brown in four minutes."

"Were you born a romantic, Renzler, or did you grow into it?"

"I think it's a congenital defect. My mother was a big believer in trying to look on the bright side of things."

"What about your father?"

"He's the one who made it necessary for her to do that."

"Do they still live out here?"

"No, they got half smart in the fifties and left."

18

"Half smart?"

"Yeah, they moved to Florida."

Harmony laughed as she popped open the six-pack that Nate had insisted we'd need for the long journey. "Are they still there?"

"No. My father died in sixty-eight. My mother passed on last year. On Christmas Eve, as a matter of fact."

"Is that why you hate the holidays?"

"No, but it gave me another reason."

She did a double take before giving me the full-treatment, double-dimple smile. "I think I'm going to like you, Renzler."

I returned the smile. "The feeling's mutual."

Paterson is in north Jersey, a twenty-mile poke west from Manhattan. It's about the twelfth dirty old town in a line of dirty old towns with names like Hackensack, Lodi, Garfield and Passaic. Although mostly an industrial area, north Jersey once held some claim to a share of the Garden State nickname. But the evidence had all but vanished during the postwar rush to the suburbs. The landscape that once sprouted cornfields and apple trees was now overgrown with shopping centers, industrial parks and neon burgers and hot dogs marking fast-food joints.

I got off the highway in Clifton, the town where I grew up. There was an exit closer to Paterson, but the only way I knew how to get there was by following the tire tracks left from my youth. Paterson was in decline even then. It's the oldest city in New Jersey, and it looks it. Its glory days were the early 1900s, and they went south with industry after the war. At one time, Paterson was the largest textile center in the country. It was also a charming place, if you could believe the city's most noted and quoted resident, William Carlos Williams. I always suspected Williams had taken some poetic license.

"Kind of grim here," Harmony said softly. I started to speak, but she beat me to it. "I know, don't tell me. This is the nice part of town, right?"

"Wrong. There are no nice parts."

"How many people live here?"

"About a hundred and fifty thousand, if you can call it living. Mostly black, mostly poor."

"Sugar, that's what living is for blacks in this country."

It took a few minutes of trial-and-error exploration along the Passaic River before I found Jasper Street. It was near the Great Paterson Falls, a landmark that Williams had rhapsodized about. In his day, it had been a delightful spot for a Sunday picnic. Nowadays it looked like the perfect spot for a Saturday-night mugging.

Sheila Love's house was a two-story wood wreck. Layers of paint peeling off the sides like sunburned skin indicated that it had been white, yellow, red and blue over the years. But no one had gotten the redecorating bug for at least a decade.

Harmony shook her head. "Jesus. Harpo living in a shithole like this."

The entrance was on the side of the house, a matched pair of battered screen doors with gaping express lanes for flies and mosquitoes. Behind the screen to the right was a dark stairway. Behind the left was one of those hollow doors with the approximate strength of a paper towel. A hole the size of a fist indicated that someone had tested its durability. Two rusted black mailboxes were propped on either side of the doors against a crumbling concrete foundation. Sheila's name was scrawled in pen on a strip of masking tape on the box to the left. Another name had been scratched out, but I could make out "J. Brown." A piece of masking tape under a doorbell button also said "Love," and beneath it someone had added "Hate." I wondered if that had been Harpo's doing.

Pressing the button didn't ring any bells, so I pulled back the screen and tried to knock on the inner door without breaking it down. In a few moments, a short, slender black woman in blue jeans and a black turtleneck sweater opened the door about six inches and peered at us with distrustful eyes. She had a small, round face with a smooth complexion. Her nose and mouth seemed very tiny, but that may have been an illusion created by a mountainous Afro hairdo. Hanging from her neck were about eight strings of beads that looked like Good 'n' Plenty candies.

"Sheila, I'm James's sister, Harmony. Remember, we spoke on the phone?"

"Yeah."

"I'd like to talk to you for a few minutes."

"What about?"

"I'm trying to find James. Can we come in for a minute?"

"Who's the pig with you?"

"Don't worry, he's cool," Harmony said.

"Did anybody follow you?" She leaned out the door and looked toward the street.

"Nobody followed us," I said.

"I wasn't asking *you*." She pronounced it "ax" and glared at me as if she'd like to split my skull with one.

"Don't worry," Harmony said. "Everything's cool."

"Okay, come on in. But you can't stay long."

Somehow, I didn't think we'd be wanting to.

F O U R

One glance around Sheila Love's apartment was enough to see that she didn't do much entertaining. Half-filled cardboard boxes were strewn about the dark, cramped living room. There was only one small window for the muted, late afternoon light to enter, and that hadn't been cleaned since the house was painted. The decorating scheme was church-sale reject, with the only furnishings consisting of two metal folding chairs and a card table that had seen one bingo game too many.

Sheila didn't invite us to sit down, and I didn't think it was because the chairs were occupied with bundles of newspapers. The paper was called *Our Struggle—The International Voice of the People's Revolutionary Front*. The headline across the top was: "SWP = Agents of Rockefeller/CIA." I made a note to ask Harmony about that one.

Sheila gave me the once-over two or three times, then asked Harmony, "You sure he ain't a pig?"

I took the liberty of answering for myself. "No, I'm not."

She sniffed at the air with her cute little nose. "Could've fooled me."

"Harpo sounded worried when I talked to him," Harmony said.

"Who's Harpo?"

"I'm sorry, I mean James. We called him Harpo when he was growing up."

"He never said nothing about that."

Harmony smiled. "No, he wouldn't have. He never liked it much. Have you heard from him since we spoke?"

Sheila shook her head. "Nope. Not since he left."

"How long ago was that?" I asked.

Sheila ignored my question, but answered it when Harmony nodded to indicate that she wanted to know, too. I decided I'd leave the questioning to her.

"About ten days ago. You got to promise not to tell anybody I talked to you. We're not supposed to talk to people outside the group about people in the group. But being you're his sister and all . . ."

"Of course, I promise."

Sheila glowered at me. I raised my hand. "Scout's honor."

"And you don't have any idea where James went?"

"I asked Hartman about it, and he says not to worry, James is in isolation."

"In isolation? What does that mean?"

"It's for ego-dismantling and creative mentation. Everyone in the group has to go through it. Hartman says it's a symbiotic process to prepare us for armed revolutionary struggle. We do combat training, martial arts." She gave me a dismissive nod. "If I wanted to, I could break his arm in three places."

"Who's Hartman?" I asked, breaking my resolution to let Harmony ask the questions.

Sheila tried to ignore me, but I guess the question was too preposterous to overlook. "Is he for real?"

Harmony smiled and shrugged.

"Hartman DeWitt is the Supreme Commander of the PRF." She spoke strictly for my benefit, but I didn't think Harmony had heard of him, either. "I can't believe you don't know that. Everybody knows that. Even pigs know it. That's why the CIA wants to assassinate him."

"Is that so?" I said.

"Yeah, that's so. The FBI followed him home and beat him up a week and a half ago."

"And why did they do that?"

"Because. They're scared shit about what's going to happen after he comes to power. They think they can frighten him, but it won't work. Nothing will deter Hartman from his master plan."

Harmony didn't inquire just what Hartman's master plan might be. "Have you been in isolation?" she asked.

"No, just the assistant commanders—Rodney, Roach, and now James. Hartman says my turn will come soon."

It sounded to me like PRF management was a little top-heavy with males.

"Do you know where the isolation takes place?" Harmony asked.

"Uh-uh. I wouldn't tell even if I did. It's a secret. If Hartman found out I even mentioned it . . ." Sheila shivered. Evidently the supreme commander kept his troops on a supremely short leash.

"Do you know how long it lasts?"

"It all depends on the person. Hartman says it can take a day or a week or a month."

"Doesn't it seem strange that James would go into isolation without anyone knowing?"

"Maybe a little. Especially being it was right after the break-in."

"What break-in?"

"James thought somebody broke in here. He couldn't find nothing missing, but he was sure somebody went through his stuff. Somebody's been breaking into all our houses. Hartman thinks it's the FBI, but there could be a snitch in the group. Rodney's in charge of finding out, but James thought it might be Rodney that broke in here. He says you can't trust Rodney."

"Why's that?"

"I don't know. I think James used to know this friend of his or something."

"What makes you think that?"

" 'Cause this friend of Rodney's was here a couple weeks ago, and James acted real nervous when he met him."

"Do you know what the friend's name was?"

"Uh-huh. His name was Bill. I don't know his last name."

"So you think James will be coming back here when he gets out of isolation?"

"I guess so."

"Honey, you don't sound too sure. Is something worrying you?"

"It's nothing." Sheila looked at the floor. "Rodney says

James isn't in isolation, that he's shacking up with Judith."

"Who's Judith?"

"She's this stuck-up white bitch. Judith Fairbanks." Sheila pronounced the name as if she despised every letter.

"That doesn't sound like James." I couldn't tell if Harmony was serious or if she was trying to win Sheila over.

Sheila smiled, but it took a lot of work. "Rodney probably just said that because he wants to get in my pants."

"Did you ask Hartman whether James was living with Judith?"

"You mean accuse Hartman of lying?"

"Where does this Judith live?"

"I forget. Oradell, Glen Rock. One of them rich-ass white towns."

"Maybe if I talked to Hartman," Harmony said.

"No, don't do that. You can't let him know I talked to you."

"No, I wouldn't do that. I wouldn't mention you."

"He'd still find out. Hartman knows everything."

"What about Rodney? Maybe he knows where she lives." Harmony was asking all the right questions.

"Yeah, he would. She was hot for him too. But you can't tell him I talked to you either."

"I wouldn't do nothing to get you into trouble. You just tell me where he lives, I'll go talk to him. I won't say a word about you." Harmony put out her hand and rested it on Sheila's shoulder. "I'll say I got his name and address from James."

"Well, okay." Sheila sounded like a kid who had just been talked into trading a Mickey Mantle card for a Tom Tresh. "He lives over on Danforth. I'll have to check the number." She went into the kitchen and returned with a pocket address book. She read off the number, then put the book down on one of the newspaper bundles. "Now you got to leave. Roach will be coming over to check on me, and I don't want him finding you here."

"Why's he checking on you?"

"Hartman says I need some security."

"I guess this is kind of a dangerous neighborhood, huh?"

"Well, now it is—with the FBI coming around and all."

"The FBI was here?"

"That's right. Two pigs. They looked kinda like *him*." She nodded at me. "They were asking for somebody named Henry Collins or something. I told them I didn't know nobody by that name, but they kept saying I was lying. They went snooping all over the place. And then they took a bunch of papers."

"What kind of papers?"

Sheila motioned toward the bundles. *"Our Struggle.* You can have one. They took a whole bunch." She pulled a paper from the stack and handed it to Harmony. "They were parked out in front on and off until a couple days ago. I told Hartman about it, and he said he'd take care of them."

"What did he do?"

"I don't know. But he must've done something, because they went away."

"You didn't tell them about James, did you?"

The lines on Sheila's forehead creased as a baffled look spread over her face. "Just that he was living here. Why?"

Harmony winced at the news that Harpo's cover was blown. I figured there was a good chance that had already happened.

Sheila noticed her reaction. "There's nothing wrong with that, is there? They said they were looking for somebody else."

"No, that's okay, honey, you did all right."

Sheila shivered. "It's getting real weird around here lately. Next thing you know, the CIA will be snooping around."

"You can bet that'll drive down the property values."

Harmony shot me a sly grin, and Sheila shot a pair of daggers at the center of my forehead. "You better go now."

"Sure, just one more thing. Do you have a photo of James?"

Sheila took two steps back and put her hands in front of her chest in a sudden, jerky motion. I think she was attempting a karate attack stance. Her tone changed to the snarl reserved for pigs. "I thought you said you were his sister."

"I am."

"Then you should know what he looks like."

"Of course I do. I just haven't seen him in a couple of years, that's all. All I got's old ones. I thought you might have an extra for me to show around."

Sheila dropped her hands to her waist and shook her head. "James wouldn't let nobody take his picture. Rodney did one time, and James jumped all over his ass—"

A knock at the door made Sheila jump almost to the ceiling. "Oh, shit. You got to keep out of sight."

Harmony and I moved to the wall as Sheila peered out the front window. "It's just Juan," she said. "But you still got to keep quiet."

From my angle I could see out to the porch, which was lit up under a bare lightbulb. A short guy with long blond hair stood with his hands in the pockets of a red down jacket. He had his tongue out to catch snowflakes.

Their conversation was brief, and we could hear every word. Juan had come to tell Sheila about a meeting of the committee.

"But I'm not on the committee," she said.

"Me neither. But Hartman said we're both supposed to be there. Tomorrow night at six, at the office."

"But I got to work."

"Call in sick, that's what I'm doing."

While Sheila pondered that revolutionary problem, I reached over to the stack of papers, picked up her address book and slipped it into my coat pocket.

"You seem real bummed, Sheila. Is there something you want to rap about?"

"I'm just cold. The pig landlord won't give us enough heat."

"That's a bummer." There was a long pause while Juan seemed to be waiting for Sheila to speak. She didn't. "Okay, well, I guess I'll see you at the meeting."

I watched out the window while Juan walked to his car. I could make out the form of a VW Beetle, but it was too dark to see the color.

Sheila leaned against the door after she shut it and sighed with relief. "Okay, now, you got to leave. I ain't answering no more questions."

I asked one more just to try her patience. "When James left, did he take his car?"

"No. He walked."

I managed to work through the sting of her sarcasm. "What kind is it?"

"None of your business."

"Come on, Sheila," Harmony pleaded. "This is important."

"Okay. He had a white Impala."

"You wouldn't happen to know the license plate," I said.

"No, I wouldn't."

As we moved toward the door, I gave Harmony a slip with her name and my phone number on it. I let her pass it to Sheila; otherwise it would have gone right into the trash.

"I really appreciate your help, Sheila," Harmony said. "If you can think of anything else or you hear from James, would you give me a call?"

Sheila nodded, but I felt sure we wouldn't be hearing from her.

When we got in the car, Harmony rapped her fist on the dashboard. "Damn, I slipped up in there, calling him Harpo."

"You did a fine job. You got a lot more out of her than this pig would have."

She laughed. "Yeah, I guess we got to work on that."

"What am I supposed to do? Wear a Nehru jacket and love beads?"

"You could start by getting rid of those khakis and putting on some jeans."

"I'll buy a pair tomorrow if you think it'll help."

"You can't wear *new* blue jeans, Renzler. They've got to be old and faded if you want to look the part."

"I'm not so sure I want to look the part. Maybe I'll just work on getting used to being called a pig."

FIVE

The snow was falling in earnest and the streets were getting slick as we drove toward Rodney's neck of paradise. Common sense dictated a hasty return to the city, but there was a sense of urgency about Harmony's search for her brother.

"So you don't think Sheila will be able to put together Harpo and James?" she asked.

"I don't think Sheila could put together a plastic prize in a cereal box."

Harmony shook her head and whistled softly. "Yeah, she's one mixed-up girl, all right. Scared, angry, paranoid."

"Every winning personality trait you could think of. Even if she could put it together, I don't think it would matter. Now the G is another question."

"Who's the G?"

"That's cop lingo for FBI." I felt a little smug being able to explain an initial to Harmony for a change.

She sighed. "Yeah, it sounds like they're right on his heels. I wonder who put them there."

"You wouldn't consider the possibility that they just caught up with him?"

"After this long? No way. Somebody tipped their asses off. You can count on it."

I figured she was right. Despite all of Harmony's talk about surveillance, the FBI couldn't assign an agent to every suspect. "So the question becomes, was it someone from inside the group or outside?"

"Yeah, that's always the question."

"It sounds like you've had experience in these matters."

"Are you kidding? SDS was crawling with informers. So were the Panthers. You didn't know who you could trust."

"So you think it's someone from inside?"

"Yeah, and it sounds like it could be this Rodney dude."

"There's a long-shot chance someone tipped the G off to protect Harpo," I said.

"What do you mean?"

"If Harpo left Paterson, it would work in his favor for them to still be looking for him here."

"I hadn't thought of that."

"It's only speculation. By sending them to his house, it also makes it easier for them to figure out he was James Brown. When you spoke to Harpo, did he mention this Hartman?"

"No. The first time, he told me he was in the PRF. The last call, he just said he was in trouble. That's why I don't buy this isolation crap." Harmony lit a cigarette for each of us. "There's a lot of questions that need answering."

"What I want to know is how a kid with blond hair and blue eyes ever got a name like Juan."

"He probably changed it to be in solidarity with the Third World movement. That's becoming popular these days."

"Beg your pardon."

30

"Sugar, you wouldn't believe how guilty some of your people feel about being white."

I shook my head. "And all these years, all I've ever felt was lucky."

"That's exactly how you should feel. 'Cause you *are* lucky."

As we peered at the house numbers along Danforth Avenue, I realized we were nearing the town of Totowa. That was hardly what you'd call ritzy, but it was a major step up from Paterson.

"Looks like this dude's doing better for himself than Harpo or Sheila," Harmony said as I pulled up to the curb in front of a green Cape Cod. The peeling paint gave Rodney's house a bleak aura, but it looked almost respectable compared with Sheila's shack near the falls.

"That's exactly what I was thinking."

"You know, I just assumed Rodney was a brother."

"You think maybe he's one of the lucky ones?"

Except for the front-porch light, Rodney's place was dead dark. I leaned on the bell for a while, but no one answered, so we were still in the dark on the question of Rodney's heritage.

"Should we break in and take a look around?"

I studied Harmony's face to see if she was serious. She looked it, but I asked just to make sure.

"Yeah, why not?"

"For one, it's against the law. For two, he might be home any moment. For three, we're not sure we have reason to break in."

"For four?"

"How many reasons do you need?"

She sighed. "I guess that's enough. But you know, Sister Shamus would just bust right in."

"How would she do that? Shoot off the knob?"

"No, she'd pick the lock."

"Can you pick locks?"

"That ain't my line of work, sugar. But I figured you could. You can, can't you?"

I didn't want to disappoint her. "Yeah, some. But I really don't think the script calls for that yet."

"What do you think it calls for?"

"There's a place near here that serves food that won't kill you." I didn't tell her it was a Howard Johnson's.

"Oh, there's a recommendation. We calling it a day?"

That's what I wanted to do, but I could tell she was anxious. "We'll stop back here before we head to New York."

It took me a few minutes to find the sad little shopping strip on Route 46 at Browertown Road in West Paterson.

"Where we going?" Harmony said as we pulled into the lot. "Shoe Town?"

"No, beyond that."

"Are you jiving me?"

"The orange roofs of HoJo's have always held a special attraction for me."

"Why? You lose it in the parking lot here?"

We had our choice of seats in the place. Either the food was terrible or the locals were all rushing home to cut off their fingers in their snowblowers. Harmony picked out a corner booth that afforded a view of the Shoe Town dumpster out one window and a drainage runoff from the Route 46 overpass out the other. For a moment I almost had her believing the torrents of water pouring down the concrete spout were the inspiration for the name of the next town over, Little Falls.

"I wish we knew where the PRF office was," she said. "I'd like to have a word with Hartman."

I pulled Sheila Love's address book from my pocket and held it up. "I think we might find it in here."

"My, my, don't you have sticky fingers." She reached across the table and gave them a rub. She had long, sharp nails, evenly lacquered in a shade that might be called black cherry.

32

"I prefer to think of it as quick hands."

The thing that jumped out at me as I thumbed through the book was that Sheila didn't have many friends. At first it looked like they were all members of the Soviet hockey team, but closer inspection revealed that she had written them in code. Fortunately, the code had a degree of difficulty approximating the brain twisters for kids on the HoJo's place mat. I cracked it by the time a gum-cracking teen in squeaky shoes ambled over to take our order. I figured she had bought them at Shoe Town.

The entries in Sheila's book were all spelled backwards. There were maybe a dozen in all. I busied myself recording them on the place mat while Harmony buried her head in her free introductory issue of *Our Struggle*. I knocked off three names before I had to stop and ask why she kept gasping.

"This Hartman, he's a madman."

"Well, you do know that the CIA wants to assassinate him."

"Yeah, yeah. I just can't believe Harpo got involved with this crank."

"I didn't understand the front-page headline. Didn't you tell me SWP stands for Socialist Workers Party? Aren't they a left-wing outfit?"

I expected Harmony to be a supporter of socialists, but she dismissed them with a wave of her hand. "Bunch of Trotskyites."

"The headline says they're agents of Rockefeller and the CIA. Do you believe that?"

Much to my relief, she snorted with disapproval. "Are you kidding?"

"I had the impression these left-wing groups were working together against the war."

"Sugar, the only thing these groups do nowadays is feud with each other. The whole movement's been splintered to pieces."

"Is that because of the draft lottery?"

"What do you mean?"

"I had the impression the antiwar movement fizzled out as soon as they started the lottery. The kids who got high numbers decided to go back to class, get their degrees and jump into the job market while their pals with the low numbers are over in Nam getting their asses shot off."

"You know what? That's kind of simplistic, but you're not very far off. There's a lot of other reasons, too. One thing you should remember, though: Most of the guys getting killed in Nam are black."

"They didn't qualify for college deferments?"

"That's right. And they couldn't afford rich-ass doctors and psychiatrists to write phony medical excuses."

"Well, I guess we won't have to worry about that, now that peace is at hand."

She choked on her fried clams. "Gimme a break."

"But Henry Kissinger said so." I was joking, but saying it left a bad taste in my mouth. I'd gotten so sick of the war myself that I'd let Nate talk me into registering to vote. A lot of good that did. Nixon got reelected by the biggest landslide in history, and Kissinger's eleventh-hour announcement that the war was over had been the icing on the cakewalk.

"So why *do* you think Harpo got into the PRF?" I asked.

"I wish I knew. This Hartman DeWitt is really scary."

"Maybe it's not the FBI that Harpo's so scared of," I said.

"Look at this! The man's a racist. He's got a story here saying Amiri Baraka is a CIA agent. They're going to bust up a black empowerment rally he's having in Newark next month."

"Who's Amiri Baraka?"

"He's a poet. You might know him as LeRoi Jones."

"Oh, yeah." I hadn't read his poems, don't read any poetry, as a matter of fact, but Nate had been to a party at his place.

"In here they call him a gutter dweller, mad dog, Aunt Jemima, Superfly."

"At least those are easier to remember than Amiri Baraka."

Harmony gave me a stare that made my temperature drop ten degrees.

The lights were still out when we swung by Rodney's. With the address book in hand, Harmony didn't suggest any more Sister Shamus tactics. Or maybe it was because she didn't feel like talking to me. We slid back to Manhattan at thirty miles an hour, but it was the silence, not the driving conditions, that made the ride difficult. Harmony had clammed up tighter than the HoJo's special, and I couldn't think of anything to say that wouldn't sound dumb. As my ex-wives will attest, apologizing has never been my strong suit.

It was pushing midnight by the time I lucked into a parking space on West Seventy-third Street at Needle Park. The neighborhood junkies had taken shelter from the storm, and the fresh blanket of snow gave the park a rare sense of peacefulness, one of those fleeting moments of perfection that make the city seem livable. By tomorrow morning, the dogs would have pissed the snow yellow, the cabs and buses would have crushed it into slush, and the place would once again look like a trash can.

Harmony took my arm as we walked along Seventy-second Street. "I'm sorry I got mad at you, Renzler. I just can't stand it when I hear you being racist."

"I wasn't being racist. I—"

"Sure you were."

"I didn't mean to be. I was only making a joke."

"Yeah, I know. That's just a sign of how inbred it all is."

After putting up with Sheila Love calling me a pig, I could feel some indignation rising inside me. But I put the lid on it

35

before any spilled out. "I'm sorry I hurt your feelings," I said.

"It ain't my feelings you hurt. When you make cracks like that, you just hurt yourself."

That was something to think about sometime, but not now. I'd had more than enough education for one day. When we got to my apartment, I told Harmony she could have my bedroom.

"No, no, I'll take the couch. I've had lots of experience crashing at people's apartments. You wouldn't believe some of the pits I slept in when I was in SDS."

A little light went on in my head that sent a little shudder down my spine. That would have been her bell-bottom period.

S I X

I hit dreamland the instant I hit the bed. I was lying on my stomach in a small, dark room. There weren't any windows, but snow was blowing around me. Music played in the distance, but I couldn't make out the melody. Suddenly the music got very loud. I was humming along, but I didn't recognize the song until I heard myself singing, "You better watch out, you better not cry, you better not pout . . ."

I stopped when I felt someone's hands on my back. My back was cold, and the hands were warm and soft and soothing. Long fingernails were tapping the melody. I looked over my shoulder and saw Santa Claus behind me. Not the real guy, but a gorgeous black woman dressed like him. She said, "Sugar, this is going to be the best Christmas you ever had." And it was, until the fingernails began cutting into my flesh. I looked again and saw Sheila Love. She was snarling like a dog, scratching furiously, and I couldn't do anything to stop her. She had my right arm pulled behind me, and I heard it snap, a sickening crunch . . .

I woke up startled, sweating and twisted up in my blankets, with my right arm tucked beneath me. Harmony stood over me in a black silk robe looking like a million bucks. She held out a cup of coffee. "Sounds like some little boy's dreaming about what he's going to get for Christmas."

I took the coffee and shook my head to get my brain defogged. "Was I singing out loud?"

She gave me a half-tilt smile. "I guess you could call it singing." She sat down on the edge of the bed and pulled a notepad from the pocket of her robe. "I finished decoding Sheila's phone directory. Guess what I found."

I've never been big on guessing games, and I'm not what you'd call a morning person. Guessing games in the morning are completely out of the question. On this morning, I faced the added distraction of having a bird's-eye view of the magnificent twin peaks that stretched the fabric of Harmony's robe. Gentleman that I am, I averted my eyes to the Utica Club beer clock on my night table. It was seven o'clock.

Harmony didn't wait for my answer. "Under F, I found an address for Judith Fairbanks. I wonder why Sheila didn't give it to us yesterday."

"Maybe she forgot she had it."

"Then I guess she forgot what she wrote beside it."

"Oh, what's that?"

"Stuck-up white bitch."

"Was that part in code, too?"

"Oh, yeah. There's only one thing in here that's not. Next to this guy Paul Weisberg, she wrote, 'fascist pig.' "

I lit my first and best cigarette of the day. "That sounds like the guy we want to talk to."

"Yeah, but first we should go see Judith, right?"

"Right. And first I've got to take a shower."

I figured it would be a while before the snow was cleared off the highways, so we postponed our Jersey outing until the afternoon. Harmony wanted to call her mother and the friend in Chicago through whom Harpo had contacted her in case he tried to get in touch that way again. I wanted to find out the license-plate number of Harpo's car. I gave Harmony a brief lesson in the fine art of private investigation by explaining how to get it. I told her to call the Jersey Department of Motor Vehicles and ask for a guy I had paid off a couple of years before.

As for me, I had a friend I wanted to see.

Randall Edwards and I didn't go back far, but we went back deep. I met him on a bad day in 1971, a bad day for me, a worse one for him. I also met him in a bad place—a saloon on West Forty-sixth Street. I was on a piss stop after getting booted off a case. If you want to take a leak in New York, your only choices are the street or a saloon. I chose a saloon, but I hadn't been real choosy.

I was finishing off a mandatory beer when a young, stocky black guy in a suit and tie wandered in. That's usually not a smart idea on a sunny day in Hell's Kitchen, and definitely not a smart idea when three loud white assholes are getting pickled.

The black guy was already pickled. He staggered to the end of the bar near the door, clutching a wad of soggy bills. When he tossed them down, they went over the bar.

The three patrons exploded with laughter. He nodded and slurred, "Afternoon, gentlemen." Then he noticed me, closer to him, and said, "Not you. You're not a gentleman, are you?"

"In a place like this, I try not to be."

He ordered Johnny Walker, and the bartender asked if he wanted the red or the black.

"Black, of course. What do I look like—a communist?"

"You look like a drunk nigger," one of the patrons said.

He looked past me through glazed eyes, then at me. "It'd be smart to ignore that, wouldn't it?"

"I would."

"Ask him if he wants a watermelon backup, Scotty."

Scotty put the shot down. "Buck-fifty." The drink prices had gone up since I got there.

"Take it out of what went over the bar."

"I didn't see nothing go over the bar." Scotty polled the regulars to make sure he wasn't mistaken. They assured him he wasn't.

I'd had enough of the friendly atmosphere, so I pushed two singles at Scotty and told him it was on me.

"Then the next one's on *me*, my friend."

I could sense the guys at the far end getting off their stools. I stood up and squeezed his arm. "Let's get it somewhere else."

Randall shrugged me away and launched himself back from the bar like a swimmer pushing off the side of a pool. "No fucking way," he shouted. "I don't take no shit from no white trash limp-dick motherfuckers." He assumed a boxing stance, then lowered his voice and asked me, "How many are there?"

"Three."

"No problem. Any more than that and I might need backup."

Randall Edwards almost proved true to his boast. The three jerks charged him, but they elected to get their shots in one at a time. He crumpled the first guy with a kick to the side of his knee and startled the second with a roundhouse right. The third guy tried to come back-door, but he caught him with an elbow.

I took care of the fourth. Scotty grabbed a sap and came around the bar. I tripped him with my foot and planted my fist on the side of his head as he fell. The sap slipped out of his hand, and I scrambled to pick it up. I had to clobber one goon who was getting the edge on Randall, then I gave it to him so he could get in a few choice whacks.

As we stumbled out, he said, "Damn, that felt good, didn't it?"

"Yeah, it felt great. But I don't think we should try it again at the next place."

That turned out to be a Chock Full O' Nuts, where Randall broke down and told me about his bad day. He had resigned from the FBI, had been more or less forced to. His fellow special agents had made a specialty of making his life miserable. It started with obscene phone calls, which soon became death threats. Dirty drawings of him and his wife showed up on his desk, with racial slurs written on them. He complained to his supervisors, who promised to look into it. He toughed it out three years until someone taped a photo of his kid onto a picture of a monkey. That was the straw that broke the camel's back. Randall wanted to stay and fight, but his wife finally put her foot down.

I bumped into Randall a few months later at a Yankees game. He said he'd gone into the accounting business and if there was ever anything he could do, just call. I fully intended to contact him when I decided to begin filing again. For now, I thought he might be able to help me find out just how much the FBI knew about Harpo Rollins.

"What's going on, Renzler?" he said when he answered the phone. "You finally worked up the balls to file?"

I wished I could say that I was calling to extend season's greetings. "No, I've got questions about the bureau for you."

"Oh great, ruin my Christmas."

"Sorry."

"Only kidding." Randall lowered his voice to a whisper. "My wife's brother's in from Detroit with his wife and kids.

I'm dying to get out of here." He said he knew a bar over in Hell's Kitchen that served a mean Bloody Mary, but we settled on the Astro coffee shop near my corner, Seventy-second and Columbus.

We talked about the holidays and what a pain it is to see your relatives over the first cup of coffee, then I hit him with my problem. "Did you follow the Black Panthers when you were at the G?"

"A little bit. But I never worked on them. That was all handled out of Racial Matters. And they didn't want a black guy messing around in Racial Matters. They didn't want any blacks, period. They got eighty-six hundred SA's in the bureau. Eighty-five hundred of them are white."

I nodded long enough to acknowledge his bitterness. "But did you have access to information about the Panthers?"

"Some, yeah."

"What about now?"

Randall cocked and dipped his head to the right. That was how he shrugged. "Yeah, probably. What is it you want to know?"

"I'm trying to check on a guy named James Brown."

"Like the football player?"

"No, the singer. Yeah, like the football player, too."

"And he was with what chapter of the Panthers?"

"Chicago. But now he's in Paterson, New Jersey."

"Oh, lovely town. One of the pricks that harassed me got transferred there. Jack Fogarty. That was his punishment. I don't think there's any Panthers in Paterson these days. Far as I know, there aren't many Panthers period. Between fighting with the cops and fighting each other, they pretty much got wiped out. There was never more than a thousand or so to begin with. They just seemed larger than life after that incident out in Sacramento."

"What was that?"

"A bunch of them marched into the state capitol armed to the teeth to protest a gun-control law. They had enough guns to start a war."

"Now that you mention it, I remember seeing it on TV."

"Oh yeah, they played it on the news for weeks. All the politicians diving for cover, hiding under their desks." Randall laughed. "Yeah, that scared some white folks, all right."

I didn't let on that I was one of them. "James Brown is now in a group called the People's Revolutionary Front."

"Who are they?"

"Some outfit run by a crackpot named Hartman DeWitt."

"Hartman DeWitt!"

"You know him?"

"No. I'm thinking of another guy. Lyndon LaRouche. Talk about crackpots."

"Before that he was in the Panthers. His name then was Rollins—Henry 'Harpo' Rollins."

Based on what Harmony had said about Harpo's notoriety, I expected Randall to jump out of his seat. Instead he calmly shoveled a trash can worth of scrambled eggs into the hopper. "Name sounds familiar. Was he around for the Hampton murder?"

"What was that?"

"Fred Hampton. A kid in Chicago. He was the chairman of the Panthers, or the minister, or whatever crazy title they had."

"Yeah, he was." I was startled that Randall thought of Fred Hampton as being murdered, too. "But he's wanted for breaking into a G office in Media, PA, last year."

"That wasn't a Panther thing. That was one of those groups with half a dozen five-dollar words in their name. It happened right before I left. That was one of those resident agencies. They've got fifty-nine field offices, but they've got like five hundred of these two-man offices. We called them ma-and-pas. Pretty much anybody who can pick a lock can break in." He chuckled. "Hoover was pissed, pissed, pissed about that one. He assigned a *hundred* SA's to it. They take it personal when you break into their house and steal their shit. And it was good shit—spying on antiwar groups, black student associations. It embarrassed them big-time. They never solved it, but you can bet the boys are still out looking. Smart move to change ID."

"He changed his whole face."

"Very smart move." Randall nodded as he picked off his fried potatoes. At the Astro they're orange, an old Greek recipe that I suspect involves goat urine. "You change your name and your face, stay out of sight and don't talk to anyone from your past, they never catch you. Now, Angela Davis, she was on the most-wanted list, and they were hot on her ass. But it still took two months to catch her. But like H. Rap Brown, the only reason they caught him was he was in on a tavern heist. He was on the lam for a year and a half."

"The G *has* caught up with this guy, Randall. They showed up at the home of James Brown asking for Rollins. He took off a day or two ahead of them."

"I hope he's a fast runner. You mind me asking why you're asking about him?"

"His sister's a friend of a friend of mine. She wants me to find him. She thinks he's in trouble."

"I'd say she's right about that." Randall swallowed a piece of toast while muttering "Rollins, Rollins." He picked at the last shard of scrambled egg on his plate. It tumbled off his fork and stuck to his bottom lip. I decided not to point it out until he was done thinking. He tapped his finger on his chin right under the egg, as if he were pointing it out to himself. "If I'm not mistaken, I think he got fingered as an informant."

"When?"

"In Chicago, in the Hampton thing."

"Why'd they need an informant? I thought it was a shoot-out."

"They needed an informant to provide them with the info to get a search warrant." Randall shook his head. "A shoot-out, huh? Yeah, there was some shooting, all right. The cops fired like a hundred rounds. You want to know how many shots were fired back? *One.* Of the hundred rounds, you want to know how many were fired at Hampton's bed? About *fifty.*"

"You're kidding me."

"No, I'm not." Randall raised his hand like he was taking an oath. "Hey, don't get me wrong. I never supported any of this black militant crap, but you don't go knocking down somebody's door and start firing. Not at five in the morning. That's what time they raided the place. The cops had machine guns, did you know that?"

"No, I didn't." My head was spinning from the possibility that Harpo was a snitch, and now I was getting an education that Harmony would have approved of from a most unlikely teacher. "Let me get this straight. You're saying Harpo Rollins was an informant for the G?"

"No, not the G. The Chicago police. The G didn't have anything to do with it. But if it's the guy I'm thinking of, he was an informant."

"I don't think so, Randall. Not this guy."

"Yeah, I'm pretty sure. Of course, he could've had a snitch-jacket on."

"What's that?"

"That's when you put out the word to make people *think* someone's a snitch. Which is just as bad as being one, far as the person who's wearing the jacket is concerned." Randall took a slug of coffee. "Anyhow, one of the Panthers got in a fight with the guy, and he killed him."

"Who killed who?"

44

"The informant, this Harpo Rollins, killed the guy."

Now my head was really spinning. It didn't help to look out at the revolving neon Astro sign that stayed lit twenty-four hours a day, 365 days a year. "What would you say if I told you the G *was* involved in the Hampton killing?"

Randall did his shrug. "I'd probably say you were full of shit. But of course I'd say that anyway."

"Did you ever hear of something called COINTELPRO?"

Randall's jaw dropped, and I got a lovely view of Astro spuds and sausage. He leaned across the table, lowered his head and whispered. "Now just how in the hell do you know about that?"

I gave him a sketch of what Harmony had told me about the Wisconsin break-in. "So this COINTELPRO thing is for real?"

"Damn straight it's for real. It's code word for the G's counterintelligence operations. I never worked any of them. That's all handled out of ISD—Internal Security Division. I never heard about them being involved in the Hampton thing, but they got into some pretty messy shit. Like that trial up in New Haven—Erica Huggins and Bobby Seale—did you hear about that one?"

I wasn't sure that I had.

"Well, they got off. It involved the murder of this kid Alex Rackley, who was a suspected informant. But I heard from a reliable source that the star witness, this guy George Sams, was a paid informant for the G. And *he* was the one that pulled the trigger. He copped a plea of second degree to testify."

Randall looked at his watch. "Damn, I got to get going. I'm just supposed to be out getting the lights for the Christmas tree." He wiped his mouth with his napkin, then took out a pen and started to write on it. "So you want me to find out what they got on Rollins and Brown. You want me to check out DeWitt, too?"

45

I nodded. "You sure you can do that?"

"Yeah, I got a brother who works in the records department in D.C."

"A brother of yours works for the FBI?"

"I mean a *brother,* Renzler. You know, a black dude. He owes me big-time. I saved his ass from the IRS." Randall handed me his business card. "I can save yours too, brother."

"This isn't the time to be thinking about that."

"No, maybe not. But something you ought to think about, Renzler: If this Henry Rollins is who I think he is, it sounds like his sister isn't being straight with you."

"Yeah, Randall, I realize that."

S E V E N

I left the Astro with a queasy feeling, and it wasn't just the usual breakfast-special payback. I was feeling uneasy that Harmony might be holding back something about her brother. But I was holding out hope that Randall Edwards was wrong about Harpo. I decided not to broach the subject until he got back to me with his report.

Harmony gave me her report when I got back. "Your friend Dominic said to wish you merry Christmas. He gave me his home address in case you want to send him a card."

"Wasn't that thoughtful? Did he give you what we need?"

"I think so. He couldn't find anything in Paterson. But there's a white 1971 Impala licensed to a James Brown on Westervelt in Passaic. PRF 666."

"That sounds like the one." It also sounded like Harpo had popped for a few extra bucks for special plates.

"He registered it six months ago. Transferred from Toledo, Ohio." She shook her head. "Beloit, Toledo and Paterson. He's been living in some choice spots."

"Sounds to me like he's been working his way down from the nation's armpit to its asshole," said Nate, emerging from the can with a bottle of beer and a copy of *Screw* magazine. He had shaken loose from the shackles of Constance and was planning on going with us to Jersey.

Harmony gazed at him tucking in his shirt. "You're a class act all the way, Nathan."

"I gave a lecture at Beloit College last year," he said. "It's a scumhole town, but not a bad school. Lots of cute young art students. Great dope, too."

"When I was in Wisconsin, all they had was this home-grown trash they called Wisco weed. Five joints and all you got was a headache."

"Not this stuff. This was primo. One hit and you were paranoid all day long."

This wasn't a subject I could discuss with any expertise, so I called to make arrangements for a car that would accommodate my partners. Angelo Albani is my bookie, and he also has a small fleet of big hulks that he comes into by odd circumstance, usually involving the dubious activities of sundry in-laws and cousins. He tried to give me one outright in lieu of a payoff the last time I had a big score, but I wasn't buying.

"Renzler, *come va?* Just in time for the *joka del giorno.*" One downside to dealing with Angelo is having to listen to his jokes. At least this was a new one.

"Guy goes to see his doctor. Doctor says I got good news and bad news. Which do you want first? Don't pull no punches with me, Doc. I'll take the bad news. Doctor sighs. Louie, you got cancer, two months to live. Louie gulps. Jeez, what's the good news? Doc's all smiles. Didya see the new receptionist? I'm bangin' her." Angelo let out a laugh. "Pretty funny, huh?" That's what he always asks.

I told him it was and what I wanted. He said he had an Oldsmobile I could borrow that would make me feel like a million lire. His nephew Eddie would drop it off in twenty minutes.

It was more like an hour later when a kid who looked about fifteen arrived, mumbling apologies about problems negotiating the slippery streets on bald tires. I gave him a ten for his trouble, and he gave me a quart of oil and a caution. "She runs good, but she's a real boyner."

She didn't run good and she did burn oil, but there was a monster heater and room for cozy, three-across seating.

The address we had for Judith Fairbanks was in Ho-Ho-Kus, a ritzy little burg about ten miles north of Paterson and ten thousand rungs up the social ladder. I expected it to be an apartment in one of the block-long commercial districts that constitute "downtown" in Bergen County, but it turned out to be a large brick house on a corner lot lined with enough evergreens to start a Christmas tree business. Judith looked to be swimming in bucks, and it looked like there was a pool to hold them in the fenced-in backyard.

"Where'd they get a name like Ho-Ho-Kus?" Harmony asked as we pulled up to the curb in front.

"It's an old Indian word that means 'close to shopping centers and schools,' " I said.

Harmony took a look around. "In this neighborhood, Harpo would stand out like a sore thumb."

"It's also the last place in the world anybody would look for him."

We began the trek up the snow-covered driveway, which

was long enough and wide enough for drag racing. "I feel like the Mod Squad," Nate said.

"Who am I—Linc or Julie?" Harmony asked.

"Yeah, I guess it doesn't exactly work out, does it?"

"What's the Mod Squad?"

Nate glowered. "Jesus, Renzler. With all the TV you watch? Just pretend you're Pete and don't ask any more dumb questions."

The name on the mailbox was Fairbanks, but the name Summerfield was penciled in on a strip of tape below it. Nobody answered our first ring. When I pushed the bell again, I thought the curtain in an upstairs window moved slightly. But after watching a few moments, I concluded it was an illusion from the reflection of the sun.

"I know Sister Shamus would break in and have a look around," I said. "What would the Mod Squad do?"

"Probably smoke a joint and build a snowman," Harmony said.

"And then they'd sit down next to it and talk about their feelings."

"What does the professional suggest?" Harmony asked.

"Go back to the car, drink a beer and wait."

We took the professional solution, pausing for a look in the garage window to see if Harpo's car was parked inside. It wasn't.

As Nate passed out beers, Harmony said, "Well, I guess I'm getting a lesson in what being a real private eye is like."

"Pretty boring, huh?" Nate said.

"You want to see boring, come watch a movie being made."

I told her I wouldn't mind doing that sometime.

"Anytime you want, you can be my guest. Just be sure and bring a book with you."

Nate yawned. "You know, Harmony, there's a whole separate culture out here in Jersey."

"Cultural wasteland, right?"

"No, I'm serious. Did you know Jersey has its own alphabet?"

"Stop jiving me, Nathan."

"Swear to God. Renzler grew up here, he can tell you."

Harmony shot me a skeptical look, and I nodded solemnly. "Fuckin' A, fuckin' B, fuckin' C . . . That's all I know."

I glanced in the side mirror and saw a green sedan pulling around the corner on the cross street behind us. I hadn't noticed the car when we arrived, but I now realized it had been parked behind a row of pine trees on the far side of the house. The car inched to a stop about twenty feet behind us.

"Things are about to get less boring," I said, handing Harmony my beer. "You're about to get a lesson in Jersey cops."

There were two of them, dressed in navy suits. They got out at the same time and walked deliberately, one on each side. The guy on my side was about forty-five. He had an orange crew cut, a jaw as square and solid as a box of bricks and a nose that looked like it had been flattened with one. His partner was younger, thin, with a long face and slicked black hair. They arrived at my window and the passenger window at the same time. These weren't Jersey cops.

I pushed the window button. "Let me handle this."

"You mind telling me what you're doing here?" the crew cut asked.

"We're waiting for Mr. Summerfield." I nodded toward the house.

"Let's see some identification."

I smiled. "You show me yours, I'll show you mine."

"Oh, a fuckin' wise guy." He flipped open his wallet to reveal a badge. "Jack Fogarty, FBI."

"Jack Armstrong, all-American boy," Harmony muttered.

"What'd you say, lady?"

"I didn't say *nothin'*."

Fogarty peered in and scowled at Harmony, affording me a capsule history of a lifelong battle with acne.

"I'm a private investigator," I said, pulling my wallet from my inside pocket.

As he looked at it, Harmony covered it with her hand. "You don't have to show him *shit.*"

Considering we were looking for a federal fugitive, I really didn't want Fogarty to know who I was. But I figured he was searching for Harpo, and I hoped to satisfy his curiosity by showing my ID and feeding him a line. I didn't want him finding out who Harmony was. That wouldn't help Harpo worth a damn.

"I want to see IDs on *all* of you."

I groaned silently as Nate got into the act. Looking at Fogarty, he hooked his thumb back toward the guy on his side. "First maybe you should tell us who Mr. Greasy is."

Fogarty's partner thrust his badge into Nate's face through the opening in the window. "Pete Wilson, asshole."

"That's funny," Harmony said. "I thought he was an FBI agent."

"Okay, that's it." Fogarty pulled a revolver from his shoulder holster. "All of you, out of the car."

As Harmony slid out, she said, "Have we broken some law, Mr. Fogarty, sir?"

"You got open beer in the car," Wilson said.

"Oh, is that a federal statute now?"

Wilson glared at her, shaking his head in disgust. "You got a real mouth on you."

Fogarty motioned us to the back of the car with his gun, then stood guard while Wilson frisked us. He did me first, a full-service effort with a few pokes in the ribs. If properly administered, that can hurt. Wilson was a good administrator.

"This guy's clean, Jack."

"Where's his ID?"

I shrugged as I turned around. "Gosh, I must have left it in the car."

"Me, too," said Nate, who had recently worked up the nerve to start carrying a small hand purse that Constance had given him. "But I don't have an identity. I'm a nonresident alien applying for political refugee status."

Fogarty stood at arm's length and measured us with that smug, all-powerful expression that some cops get. "You're a pair of fuckin' wise guys, is what you are." As Wilson began to grope Harmony, Fogarty's mouth curled into a smirk. "How do those nigger tits feel when you squeeze 'em, Pete?"

I could feel Nate tense up beside me. An instant later, his fist was pushing Fogarty's nose a few inches closer to the back of his skull.

"Like a sack of—aw, fuck!" Wilson screamed loud enough to be heard in Manhattan.

As Fogarty fell back, I kicked at his hand and knocked the gun loose. Nate landed on top of him, knee on his chest. I pounced on the gun and came up poised to fire, expecting to see Wilson taking aim for my head.

He wasn't. Sister Shamus hit him with an elbow, knocking him off balance long enough to stack the deck in my favor.

"Freeze!" I yelled, melting any hope he had of pulling out his gun. "Now take the heater out real slow, put on the safety and throw it as far as you can."

He followed the first two orders but balked a bit on the third. The throw was barely a Little League effort. The gun landed in a snowbank about ten yards away. That was far enough.

"Do you realize what the fuck you're doing?"

"Did anyone ever tell you you throw like a girl?"

As Nate got off Fogarty, I ordered them to lie in the snow, facedown. Harmony planted her boot between Wilson's legs and gave him a kick that made him groan in pain. "Now you can tell your partner how honky nuts feel when you crack 'em."

I held the gun on them while Nate and Harmony got in the car. "Count to fifty before you think about getting up."

"Have them recite the Jersey alphabet," Nate suggested.

I climbed in and pressed the accelerator to the street. I took a left at the first corner, then alternate rights and lefts. Both my hands were shaking—one from anger, one from fear. I tried to steady them by gripping the wheel as tight as I could. When we hit County 507, I turned north. I knew that would take us to the New York border, and the quiver in my frightened hand subsided enough to have a cigarette.

"I take back everything I said about detective work being boring. That was fantastic!" Harmony raised her hand, and she and Nate shook the new-fashioned way, with thumbs locked high and palms straight up. Nate had started shaking like that after a recent lecture tour of college campuses.

I played out my angry hand and let Harmony have it with both barrels. "You listen to me and listen good. This isn't the goddamned movies. It's real life. Those guys carry real guns with real bullets. There's no retakes, no trick photography, no stunt men. Next time we have to deal with cops, keep your mouth shut and let me handle it. I know how to talk to these guys."

"Talk to them. Who you kidding? You can't talk to them. Far as I'm concerned, I saved your ass."

"Are you crazy? You almost got us killed."

"Don't forget me. I helped."

"Yeah, that's right. Give Nathan some credit, too."

When we hit a town called Waldwick, I headed west on County 502 toward Wyckoff and gave it another try. "I turned forty last year. If you don't mind, I'd like to make fifty. Now

I've got to tell my bookie, who was nice enough to lend us a car, that the FBI will be coming to see him. They could be coming to see me!"

"Don't blame that on me, sugar. You're the one that showed them your ID. I tried to cover it up."

"I showed them mine hoping they wouldn't ask for yours."

"Well, I appreciate the gesture, but I assure you they would have."

"I don't think you need to worry about Fogarty knowing your name," Nate said.

"Why's that?"

"I was watching when he looked. His lips never moved."

I took a deep breath and tried to concentrate on driving. We went through Franklin Lakes, Pines Lake, Pompton Lakes and Pompton Plains.

"He ain't laughing, Nathan. I think he's pissed at us."

"Yeah, I think maybe you're right."

"He looks awful cute when he's pissed."

When we hit Route 23, I finally had an idea where we were. I pulled off at a Getty station, and Nate asked why we were stopping.

"To get a goddamn map and find a rental car place."

As I got out, Harmony put her hand on mine and gave me a look that would melt an iceberg. "Sugar, there's something really important I have to tell you."

"That's all right, don't worry about it." I figured an apology was finally coming now that I was no longer mad.

"No, I have to tell you this. I don't want you to get the wrong impression about me."

"Okay, what is it?"

She lowered her voice to a whisper. "I just want to make sure you understand that . . . *I do all my own stunts.*"

She let out a squeal, and Nate joined in. I could hear them laughing all the way to the garage, where a mechanic was cussing out a Chevy engine block. When I got back to the car, they were doing a lousy job of suppressing grins.

"Do you have any idea where we are?" Nate asked.

"Yeah, I know exactly where we are. We're in Deep Shit."

EIGHT

"Oh no, not again," Harmony said as I pulled into a Howard Johnson's Motor Lodge in Wayne. My parents had lived in this area for a few years before packing it in for Florida, so I now knew exactly where I was. Paterson was a five-mile poke down Ratzer Road.

"Yeah, these places are an obsession with the guy," Nate told her. "What's up, Renzler? You feel a craving for clams coming on?"

"New wheels," I said. "There's a car rental joint across the highway." I pulled the car around back. As I got out, I asked, "You kids want to stay here or go inside for a sundae?"

"Are we allowed to listen to the radio, Pop?" Nate asked.

"Just don't play with the horn. I'll be back in ten minutes."

While a teenager with teased hair and a name tag that read "Tammy" grappled with the car rental paperwork, I gritted my teeth and dialed Angelo Albani from a pay phone.

"Hey, Renzler, do I ever got a *joka del giorno* for you."

"I already got mine today, Angelo."

"Oh, that's right. Then I'll give you the bonus."

"Not now, Angelo. This is serious."

I gave him a capsule summary of our encounter with Fogarty and Wilson. I expected to hear bricks hitting the floor as they dropped from his pants, but I got an earful of laughter instead.

"Hey, this ain't funny, Angelo."

"You kidding? It's hysterical. Wait till I tell my cousin Dino about it. He hates the lousy fucks."

Dino, I vaguely recalled, had been acquitted of some federal charge a while back, but it had been a close call. His defense had been aided by the sudden disappearance of a key prosecution witness.

"I don't have time for this right now, Angelo. I'm just calling to let you know you better report the car boosted. Bad enough I'll have the FBI coming down on me. I don't want them going after you."

"Thanks a lot, Renzler, but don't worry about it. I think it already was boosted."

"What!"

"Maybe boosted's too strong a word. Borrowed's more like it. Let's put it this way: It ain't registered to me. So the only thing I'm worried about's them getting you on two beefs—beating on a fed and doing it in a stolen car. The stolen car, that's the one they'll get you on. Those lousy fucks love their stolen-car stats. But I can have it taken care of, if you want."

"How?" I glanced at the counter to see that Tammy the teased-hair teen was pulling my order form out of the typewriter.

"Fire up the hibachi, baby."

"But I'm way the hell out in Jersey."

"No problem. When your name ends in a vowel, you can do anything in Jersey. You ought to know that. Shouldn't cost more than two C's."

"Really?" I wasn't up on the going rates for a torch job, but that sounded like a bargain to me.

"Uh, Mr. McGuire." Tammy beckoned me to sign the rental papers as I placed my barbecue order with Angelo. Pat

McGuire was the name on the backup driver's license I had given her. I probably should have shown that to Fogarty instead of my PI badge.

Mr. McGuire's car was a black Camaro. It handled nicely on the half-mile ride around the traffic circle required to get back across the street to HoJo's. I told Nate to park the hot box in the farthest space from the building, as Angelo had instructed. Harmony helped him remove the plates while I smoked a cigarette and tinkered with the dashboard dials. I had a feeling she didn't want to be left alone with me.

"Now where?" Nate said as they climbed in.

I smiled at Harmony. "Have you ever been to Paterson?"

"Yeah, once too many times."

We had some time to kill before the PRF meeting, so we stopped by Western Union. Harmony had to collect her refund, and there was a chance we might be able to collect some information about her brother. The office was on a block with fewer discarded pint bottles than the previous one. But that had the Trailways station and a store called Prestige Liquors.

Nate stayed in the car while Harmony and I went in. The clerk behind the windowed cage rivaled Sheila Love in overall graciousness, but I figured she had earned her attitude. She was twice Sheila's age and three times her size. When we entered she was alternately trying to cajole and bully two winos back out into the freezing drizzle. They did a good job of ignoring her until she called the cops.

"Let them go to the damn bus station if they want to stay warm," she muttered as Harmony approached. Harmony didn't encourage her with a response, but she continued anyway. "This neighborhood gets worse and worse every day. Last week a gang of teenagers started beating the hell out of each other across the street. The week before that, a white guy and a black pulled out a gun and dragged some black guy away right in the doorway."

"Really?" My ears piped up at that one. There was a chance she was answering one of my questions before I got around to asking any. "Was the guy on his way in here?"

"Well, what do you think he was doing in the doorway?"

I didn't bother to point out that he could have been loitering. "Do you remember when this happened?"

"A couple weeks ago, I just said that."

"You don't remember which day?"

"Are you kidding? The days all run together around here."

Harmony shot me a knowing glance and joined in the pursuit. "What he's asking you is important," she said, pulling a crumpled receipt from her purse and pushing it under the cage. "You see, I tried to wire some money to my brother, but he never picked it up. We think something might've happened to him."

The lady studied the form as if it were the first time she'd ever seen one. After half a minute of inspection, she shook her head and chuckled. "If I sent somebody five hundred dollars and they didn't come get it, I'd think something might've happened to them too."

"Do you remember what they looked like?" I asked.

"Well, the one black guy, the one that was being dragged away, he looked scared. The others, nothing special that I can recall. They were all big, though, I remember that. And I remember thinking it was strange to see a white guy and black guy being together, instead of the two blacks against the white. People mostly stick with their kind."

"About how old were they?"

"Twenties, I guess."

"Do you remember anything else—what they were wearing, what they said?"

"Mister, I can't remember what I was wearing yesterday. They was yelling at each other, mostly cussing and whatnot."

"Did you call the police?"

"Police? Sure, I called the police. A couple of them come out asking questions and wrote some stuff down in their little book. They said it was probably dope dealers. I've been calling every day since trying to get his car towed away. It's the little Volkswagen out in front. I keep calling, but they don't take it. They'd rather keep piling tickets on the windshield. Pretty soon they'll be blowing all over the damn street."

I stepped outside to check out the car while Harmony waited for her refund. She came out holding a check, but I came up empty-handed. There wasn't any Volkswagen on the block, and the windshields of the other cars nearby were conspicuously devoid of tickets.

I went back inside and asked the lady if she was sure the car had been a Volkswagen.

"Positive. I've been looking at it every day for over a week now."

"Do you remember what color it was?"

"Color? I think it was red. No, it might've been blue."

"Well, whatever color it was, it's not there anymore."

"They must've towed it, then. It's about time something good happened for a change."

As I was heading out, a puffy-faced cop came puffing along the sidewalk. I tried to ask if he knew anything about the abduction of the VW or the black guy, but he had other things on his mind.

"Not now, pal. I'm responding to a call."

When he opened the door, I heard the clerk say, "Well, you sure took your sweet time getting here. I could've been raped, robbed and ransacked by now."

"But you weren't, right? So just take it easy and tell me what happened."

If they'd had a chance to start out on solid footing, the two of them probably could have grumbled their way into each other's hearts. Instead I figured they'd each go home from work with one more person to bitch about.

NINE

The "eciffo" of the People's Revolutionary Front, as it was identified in Sheila Love's coded address book, was housed in an old textile mill on Market Street that some big-dream developer had converted into office space. A faded sign over the doorway indicated there was still space available. A glance at the sparse listing of tenants on the lobby directory suggested there would be lots of space available for a long time to come.

The PRF headquarters was on the third floor. We probably would have taken the aluminum stairs even if there hadn't been an OUT OF ORDER sign hanging on the elevator. As we started up the first flight, Sheila Love came bounding through the door.

"What the hell are you doing here?"

"We came for the meeting," I said. "Nice of Juan to tell us about it."

Sheila shot a glance back toward the door, calculating whether she'd be better off leaving.

Harmony tried to help her decide. "Sheila, we're going to the meeting whether you do or not."

"And if you don't show," Nate added, "the wacky commander will probably think you're the rat who told us about it." The comment earned him a scowl I thought only I could provoke.

Sheila put her head down and started up the stairs. As she passed us, she glowered at Harmony. "You sure like white boys, don't you?"

"We're just trying to find James, Sheila. We won't say anything that compromises you."

I wasn't feeling as considerate, but I didn't see anything to be gained in giving up Harpo's girlfriend. There was a chance she would prove helpful, even if unintentionally.

When Sheila pushed open the door, I caught a glimpse of a short, chubby bald guy standing behind a gray metal desk. I figured him for Hartman as soon as he started scolding her.

"You're late again, Sheila. One more time, and I'm going to have you leafletting the projects." Hartman's voice was radio smooth and schoolteacher stern. Maybe that explained something of his appeal. It certainly wasn't his physical presence.

Sheila tried to slam the door, but I stopped it with my foot in time to hear her say, "I've got some pigs trailing me."

"What? What's going on here? And where's Judith? Why isn't she here?" Hartman was moving toward the door as I pushed it open.

"Maybe it's because her house is being staked out by the FBI," I said.

"What? Who are you?" There was a hint of alarm in Hartman's voice, but it was well controlled.

Sheila sniffed the air. "Smells like a pig to me."

Hartman didn't laugh, but her comment earned snickers from the three other people in the room. One of them was Juan. He was seated on a folding chair. The other two were standing. Both were tall and muscular, one white, one black. The white guy had long blond hair that could have benefited from a little shampoo. The black guy had an Afro the size of a basketball and shades that wrapped halfway around his head. I assumed they were the assistant commanders, Roach and Rodney.

"Private pig." I smiled as I handed my license to Hartman.

Roach and Rodney unfolded their arms and moved in behind him for a look. He passed it to Rodney, who said, "Pig with a capital P."

Hartman sized me up with cold blue eyes framed by thick black eyeglasses. The lenses may have enhanced the effect, but his glare made me shudder, the challenging stare you occasionally encounter from guys who mutter on the subway. I now noticed that he had chosen to fight the battle of baldness with a retreat to a graying-ponytail defense.

"Who are your friends, Mr. Renzler, and what were you doing at Judith's house?"

"We're looking for James Brown."

"Who?"

"My brother." Harmony stepped forward.

Hartman offered his hand. "That would make you Ms. Brown, I presume."

Harmony shook his hand. "Yeah, that's right."

"It's a pleasure. I'm Hartman DeWitt."

"I know who you are. Where's my brother?"

Hartman let out a little snort that was half chuckle and half cough. "I'm not sure I even know *who* your brother is."

"Yes, you do," I said. "We know that for sure, so there's nothing to be gained by pretending you don't."

Hartman held up his hand. "First things first. What's this about the FBI being at Judith's house?"

"They were there when we were this afternoon," I said. "That's all we know."

Hartman frowned, causing his glasses to slide down his nose. He didn't have much nose to speak of. "Roach, call Judith, see what's going on."

62

The burly blond guy moved at once, out the door and down the stairs. I thought maybe the PRF couldn't afford a telephone, but Hartman explained that he'd had it pulled out when the feds put on a wiretap. "When you're the leader of a revolutionary movement, you can't be too careful. The United States government will not tolerate the slightest threat to its hegemonous authoritarianism."

I nodded, as Hartman's followers were solemnly doing. I didn't see a gain in observing that any threat his movement posed appeared very slight indeed. You don't mutter back to guys who babble at you on the subway.

"This is the reason for the secrecy surrounding your brother," he said to Harmony. "We have to maintain security."

I could feel Harmony tensing up beside me, but she was doing a good job of biting her tongue.

"Your security's not so hot," I said. "It didn't take much effort to find you."

"Yes, I'm cognizant of that. And not unperturbed, I might add."

"Well, why don't you just tell us where Harmony's brother is, and we'll stop perturbing you."

"I simply can't do that."

"Can't or won't?" Harmony said.

Hartman let out a long sigh. "Perhaps you should explain why you're looking for him in the first place."

"Perhaps you should just tell us where he is," Nate said. "That way you can get right back to the revolution."

Hartman looked sharply at Nate. "Do I detect a hint of sarcasm, Mr. . . . . ?"

"Moore," Nate said. "I don't know what you noticed, but it's there to be detected."

Behind Hartman, I could see Rodney's gaze shift, slowly sizing Nate up. Even without a machine gun, he was as scary-looking as Harmony's brother. The effect had something to do with the feeling that he was incapable of smiling.

Hartman looked to the ceiling. "I suppose I could poll the members of the group. I'm a proponent of democratic decision making. Rodney, do you think I should tell them where James is?"

"I wouldn't tell nobody nothing."

"What about you, Juan?"

"Unless there's something to be gained, I don't see any reason to compromise the sanctity of the group."

"Sheila?"

"I think you should give me permission to break their arms."

"Violence is the last line of solution, Sheila. Negotiation, as Juan suggests, is the preferable option."

"Can you believe this shit?" Harmony shook her head as she polled the members of our group.

"I'm trying to be reasonable, Ms. Brown. Call it shit if you wish, but I assure you, your brother would think otherwise."

"You don't know shit about my brother."

"On the contrary. I know considerably more than you do at the moment."

"Being a proponent of democratic decision making, why don't you ask James what he thinks," I said. "We've alerted you to a security breach in your group and told you one of your members is under FBI surveillance."

"You raise a worthy point, Mr. Renzler. And I do believe in fairness. For which reason I am going to offer the following compromise. Ms. Brown, I will give you my personal assurance that your brother is entirely safe. He is in studious isolation, a program of spiritual and intellectual cleansing that is a prerequisite for promotion to the position of assistant commander in our organization. He entered into this willingly. For some reason, you seem to think he's in danger, but—"

"The reason she thinks he's in danger is because he called her and told her so," I said.

"I don't like to be interrupted, Mr. Renzler."

"Yeah, who does?" Nate said.

Hartman gave him a dismissive glance, then returned his spooky gaze to Harmony. "Your brother *is* in danger, Ms. Brown, though I'm frankly surprised he told you, because we maintain absolute secrecy and James is trustworthy beyond doubt. But the danger he faces is not posed by us. He is being pursued by the FBI in connection with an incident about which I cannot divulge any details. In fact, this is the most I've said about the situation to anyone in our group. As soon as James became aware of this circumstance, he informed me. He thought he should leave the area, not for his own safety but because he did not want to jeopardize our operations. I persuaded him to stay, because he is a vital member of our organization. I doubt you understand the subordination of individualism required for a revolutionary movement such as ours to succeed."

"I've read your rag of a newspaper, and I wouldn't wipe my butt with it. You're a charlatan and a fascist."

"Girl, you watch your mouth." Sheila took a step toward Harmony, but Hartman restrained her by holding up his hand.

"Your brother does not share your opinion, Ms. Brown. Now, I am willing to do this: If you write a message to him, I will see that he gets it and arrange for him to send a prompt reply. This is normally not permitted, but I will make an exception for you, despite your rudeness. What do you think of that?"

"What do you think of *this?*" Harmony had a gun out of her pocket and pointed at Hartman's head before I had time to blink. We had made a plan to coerce Hartman if conversation failed, but this wasn't part of it.

"Tell me where my brother is or I'll put a slug right between your eyes." It was a peashooter, but she was gripping it with two hands in a TV cop pose.

Hartman's hands went right up. So did Sheila's and Juan's. Rodney just glared, arms folded.

"Shooting me is not a smart idea, Ms. Brown." Hartman's voice had lost some of its smoothness, but it wasn't betraying panic yet. "I'm the only one who knows where James is."

I was inclined to agree with his first statement, and there was a good chance his second statement was true.

"Harmony, put the gun away," I said.

"How long are we going to play patty-cake with this blowhard?"

"Hey, I know you." Rodney slowly unfolded his arms and pointed at Harmony. "You're in the movies."

"I don't know what you're talking about, but this ain't no movie. So raise your hands like your sanctimonious guru."

Rodney followed her directions in a halfhearted manner. As he did so, he muttered, "Man, what's the name of that movie?"

I tried to conclude the negotiations by tossing a business card on Hartman's desk. "If you guarantee that you'll have James call Harmony at this number tonight, I think I can persuade her to leave right now."

"Tonight, possibly," he said. "Tomorrow morning for sure. Is that acceptable?"

"Don't ask me." I nodded to my left. "She's the one with the gun. Harmony?"

"I want to know where my brother is right now."

"Put down the gun!" The command came from the doorway. It had enough volume and authority for me to realize without turning that Roach was holding a gun of his own.

Harmony was angled in such a way that she didn't need a full turn to make eye contact with Roach. I could feel her shudder beside me as she glanced his way, but she managed to keep up a good front, still pointing her gun at Hartman. "You think you can do me faster than I can do him, you're wrong, sugar."

I took the risk of turning slowly to face the guy in the doorway. "If you start shooting here, Roach, the revolution's over. The cops and the FBI would love an excuse to bust someone at the PRF office. Tell him, Hartman."

"He's right. Don't shoot. Please, don't anyone shoot."

I could feel my heart starting to slide back down my throat. "Let's negotiate a little disarmament treaty," I said.

Hartman nodded. "What do you suggest?"

"Have Roach come in to my right and move around the desk next to you. When he gets there, we'll back out."

"Agreed."

"Harmony?"

"Yeah, fine."

As soon as Hartman nodded to him, Roach stepped inside and slid past Nate. When he got alongside me, I could see that his weapon had fallen off the same truck as Harmony's. If they started shooting, the odds of surviving were pretty good.

"Okay, let's go," I said, as Roach reached the desk.

Harmony adjusted her aim to Roach's head as we started our retreat. Nate went first, I went second. The whole process couldn't have taken more than thirty seconds, but it felt longer than a folk mass.

As Harmony backed out the doorway, she said, "If I don't hear from my brother tomorrow, you're dead meat, fat man." When we reached the bottom of the stairs, she said, "Whew, that was kind of a close one, wasn't it?"

"I could certainly use a fresh pair of trousers," Nate replied.

I didn't say anything until we got to the car. I started almost in a whisper, knowing I'd hit top volume by the time I reached the end of my first sentence.

"We had a goddamn plan, do you remember?"

"Yeah, I remember." Harmony nodded with her eyes closed.

"Tell me what it was."

She let out a long sigh. "We go in there and talk to Hartman."

"*Talk* to Hartman. Just talk to him, right?"

"Right."

"For what purpose?"

"To find out for sure if he knows where Harpo is." She spoke as if she were reciting something she'd heard a hundred times before.

"And what else? To get a sense if anyone else at the meeting might know where he is too, right?"

"Right, right."

"And if they won't tell us where Harpo is, then what?"

"We leave, we wait here, then we follow Hartman home."

"And that's when we start the strong-arm stuff, right? *After* we find out where Hartman lives. For all we know, that's where Harpo could be."

"Yeah, I know, I hear you."

"So what the hell happened?"

"I got a little impatient."

"A little impatient! You almost got us killed!"

"Stop yelling at me. Please."

"Yeah, you're coming in loud and clear," Nate said.

"I certainly hope so." I cranked the engine and started to pull away. "Because now you've blown it."

"What do you mean? How did I blow it?"

"Following Hartman's out of the question."

"Why?"

"Because now he expects us to follow him. He won't be going anywhere without one of his lackeys. Or maybe two of them. Or all of them. And they're going to be armed."

"Don't tell me you're scared of any of those mopes."

"I'm scared of anyone with a goddamned heater, and you should be too."

"Well, where's your heater?"

"It's at home, resting comfortably in my dresser drawer."

"Lot of good it's going to do you there. You mean you don't carry a gun?"

"Only when I go to the Bronx." That got a little laugh out of her. I found it hard to stay mad at her for too long. "Now, Sister Shamus, I'll bet she takes hers into the shower."

"What, have you seen the movie?"

I didn't know if she was kidding or not. "No, but Rodney has. And it's only a matter of time before that monkey remembers the name of it and finds out your name and figures out that your brother's name is actually Harpo Rollins."

"Come on, you don't have be racist about it."

"Racist? How am I being racist?"

"Calling Rodney a monkey."

"Nate," I said, "can you help me out a little here?"

"He uses that all the time. He picked it up from a Bogart movie. Renzler's an equal-opportunity monkey caller."

"Okay, I'm sorry, I'm just a little sensitive about that kind of stuff."

"It's all right. I'll try and be more sensitive about it myself. One thing I am sensitive about, though, is you ignoring everything I tell you to do. You've got to decide whether you want me to help you find your brother. Because right now, you've got me playing your movie sidekick, and that ain't a role I want to play."

"I know. I screwed up. I'm sorry. And I promise: I won't do it again. I'll start listening to what you say. Unless it's really stupid."

I held out as long as I could before shooting her a look. We locked good eyes for an instant before she dodged my glance, just long enough to catch her smile.

"I just couldn't listen to that preacher bullshit and those lies about Harpo being in isolation of his own volition. We know damn well he got snatched by those jerks. You heard what the woman at the Western Union office said."

"The guy who got mugged at Western Union had a Volkswagen. Harpo has an Impala."

"Yeah, but you've got to consider the possibility he was borrowing someone's car. Or maybe he got a new one."

"I'm trying to consider all the possibilities. And there's a possibility I want you to consider."

"What's that?"

"Is there any chance Hartman was telling the truth?"

"No way, baby."

"After all, your brother did join this group."

"Yeah, but Harpo doesn't believe in the crap this guy's selling. I'm sure of it." She paused to light a cigarette. "Nathan, what do you think?"

"I think I wouldn't believe a word the guy says unless I had one hand on his ponytail and the other on his nuts."

"Yeah, there you go."

"Well," I said, "we're not going to have that chance tonight. Maybe tomorrow."

"So what're we going to do now?" Harmony gave me a love tap with her elbow. When I looked at her, she smiled. "Boss."

"We're going back to Judith's. Hartman covered pretty well, but he was definitely alarmed she didn't show up at the meeting. We didn't stay long enough to find out if Roach talked to her."

"What about those clowns from the FBI?"

"If they're still there, we ain't stopping."

It took me half an hour to find my way back to Judith Fairbanks's neck of the 'burbs. I thought that was good work in the dark on sloppy streets. The sleet had given way to rain. It promised to be a brown Christmas, just like the ones I've always known.

I circled the blocks around Judith's house twice—enough

to convince myself it wasn't under federal attention and not enough to attract attention to ourselves. The only thing that gave me an itch was a gold Dodge Dart two blocks away. It was parked near a driveway filled with cars. That's the kind of space you look for to attract the least attention. I found one just like it around the corner from Judith's backyard.

I put up my hand as Nate opened his door. "Guys, I'm doing this one alone."

"Damn, you get to have all the fun." Harmony touched my wrist. "Just kidding, sugar." She circled the top of my hand with her fingers and squeezed. "You be careful now."

"Thanks, I will."

"You sure you don't want me to stand guard outside?" Nate asked.

"No, better not. Some busybody will see you and call the cops."

As I started to swing the door closed, Harmony held out her hand and showed me her gun. "Renzler, you sure you don't want to take this along?"

I gazed at the fence behind Judith's house and thought about the gold Dodge Dart parked two blocks away. I held out my hand. "Thanks," I said. "I think I will."

TEN

When I reached the backyard fence, I could see an inside light on in the rear of the house. Suburban trespass isn't my racket, but I was reasonably sure there wasn't an outdoor security system. While attempting to gauge the least visible spot to climb the fence, I noticed that the gate near the house was ajar. I took that as an invitation.

As I started up the steps, I could see that the door to the house was also open. Whoever opened it had not used a key. The frame was splintered near the knob.

The back door faced into the kitchen. Through the window I could see that breakfast had been the last meal eaten at the table. Someone had finished half a grapefruit but hadn't made it through scrambled eggs. I waited outside for a moment, making sure I didn't hear anything. As I slipped into the doorway, I thought I did. I started to reach into my pocket for Harmony's peashooter, then realized I was already holding it in my hand. It had been a long day.

I moved along the far wall to a doorway that opened into a formal dining room. An overhead light revealed a large oval oak table with a place setting consisting of an ashtray filled with butts, two coffee mugs with smiley faces, a pack of matches and half a dozen issues of *Our Struggle*. An arched doorway across the dining room led to a front room. I figured it for the living room, but I couldn't be sure. Beyond the doorway, the place was a cave.

I paused to listen for possible sounds from the intruder who had preceded me. I couldn't hear anything, but I saw a crowbar propped against a corner hutch. The bottom few inches of the crowbar were shiny and crimson. Some of the blood had dripped off the crowbar and congealed on the gray wall-to-wall carpet. Judith, or maybe her parents, was in for a hefty cleaning bill.

My stomach turned a notch at the thought of someone's head meeting the tip of the crowbar. But mostly I was relieved by the discovery. If someone was still in the house, he had put down his weapon.

I darted across the dining room in four tiptoe steps and took cover along the wall near the arch. I straddled the doorway and peered into the blackness, trying to accelerate the process of making my vision adjust. When I could make out the vaguely parallel lines of drapes on either side of a large window, I stepped into the next room.

To the right, I could see a hallway leading to a door about thirty feet away. The door was shut, but a dim light crawled out from behind it. After taking a cautious first step toward the door, I heard footsteps behind it. I took two quick steps in reverse.

I froze as the door opened, standing still long enough to steal a glimpse of a big guy in a long leather coat. He bore an uncanny resemblance to our recently reelected president, and it took me a moment to realize that the similarity had to do with the mask that covered his face. Nate had one just like it, but he made for a more convincing Nixon. It's a little tricky to do Dick with an Afro hairdo.

By the time I made these connections, I was back in the dining room, stationed near the doorway and poised for a surprise attack. I still had Harmony's gun in my sweaty right hand, but I had no intention of using it.

I could feel him at the doorway before I actually heard him. The instant he crossed the plane of the door, I kicked out my foot, cutting him off at his shins. My reflexes have lost a step or two over the years, but my timing this time was perfect. Too perfect, perhaps.

He tumbled forward so quickly, I was unable to whack him on his way down. He let out a heartfelt grunt, followed by an impeccable rendering of "motherfucker." He had a bulging file folder in the hand nearer to me, and the papers inside it spilled onto the carpet. He landed a foot from the table, Nixon beak buried in the carpet. I kicked his ribs as hard as sneakers would allow, then backed off a step and aimed Harmony's Cracker Jack prize at his head. I wasn't sure a guy who cracked skulls with a crowbar would be deterred by so little firepower, but it was definitely worth a try.

"Move a fucking muscle, and I'll put a slug right between your beady eyes." As the words spilled off my tongue, I felt like I was imitating Harmony doing Sister Shamus.

"Fuck you."

He was quick, much quicker than me, and stronger, too. In my defense, I might point out that I hadn't seen the long thin club in his right hand when I had put him down. More cautious people than I would not have considered the possibility that he carried a spare crowbar.

He swung it from underneath his stomach, lifting himself off the floor with a one-handed push-up at the same time. His aim was excellent, assuming he was aiming for my knees. The blow knocked me backwards, through the doorway and into the darkness. My right arm bumped the wall as I fell, making me lose my grip on the gun. I could feel it graze my shoulder as it flew deeper into the darkness behind me.

I looked up in time to see Dick Nixon under a mountain of black curls readying himself for another swing. This time the crowbar was coming toward my head. I rolled away just far enough to take it on the shoulder. I heard myself grunt in pain. It hurt, a lot.

It's amazing how fast your brain works, even when you're terrified, maybe especially when you're terrified. In the fleeting moment that I was left to wonder whether I would be struck again, I was also able to think through a strategy. I calculated the relative odds of groping in the darkness for the gun versus playing dead and hoping my attacker would stop at two blows. It came out a one-to-one shot on both counts. I opted for the turtle approach. He couldn't see me in the darkness, so for all he knew he already had crushed my skull. Plus I figured he was in a hurry to get going.

I called it right, but he took his sweet time about hurrying. I covered my head with both hands and tried not to breathe. He stood over me for what seemed like a full minute before wheeling into the dining room and scrambling to pick up the papers he had dropped. Through my fingers, I could see him leave one behind.

As he made his exit, my brain was still cooking. It occurred to me that I might have met Harmony's brother. But I wasn't about to call out his name to test that possibility. It also crossed my mind that he might not have not brought both weapons. The one with the bloody tip might have come courtesy of an earlier visitor.

I waited until I heard the back door shut before getting up. I wanted to split fast, but I also wanted to have a quick look around. My right knee and left shoulder were not cooperating much in that effort, but I managed to limp down the hall to the room with the light on.

The stain on the carpet in the dining room was merely an appetizer compared with the main entrée served up beneath Judith Fairbanks's head. But the floor in this room was hardwood, which is more conducive to spreading blood—and to spelling out words with it.

"*BITCH SNITCH*" was the phrase someone had chosen to write.

I assumed the dead woman was Judith, because the battered face had a vague resemblance to a girl in a framed photograph on the dresser. In the picture she was beaming, the fresh sweet smile of a carefree coed dressed in shorts and a Beloit College T-shirt; in person, on the floor, her expression was anything but cheerful.

The person who killed her must have been very pissed or very sick or both. Her hands had been tied behind her back with an extension cord, and her T-shirt, an orange and blue tie-dye job, had been ripped off. She died in bell-bottom jeans, which she had soiled during her ordeal. It was a sure bet this would put an end to my infatuation with bell-bottoms.

Judith's body was cold to the touch, and her limbs were rigid. She had been dead a few hours, long enough to make me believe the guy who whacked me was not responsible. Unless he had decided to hang out there for a while.

In the corner of the room near the doorway, some floorboards had been pried loose, revealing a space big enough to hide a bundle of papers. There were no papers there anymore. Next to the photo on the dresser, I noticed another framed picture, this one of a middle-aged man and woman standing arm in arm on a grassy lawn next to a sign that read BELOIT COLLEGE. I didn't recognize the woman, but the man was immediately identifiable, despite the additional hair loss he had suffered by the time I met him. The photograph proved that Hartman DeWitt was capable of smiling.

I tucked the picture into the pocket of my coat and made my way back through the house. I had to flip on the light in the living room for a moment to recover Harmony's gun. It looked like the carpet cleaning bill would be larger than I originally thought. The beating of Judith had started here and moved down the hall to the bedroom.

Back in the dining room, I picked up the sheet of paper that my assailant had left behind. Judging by the faint type, it was a copy of a photocopy. The heading was "United States Government Memorandum." The memo was dated 11/29/69 and was from SA Roy Martin Mitchell to SAC, Chicago. In FBI lingo, that's Special Agent and Special Agent in Charge. The subject was "Black Panther Party." Most of the page was taken up by a hand-drawn floor plan, with tiny print indicating the location of rooms, doors, closets, beds and other furniture. A typewritten note ran vertically on the left side of the page: "Attached is a detail of the address at 2337 West Monroe Street, first floor apartment, as furnished by William O'Neal on November 19, 1969, which information was orally furnished to the Chicago Police Department and Illinois State Attorney's Office."

The memo didn't mean anything to me, but if it was important to the guy who had broken into Judith's house, I thought I should take it home.

Before leaving I glanced at the clutter on the dining room table. The newspapers were mostly duplicates of the issue of *Our Struggle* that Sheila Love had given us. There also were copies of the *Village Voice,* the *New York Times* and a suburban paper, the *Bergen Record.* The local rag was open to page six. I took note of that because someone had circled a short item about Happy Rockefeller, the First Lady of my home state. The story said she had agreed to be a guest model at an upcoming fashion show for charity at a Paramus shopping mall on December 29th.

The ashtray was piled high with Virginia Slims, but there were a few Kool butts in there as well. One of the coffee mugs had dark red lipstick on the rim. The matchbook turned out to be the most interesting item on the table.

It was from Friendly Ice Cream, a family restaurant chain with twenty-four convenient locations, according to the ad on the back. The cover was open, but it was a brand new pack. Inside the flap, someone had neatly printed the name, address and phone number of Harmony's little brother, James Brown.

I didn't know whether James had left the matches there out of carelessness or if someone else had put them there with great care. But I was sure Harmony would not want that info left at a house where a woman had been brutally beaten to death. I added the matchbook to my souvenir collection and beat it back out to the car.

ELEVEN

When I told Harmony and Nate what had happened, it was their turn to accuse me of being reckless for insisting on going solo. Mostly it was Harmony applying the pressure. I had an easy time explaining why I hadn't used her gun.

"I didn't want to run the risk of shooting your brother."

That sounded much better than saying my attacker was too damn quick.

"Harpo's in isolation," Nate reminded me.

"There's always a chance he got out," I said. "And Harpo's not my first choice of suspects."

"It was Rodney," Harmony said.

"That would be my guess. Hartman sent him over to check on Judith. And to retrieve some papers he had hidden in the house."

I gave Harmony the FBI paper as I pulled into a diner on Route 9. From a pay phone, I called in a report of a woman beaten to death in Ho-Ho-Kus. The dispatcher asked if she needed an ambulance. I told him at this point all she needed was a few prayers and a clean sheet.

I returned to the car armed with coffee for three. Harmony was shaking her head and still studying the memo.

"I don't believe it."

"What's wrong?" I asked.

"Nothing, everything. I just can't believe I'm actually look-ing at this."

"I guess that paper means something to you."

"Means something? It means everything. This *proves* the FBI was behind the murder of Fred Hampton."

"How do you figure that?"

"Because Twenty-three-thirty-seven West Monroe was his address. I've been at this place. Look at this! Nathan, look at this!"

Nate and I leaned in from either side to read the tiny notation at the tip of Harmony's finger. In the dim light of the parking lot I couldn't make out what it said, but she read it out loud: " 'Room of Hampton and Johnson when they stay here.' " She angled her head to look at Nate. "Deborah Johnson was Fred's girlfriend. She was eight and a half months pregnant when those motherfuckers busted in and started shooting."

Harmony pulled her head up from the paper and lit a cigarette. I asked her to light one for me and started the engine.

"We always suspected the cops had a map or something, because everybody there said they knew exactly where they were going. They fired through the walls right at Fred's bed and just kept shooting. After they stopped, one of the pigs went into Fred's room and asked the other, 'Is he dead yet?' Then they heard two more shots, and the other pig said, 'He's good and dead now.' "

Harmony took a long drag of her cigarette. "And then, as if that wasn't bad enough, they hauled everybody else down to jail and charged them with attempted murder! Can you believe that? Fourteen cops barge into your house at five in the morning; they murder your boyfriend, and then you get charged with trying to kill them."

I figured Harmony had to be exaggerating, but I wasn't about to suggest that just then. She was starting to cry. I reached out to take her hand, but Nate beat me to it on the other side.

"I'm okay, Nathan. I just get so furious every time I think about it."

"I don't blame you," I said. "I can't believe this really happened."

"Oh, believe it, sugar. And they all got off. Three so-called investigations, but they all walked. This pig state's attorney Hanrahan, his assistants, all the cops, they walked." She held up the paper. "Of course they walked. The FBI was behind it, and they were the ones doing the investigating."

"Who was William O'Neal?" I asked. "The memo says he provided the FBI with the floor plan."

"Bill O'Neal. Brother, would I ever like to strangle that boy. He was crazy, always wanting to blow things up, start trouble. I never liked him. Harpo, he hated the guy. And it turns out he was right. O'Neal was the rat, after all."

After Harmony fell silent for a few moments, I decided it was time to broach the subject that had been bothering me all day.

"This morning, I went to see a friend who used to work for the FBI," I said.

"You've got a *friend* who works for the FBI?"

"*Used* to work for the FBI. A black guy."

"That doesn't make any difference, whether he's black or not. A pig's a pig, no matter what color he is."

"Well, he's not a pig anymore. Anyway, I asked him some questions about what you told me."

"You've been checking up on me?"

"Not on you. On your brother."

"And what'd he tell you?"

"You're not going to like this, but he told me he thought Harpo had been fingered as an informant for the Chicago police."

"What! That's ridiculous," Nate said.

"No, Nathan, that's right, he was." Her voice was surprisingly calm. "You've got to understand, this was a terrible time. Everybody was suspicious of each other. After Fred was murdered, it just got worse. Everyone knew there had to be a snitch. Some of them probably thought it was me. If you weren't one of the nine people in the apartment that night, you were suspected. That's just the way it was. But Harpo, he's the one people thought of the most. He was supposed to be there that night, but he was sick. But it wasn't like he had a note from his doctor, you know what I mean?"

Harmony turned her head, and I could feel her gaze fall on me. "This friend of yours, did he tell you anything else?"

"Yeah. He said he thought Harpo killed a guy, another Panther."

"Oh come on, now that's crazy," Nate said.

"Only half crazy," Harmony replied. "It was self-defense. He didn't have any choice. It was Leroy Martin. He challenged Harpo. He had him cornered. O'Neal put him up to it. He had Leroy convinced Harpo was the snitch."

"What happened?" Nate asked. "Did Harpo shoot him?"

"No, they just had a fight. Harpo hit him. He fell and cracked his head on the sidewalk. That's the reason I had to get out of Chicago. I thought someone might come after me."

"What about Harpo?" I asked.

"Oh, he got out of town in about ten minutes. He would've been dead. There must've been half a dozen people wanting to kill him. He went to Milwaukee and changed his name to Noah Dark."

"Noah Dark?" I asked.

"Yeah, he thought that was kind of cool, like he was starting a new life. That's why Harpo was so excited about stealing these papers, see. He wasn't just interested in exposing the FBI. He wanted to clear his name."

"Why didn't you tell me any of this earlier?" I asked.

"You said you didn't want me to bore you with politics."

"Harmony, this ain't politics. This is about murder and dirty tricks. The kind of stuff that doesn't bore me a bit."

"Okay, you want to know the real reason?" She let out a heavy sigh. "It's because up until a few minutes ago, when I saw this piece of paper, I wasn't entirely sure Harpo was telling the truth. I wasn't certain my brother wasn't the snitch who set up Fred."

"Wow," Nate said.

I nodded and glanced at Harmony. With the car illuminated as we approached the George Washington Bridge, I could see tears welling up in her eyes.

"You're not going to like the question I want to ask you," I said.

She shrugged. "That ain't going to stop you from asking it."

"Any chance Harpo killed Judith Fairbanks?"

"None whatsoever. Absolutely not. Harpo wouldn't do something like that to anyone, especially a woman. Unless . . ."

"Unless what?" Nate asked.

She closed her eyes again. "Unless he's gone completely, totally over the edge."

I didn't think that was out of the question, but I wasn't about to say it. I was still considering the possibility when we got back to my apartment. As I unlocked the third and last dead bolt, I could hear the phone ringing inside. I was short of breath when I answered.

The voice on the line was deep and soft, but definitely not friendly. "Are you the honky my sister's hanging with?"

"Is this James?" I thought I showed great restraint in not calling him Harpo. As Harmony grabbed at the phone, I covered the mouthpiece and reminded her to do the same thing. I would have laid odds that Hartman was listening in.

She nodded as if the caution was completely unnecessary.

Their conversation was short, three minutes tops. Every time Harmony started to ask a question or make a comment, she stopped dead and listened. Except for telling him I had found the floor plan to Fred Hampton's apartment. On that one, she managed to get through a full sentence.

When she put down the phone, she was shaking her head. I waited a moment for her to speak, but she remained silent.

"What did he say?" I asked.

He kept saying, "Everything's cool, baby, everything's cool."

"And you don't believe that."

"No." She stared me down with her soft brown beams and spoke in a whisper as she shook her head. "Not for one second."

TWELVE

I was saved by the bell from committing a lewd act with my houseguest at seven o'clock in the morning. In my wildest dream in memory, naturally.

Harmony beat me to the phone by several strides. At that hour it couldn't be Nate, but I figured Randall Edwards was a likely possibility. From what I hear, once you've got kids, you lose all perspective on when right-thinking people might be asleep.

I hovered guiltily, savoring the husky strains of Harmony's morning voice while waiting for her to hand me the phone. When I realized the call was for her, my feelings of guilt doubled, because I had a box-seat view of the playing field under the T-shirt she was using as a nightgown. But guilt turned to sheepishness when I realized that if she glanced in my direction, the telltale bulge under my robe would clue her in about the kind of dream I'd been having.

I retired to the john to get my house back in order. When I emerged, she was just hanging up.

"That was Rodney. He says he knows where James is, but he won't tell me over the phone. He'll only do it in person."

"Where and when are we supposed to meet him?"

"Not we, sugar. Me."

"No way."

"I've got to. He wants me to come alone."

"Of course he does. But this is probably the guy who slugged me with a crowbar last night. There's a real good chance he's trying to set you up."

"Well, that's a chance I'll have to take."

"Uh-uh. Rodney's not calling the shots."

"And *you* are?"

Arguments before morning coffee have a way of ruining my mornings. Bad morning coffee can ruin entire days. It's a pattern that ruined both my marriages. As Harmony glared at me with hands on hips, I stifled the urge to pressure her into doing what I said. For one thing, I knew it probably wouldn't work. For another, a surreal memory flashing across my brain pan made me realize that in my dream she had not been a consenting participant.

"Let's have some coffee before we talk about it," I said. Temporary surrender was a technique suggested by the counselor Katie and I had gone to. It wasn't a bad technique, but at a cost of a thousand bucks, it was a bit overpriced.

"We can have all the coffee you want. But you're not going to change my mind."

My teeth clenched, but I managed to let that one go by. Maybe I was developing the charm to give marriage a third try. "Where does he want you to meet him?" I asked.

"Six o'clock this evening at Friendly Ice Cream in some town called"—she looked down at the slip of paper she had written on and spelled out the name—"T-O-T-O-W-A. Do you know where that is?"

"Sure, Totowa. It's not far from his house. Did you ask if he collects matches from there?"

She gave me a quizzical look.

"The matchbook I picked up with your brother's address last night was from Friendly Ice Cream."

"You're right. I didn't even think of that." She shrugged. "It's a little early for me."

"It's early for me, too." I smiled as I handed her a coffee mug.

A grin began to spread over her face. "You like to think you know everything, don't you, Renzler?"

"I do know everything. At least most of the time."

"Shit."

Her response would have gone longer if it weren't for another phone call. This time it was for me.

Randall Edwards did fast work. And so did the former colleague who owed him a favor. He didn't uncover a lot of information, but the little he had learned told me quite a bit. Fortunately, Harmony decided to take a shower while we were talking. After hearing what Randall had to say, I decided it was wise to share only part of his report with her.

Randall's pal found out that Harpo Rollins was on the FBI's rabble-rouser index. "That," Randall explained, "means the G has a very special interest in nailing his black ass. Of course, we already knew that."

Randall said his friend had also determined that the last sighting of Harpo had been in Beloit, Wisconsin, more than a year before. There was no mention of him being spotted in Paterson, but Randall said that had occurred so recently that it wouldn't make it into Harpo's file until the next monthly reports were filed. With Harpo's trail so cold for so long, Randall was sure the only way he could have been traced was from a tip.

"Now, you want to hear the interesting stuff?" he asked. "My buddy ran a check on both James Brown and Hartman DeWitt. But he couldn't get anything on either of them."

I could tell Randall was waiting for me to ask why that was so interesting. I didn't make him wait long.

"The reason he couldn't pull anything is because both of them have protected status. You know what that means, don't you?"

I thought I did, but I let him tell me just to be sure I was right. It turned out I was, but I had trouble believing it.

"It means both your boys are informants for the G."

"You're kidding."

"Hey, I didn't make it up. Blame the FBI computer."

"Any chance the computer made a mistake?"

"There's always a chance of that. But in this type of case, the chance is somewhere between slim and none. And the chance of it happening with two people is somewhere between none and none."

"But that doesn't make any sense."

"Not to you right now, it doesn't. But somehow, some way, pretty soon it will."

With my head doing spins from Randall's discovery, I didn't do justice in relating our encounter with special agents Jack Fogarty and Pete Wilson. But he took special delight in hearing about his former nemesis Fogarty being left on the side of the road to suck snow. He didn't know Wilson, but he'd heard of him. Around the New York office, he was known as "Peter Piper," for having once beaten a bank robbery suspect with a lead pipe.

As soon as he finished cackling, Randall's mood turned sober. "You better watch your ass now, Renzler. If those guys find you, they'll make you pay big-time."

86

When I told Randall about the floor plan memo I had found, it was his turn to act stunned.

"Jesus Christ. Now *that* I'd like to see."

"You're going to get your chance. Today, if you don't mind."

With the likelihood that Hartman was listening in on the phone conversation between Harmony and her brother, I thought there was a good possibility he'd send one of his monkeys to my place to retrieve it. I had decided to make a copy for myself and leave the one I had found with Randall. He said that was fine with him.

Harmony reappeared wearing a towel on her head and her silk robe. The towel gave her kind of an exotic look, and her legs swishing through the robe gave me kind of an erotic sensation.

"Do you mind if I use your phone to call Chicago?" As she dropped onto the couch and crossed her legs, I did the genteel thing and averted my eyes. It was like detaching a beer can from a drunken frat boy. "I've got to call Brendan and tell him about that floor plan."

"Who's Brendan?" I could feel myself trying not to sound too interested.

"Brendan O'Malley. He's a lawyer who's handling the civil suit for the people who survived the raid on Fred's apartment. Brendan's the best damn guy you'd ever want to meet. When he hears about this memo, he's going to kiss me until I swoon."

"Lucky guy."

She shot me a smile that almost made me swoon. But I rode it out like the professional I am and shifted into business gear.

"Did Harpo know Brendan?"

"Oh sure. There was a time when they were almost brother-in-laws."

"Is there any chance Harpo might have gotten in touch with Brendan?"

"He should have, but I doubt it. Harpo wasn't real keen on his sister doing it with a white guy, no matter how brilliant or handsome he was. But I'll be sure and ask him."

I filed it away that O'Malley fit Harmony's notion of handsome. Like her brother, I didn't particularly care if he was brilliant.

Giving Harmony some privacy to talk to her ex seemed like the mature thing to do. I did it in the hope of scoring a few points. I went off to the shower to soak my bruises, starting with my throbbing shoulder and working my way down to my slightly wounded ego.

"Come over and sit down here," she said when I returned. "Let me rub that shoulder for you."

"Yes, ma'am." Within about two minutes, she managed to cure just about everything that had been ailing me since I turned forty. "Were you able to reach O'Malley?"

"No, there was no answer."

"Two days before Christmas. If he's like any of the lawyers I know, he's probably on vacation until Easter."

She pressed her nails so hard that I winced. "Not this lawyer, sugar. He ain't like anyone you've ever met."

A few minutes later, Nate arrived bearing bagels and newspapers. With his avuncular backing, I managed to strike a compromise with Harmony on her meeting with Rodney. She agreed to let Nate go with her, as long as he hid outside in the car.

"I've got another assignment for you, Nate," I said.

"Oh yeah, boss, what's that?"

"Didn't you say you gave a lecture at Beloit College a couple of years ago?" I was holding the picture I had found in Judith Fairbanks's bedroom.

"Yeah, the land of Wisco weed. You want me to call the woman who hired me and see what I can find out about Judith and Hartman DeWitt?"

"Exactly."

"I already did." He winked at Harmony. "Renzler and you ain't the only great detective minds here, sweetheart."

"Good boy, Nathan." She patted his head as you would a small dog.

"What did you find out?" I asked.

"Her name's Cynthia Moses. I found out she wasn't home and she's got a husband who sounds like Grandpa Moses. I left a message with him, but I'll call her back later on."

"What about you?" Harmony asked me. "What are you going to do?"

"I'm going to see Paul Weisberg."

"Who's that?"

I picked up Sheila Love's address book off the table and showed Harmony the notation next to Weisberg's name. "According to Sheila, he's a fascist pig. I've got a feeling I just might get along with the guy."

THIRTEEN

The ride to Jersey seemed a lot longer without Harmony, but it gave me time to think over what we had found out so far. I spent most of it daydreaming about her.

The fact was, I was starting to fall in love. I could tell it was happening because I kept repeating her name. A couple of times, I said it out loud. When I start doing that, you can stick the fork in me.

Naturally, sex had a lot to do with it. But it was more than that. I can be pretty domineering, but with Harmony I felt like

I had met my match. I felt overmatched, as a matter of fact. Being attracted to someone I didn't think I could control was new territory for me. And I figured it was healthier ground to be walking on, even if it made me feel shaky.

I kept telling myself I was crazy to be entertaining the possibility. I didn't have any idea what her status was, but I felt sure there was no shortage of guys lining up to meet her. A beautiful young black movie actress could take her pick. She was probably fending off invitations from Wilt Chamberlain or Bill Cosby, and that was just the C's. Whatever her situation, it was unlikely she'd have any interest in a guy fifteen years older than her. And a white guy at that.

The racial part complicated things. I didn't feel any reluctance to get involved with a black woman. In fact, I found the idea intriguing. But I had never dated a black woman, and I didn't really know any black women. For that matter, I didn't really have any black friends. Randall was probably the closest, and we rarely saw each other. This all had come about more by circumstance than choice, but when you grow up a white kid in a white town like I did, you don't imagine yourself being involved with someone who's not white. There's almost a built-in barrier against mixing.

I wouldn't dare say any of this to Harmony. She'd probably say I was being racist. And I suppose in some way she'd be right.

In addition to that, there was the whole problem of politics. It wasn't that we'd have such intense political disagreements—I'd gladly give in on my opinions if it made her happy. It's just that I'd get sick of the whole subject.

My reverie was interrupted by a report on news radio about a murder in the quaint little town of Ho-Ho-Kus. It turned out the victim was indeed Judith Fairbanks. The report said Judith had attended college in Wisconsin and was living at her father's house while he and her stepmother spent the winter in

Florida. I thought that explained why there were two names on their mailbox.

The report added that Judith was associated with a radical political group called the People's Revolutionary Front and that police suspected she might have been involved in a plot to kidnap Happy Rockefeller. I figured that meant the cops had found the newspaper on Judith's dining room table.

The one thing that startled me was the news that the police, acting on a lead from the FBI, were seeking a man for questioning in connection with Judith's murder: Henry "Harpo" Rollins.

Although I hadn't had time to search the entire house for evidence of Harmony's brother, I doubted the police had found any. The matchbook I had lifted contained the name and address of James Brown, not Harpo Rollins. Since the news report didn't mention James as an alias, it appeared that whoever had tipped off the FBI didn't know James and Harpo were the same person. Or maybe the tipster had deliberately left out that information. Or maybe the FBI had deliberately withheld that information from the local police.

As I mulled that possibility, it occurred to me that I was starting to think just like Harmony or Nate. Or, God forbid, Hartman DeWitt. The only thing I felt certain about was that the *Post* and *Daily News* would have a field day speculating about a plot to kidnap New York's First Lady.

I heard the report twice more before I pulled up outside Paul Weisberg's house on Godwin Avenue in Ridgewood about four o'clock. I was taking a chance that Weisberg didn't work a regular job. If he did, I didn't mind killing an hour on the sports pages and making acquaintances with his neighbors.

Ridgewood was a wealthy town, the sort of community where you might expect a fascist pig to take up residence. But the size and condition of Paul Weisberg's house suggested that he hadn't reaped any of the financial rewards you might expect to accrue to someone with that disposition. His was the smallest shack on the block, a modest box wedged between a pair of dolled-up Victorians. It looked as if it hadn't been painted since it was built. Judging by the aluminum storm door with the swirly *W* in the center of rusted latticework, I figured that had been the fifties.

Unlike the other houses, Weisberg's place didn't come with a driveway. That was the first thing that made me think the car parked out front went with his house. The second thing that led me to that conclusion was the make and license plate of the car. It was a white Impala, PRF 666.

I could've predicted the doorbell wouldn't work, but I gave it the old college try before knocking on rotted wood along the inside door. It took three knocks to raise a sign of life. That came in the sound of footsteps nearing the door. I noticed a curtain move near the picture window to the left and tightened my grip on the cold steel hand-warmer in my pocket. After my run-in with the crowbar, I'd decided to heed Harmony's advice, but I had my .38, not her toy.

The door opened a bit, not wide enough to fit an average face, but the one that peered out at me did not fit the law of averages. It was long and narrow, a rectangle. If someone were doing a caricature, this was a face that could end up as a hot dog. The top part of the bun came up to my chin.

"Yeah, what do you want?"

I flashed my license. "I'm a private investigator helping a woman who's looking for her brother. Are you Paul Weisberg?'

"Yeah, that's right." The door opened wider, unveiling tiny ears that were pointed at top and bottom. "What is it you want to know?"

I hadn't expected Weisberg to be so accommodating. I remained standing outside the storm door so he wouldn't feel threatened. With the inner door wide open, I got a full fix on his face. He had dark skin, but there was a quality of paleness about him, especially around the eyes. He had blond hair, tied tightly in a ponytail. It took me a few moments to realize that Paul Weisberg had a Jewish father and a black mother. But my gut told me right away that this was his parents' house. I figured him for about thirty-five.

"The guy I'm looking for is in the PRF," I said through the glass. "His name is James Brown. Do you know him?"

Weisberg made a point of repeating the name a couple of times before saying, "You mean like the football player?"

I put my hand on the storm door and casually pulled it open. "No, I mean like the singer."

He got that one right away, relieving me of the need to try humming a few bars. Then he shook his head. "Sorry, I don't know the guy."

"Then you want to tell me what the guy's car is doing parked outside your house, Paul?"

He sighed, a breathful of defeatism that steamed a ring on the door pane. "You said you were working for his sister?"

"That's right. She thinks James is in some kind of danger. All she knows is that he belongs to the PRF."

"OK, step inside, I'll talk to you." It surprised me that Weisberg was rolling over faster than a hungry puppy. "Anything I say to you is private, though, right? You're not going to repeat it to anyone."

I shook my head. "All I want to do is find out where he is so his sister can talk to him. She's really worried."

"He left town. Last week. She's right, he was in trouble. With the PRF. Do you know anything about them?"

"A little."

"Man, those are twenty-five of the most fucked-up people in the world, man."

"Is that how many members there are—twenty-five?"

"In this cell, and this is the primary cell, yeah, I'd say about that. There used to be about fifty. There's a few other cells. One in Germany, that's a big one. They've got about twenty over there. There's one in Greece and Sweden, too. Hartman DeWitt has people convinced the PRF is going to take over the government of the United States by the end of the century. But the first step is taking over the trade union movement. The target date for that is 1984." Weisberg's tone was mocking, but he didn't crack a smile.

"I was under the impression you were a member."

"I was. That was before they went weird. James was a member, too, but he couldn't take it anymore either. Hartman freaked out on him, accused him of treason. Have you met Hartman?"

I nodded. "Once."

"These days once is enough. He used to be okay. He's a brilliant guy, as a matter of fact. But about six months ago, he went off the deep end. He hasn't been right since. He went from a Marxist to a Trotskyite overnight. Now he's turned into a raving fascist."

"What happened six months ago?" I wasn't interested in hearing the evolution of Hartman's political ideology.

"I don't know. He just started getting really paranoid all of a sudden. I mean *really* paranoid. He accused me of being a mole for the FBI and CIA. Out of the blue. He was coming after me, too. He has these two guys, Rodney Jones and Roach Zimmer."

"Yeah, I've met them."

"Bad dudes, man. You don't want to piss them off. They'll do anything Hartman says. Anything. Especially Roach. He's the number-one man in the group. That's because he and Hartman have a thing going."

"You mean they're homos?"

Weisberg held up his hand. "I don't know where you're coming from, man, but I call them *gay.*"

94

"Right, sorry." I don't have anything against anyone doing whatever they want as long as everyone's willing. I just find "homosexual" to be an unwieldy word. "So what do you mean when you say Hartman was coming after you?"

"He sent them over here to beat the shit out of me. Or something. It could be he was going to put me in the chair."

"The chair?"

"An electric chair. Rodney designed it. Rodney would just as soon kick your ass as say hello. Everyone in the PRF's gotten really paranoid about informants. Especially Hartman. All he does anymore is rant about people infiltrating the group. So Rodney built this chair to give people shocks with. They use it to interrogate suspected informants."

"Have you ever seen them use it?"

"I've never actually seen it. I think they keep it in Rodney's basement, but they might've moved it to Hartman's."

"So what happened when they came after you?"

"I booked, man. I went away for three weeks. I lost my job on account of it. James is the one who warned me they were coming. We got along, James and me. We both realized things were getting weird. Nobody else seemed to. Except for this one girl, Judith. She knew he was getting weird, too. If you listen to Hartman's rap, he's really anti-Semitic and racist. But he's got Jewish kids and black kids hanging on his every word. He calls himself the supreme commander, and they believe it."

I considered telling Weisberg that Judith was dead, but I decided to hear him out a little more first.

"I viewed James as my friend. That's why I was happy to help him when he decided to split."

"When was that?"

"What's today—Wednesday? It was on a Friday, so that would have made it like, what, twelve days ago. He came to see me right before he left."

"What is it you did to help him?"

"I let him have my car. He was afraid they'd follow him. So we swapped. I shouldn't make it sound like I was any big help, actually. It was a good deal for me. I got a '71 Impala for a '66 Volkswagen and a couple of stamps."

"A couple of stamps?"

"Yeah. James said he wanted to send out a couple of Christmas cards. I thought that was weird. James doesn't seem like the Christmas-card type."

"What did James do that Hartman accused him of treason?"

"He didn't tell me. James is a very private individual. You don't force yourself into his space. But you don't have to do much to have Hartman accuse you of treason. Excuse me, it's not treason. The word he uses is . . . *sedition.* Yeah, that's it, sedition."

"Hartman told us James was in isolation. Does that have something to do with this electric chair?"

"No. At least I don't think. I don't really know what the isolation program is. I think you have to fast for a few days and read a lot. Mostly you've got to read Hartman's writings. He says the process is for achieving creative mentation. You don't get to do it until he thinks you're ready. He never thought I was ready."

I must have looked as baffled as I felt, because Weisberg grinned. "Yeah, I know, man. It sounds really weird, doesn't it?"

I nodded. It was beyond weird.

"But let me tell you something. You've got to be careful with Hartman. Don't believe anything he says. He's the world's best liar. James isn't in isolation. I'm sure of it."

"Where does Hartman get his money?"

"Oh, that's a good one. The PRF gets a share of everyone's wages. First it was like ten percent. But he kept increasing it. Now I think you've got to turn over like half of what you make. But that's not where most of the money comes from."

Weisberg paused, as if waiting for me to pop the big question. I obliged him.

"He sells pot. He's got a farm out in Wisconsin where they grow it, in this huge barn. Roach and James drive out there once a month to harvest the stuff and bring it back to sell. There's only a few people who know about that. I only know because James told me. This girl Judith that I mentioned, she goes to college out there. She does a lot of the selling."

"Not anymore she doesn't." I decided there was nothing to lose by telling Weisberg about Judith. I thought it might prompt him to recall something useful.

"What makes you say that?"

"Because Judith was murdered yesterday."

"What!"

"That's right. She was beaten to death in her father's house. It's being reported on the radio. Do you know anything about the PRF plotting to kidnap Happy Rockefeller?"

"Huh? Why do you say that?"

"Because that's what they're reporting on the radio."

Weisberg shook his head, and his ponytail came loose. "The PRF has gotten so weird, I wouldn't discount anything. But you can't believe what the media says either. They're all controlled by corporate power interests." Weisberg paused to retie his ponytail. "But man, that's too bad about Judith. She had great tits."

"Did James ever say anything to you about FBI documents?"

The question seemed to catch Weisberg by surprise, but I couldn't tell whether he knew something or if he was thrown by the sudden change in subject.

"Not that I can recall. Why do you ask that?"

"I'm just wondering what caused the rift between him and Hartman."

"Like I said, Hartman doesn't need a reason to turn on you. But if I had to guess, I'd say it probably had something to do with the dope operation. I think James might've been pulling out a little stash for himself to sell on the side."

"What makes you say that?"

"That's what I would've done."

"Did James give you any idea where he planned to go?" I was sure James hadn't gotten away, but if I could find out where he hoped to get to, I thought Harmony might know someone there he might have contacted.

"No, he never would've told me that."

"Why not?"

"Because James didn't know if he could trust me. The thing you've got to realize is, there definitely is an informant in the PRF. It's just that no one knows who it is. James told me he suspected it was Rodney. He thought Rodney might really be this guy named Harpo Rollins. He's a guy from Chicago who infiltrated the Black Panthers a few years ago."

"Do you think he's right?"

Weisberg turned his palms up. "Let's put it this way: Nothing would surprise me anymore."

"Well, don't be surprised if he comes back looking for his car."

"Why's that?"

"Because James never made it out of town. Rodney and Roach picked him off down at the Western Union office."

"Tell me you're kidding."

"If I did, it wouldn't mean I was. Anyway, your car got left there on Market Street. The cops towed it away yesterday."

"That's a bummer, man. That's bad news for James, very bad news."

"Where do you think Hartman would keep James?"

"I don't know, man. Could be at several places. There's Rodney's house. He lives in Paterson. Then there's the farm out in Wisconsin. Or maybe he'd just keep him at his house. Yeah, that's probably where he'd be. Roach lives there, and he could guard him."

"Do you know where Hartman lives?"

"As a matter of fact, I do." Weisberg grinned. "I followed him home from a meeting one night."

I wrote down the address Weisberg gave me, then handed him a card. "If you hear anything you think I might find interesting, would you give me a call?"

"Sure, but I doubt I will, man. I plan to stay as far away from the PRF as I can."

FOURTEEN

I found it curious that Hartman DeWitt lived in Clifton, my hometown. Not because of that coincidence, but because Clifton is a white enclave between Paterson and Passaic. For decades, Clifton was one of those towns that had secret land covenants barring the sale of houses to blacks. That changed in the early sixties, but it was still a white town and people knew it. I thought it was interesting that a guy who wanted to unite people and overthrow the government didn't live among his potential followers. Not that I was surprised. When a guy calls himself the supreme commander, you don't expect consistency.

In the twenty years since I had lived there, the town had changed quite a bit. Mostly it had just kept getting bigger, as all the wooded land was bulldozed to make way for subdivisions. Hartman's house was in a subdivision on the west side, in the hills near Garret Mountain. When I was kid, we used to sled there. A kid who tried that now would end up in someone's rec room.

Dusk was falling and weary dads in ties were returning home from the office when I got there. I parked a few doors down and watched the Christmas lights popping on all around me. The only evidence that Hartman was not living a totally conventional existence was the absence of any attempt to dress the house up for the season.

Although the shades were drawn, I could see that lights were on in almost every room. The driveway had two cars in it—a blue Volkswagen and a white Mercedes. I assumed that Hartman owned the Mercedes and the bug belonged to one of his drones.

Now that I was there, I wasn't sure what to do. If there had been no sign of life in the place, I would have considered another flirtation with suburban trespass. But with the supreme commander nestled in his fort with an enforcer or two at his side, that wasn't an option. I thought about ringing the doorbell just to press Hartman's paranoia button, but I decided it was more of an advantage if he didn't know I knew where he lived. I waited an hour to see if anyone left. No one did, so I called it a day.

The access roads to the highways had been shuffled since I was last there, and I had a devil of a time getting the car pointed back to Manhattan. Three bad hunches landed me on Main Street in Passaic, a town to give a pass to if you ever have the opportunity. I was all for passing through as quickly as possible until presented with an opportunity I couldn't resist. The twin bill at the Capitol Theater was *Chained Cheerleaders* and *Sister Shamus*.

When I got to the box office, I had already missed the first fifteen minutes of the movie I wanted to see. I didn't waver about putting down my buck, though I did pause a moment

100

to marvel at the giant poster in the lobby. I would have lingered longer if there hadn't been three teenage black kids doing the same. Standing next to them, I felt like an old lech.

The poster made Harmony look about seven feet tall. She was wearing a torn shirt that had been retied under her breasts and a pair of denim bell-bottoms that clung to her thighs like masking tape. The heater she was holding had a silencer that extended about half the length of her arm. She was blowing on the tip of it and seemed by her expression to be immensely satisfied. The source of her satisfaction seemed to be four dead guys sprawled around her high-heeled sandals. They were all white.

SISTER SHAMUS, the poster said. SHE'LL BLOW YOU AWAY.

I passed on the popcorn and Milk Duds and went right into the theater. On-screen, a fat white guy with a towel around his waist and a cigar in his puss was sitting by a pool getting a massage from a pair of bleached blonds in bikinis. Two guys with bad skin in cheap suits stood before him taking orders. His orders were simple and delivered at thirty decibels: "THE BITCH STOLE MY DRUGS! I WANT THE BITCH DEAD!"

As my eyes adjusted to the darkness, I could see that the house was close to packed. Slipping into one of the back rows was out of the question. They were filled with kids who should have been home eating dinner. I made my way down to the first available aisle seat. That put me in the third row. I had a feeling that except for the three stooges on the screen, I was the only white guy in the place. Before I sat down, I checked for the nearest exit.

Harmony was naked in my first glimpse of her on-screen. Although her body was obscured by an artful combination of steam, soapsuds and a sliding glass shower door, the libidos of teens in the theater exploded in a chorus of appreciative hoots. While she showered, the cheap suits were prowling through her darkened apartment, which had a suspicious resemblance to a suite at a Holiday Inn. The suspense built as the thugs closed in on the bathroom, until they were licking their chops and exchanging hungry looks outside the tub. As soon as each guy slid back a door and popped his head inside, Sister Shamus, who until now had seemed blissfully unaware of their presence, wheeled and slammed the doors shut, pinning each goon to the wall at the neck and causing the audience to erupt with applause. The cheering got louder as she emerged from the tub, still strategically covered with suds and holding a gun just like the one she had pulled on Hartman De-Witt the night before. Amidst the noise around me, I felt fortunate to hear Harmony's single line of dialogue as she put a slug into each thug's forehead.

"There! Two new assholes for two big assholes."

As the theater went up for grabs, Harmony calmly put on a sequined robe, wandered out into her living room, poured herself a glass of wine and turned on the TV. She looked stunning, but I was also stunned by the reaction of the audience. The woman I was falling in love with had more admirers than I could have imagined, and most of them weren't old enough to drive. Still, it was a kick to see someone I knew walking and talking on the screen. I didn't know any actors or actresses, and the only other experience that came close was an appearance by Nate on the Joe Franklin Show, a local TV talk show that aired at erratic hours.

It wasn't necessary to ask anyone for a plot briefing. It quickly became clear that Sister Shamus was a one-woman wrecking crew on a kamikaze crusade against drug pushers. Over the course of the movie, she left more carnage than Hurricane Donna, shooting, booting, sticking and kicking an assortment of deserving slimeballs into oblivion. Most of her victims were white and fleshy, but there was a handful of black collaborators who made the audience hiss and boo. Along the way she dodged a blizzard of bullets and took some punches, all the while modeling and unmodeling the latest fashions. During one sequence she was held prisoner in a cheap motel and shot up with heroin by a pair of rednecks. But she managed to escape, and by the end of the movie there were no more drugs and a lot fewer cars on the streets.

I didn't stay through the credits. I wasn't sure my head could survive the theme song, which featured an electric guitar that sounded like buzzing mosquitoes. But my real concern was that I might be a target for the cheap anger generated by the movie, a lonesome honky pummeled by a gang of rowdy black teens.

When I got home, Harmony and Nate were still out. An hour and a couple of beers later, I was pacing the apartment, dividing my attention between worrying something had happened to them and imagining they were having a great time without me. I decided to tackle the stack of clips that Harmony had brought. Most of them had to do with the raid on Fred Hampton's apartment. Now that I had seen the floor plan memo, I was interested in learning more.

The raid took place three years earlier, on December 4, 1969, around five in the morning. It was carried out by fourteen special-unit Chicago cops working for the Cook County state's attorney. One of the things that made them special was that they were armed with shotguns, a carbine and a Thompson submachine gun in addition to their regular sidearms. But none of them thought to bring tear gas, floodlights or a loudspeaker. The reason for the raid was that the cops had gotten a tip there were illegal weapons in the apartment. They did find a ton of guns, but all but two had been legally purchased.

Hampton was shot twice in the head at close range in his bed. A kid named Mark Clark also was shot dead, and three other people were wounded. Clark was in the living room standing watch, and the cops said he started firing when they knocked. The Panthers said the cops kicked in the door and started shooting.

Just as Harmony had said, the seven people who survived were all charged with attempted murder. At a press conference that morning, the state's attorney, Ed Hanrahan, said there had been a fierce gun battle started by the Panthers, and he held up a gun that he said Hampton had fired. Hanrahan arranged to have the cops reenact the raid on the CBS-TV news, and the *Chicago Tribune* carried their exclusive story, complete with photos showing bullet holes from shots fired by the Panthers. The next day the rival *Sun-Times* ran photos showing that the *Tribune*'s bullet holes were actually nail heads. When independent ballistics evidence was finally developed, it showed that at least eighty-two shots had been fired by the police and only one could have been fired by the people in the apartment.

Within hours after the raid, people from the neighborhood began touring the apartment to see what had happened, and soon there was a line stretching down the block. An outcry arose that led the Justice Department to open an investigation into the conduct of the cops. Along the way, it was revealed that the police autopsy and ballistics reports had been falsified. A later autopsy indicated that Hampton had been dosed with barbiturates. But instead of bringing indictments, the reds issued a report blaming both sides, and Hanrahan was finally persuaded to drop the attempted-murder charges against the seven survivors.

The thing that interested me most was noteworthy for its absence: In all of the articles, there was no mention of any FBI involvement in planning the raid, except for a wild accusation by a Panther named Bobby Rush. The only other references to the FBI had to do with the bureau's investigation of the cops after the raid. But if the FBI had supplied the floor plan before the raid, it was doubtful their investigation was very thorough.

I was so dazed and tired that I dozed off in the easy chair with Fluffy on my lap. I awoke to the sensation of a sharp object being jammed into my ribs. Fortunately, it was Harmony's finger.

"Wake up, Renzler," she said. "It's time to go to bed."

"What happened with Rodney?"

"It's a long story."

I yawned, stretched and got to my feet. "For you, I've got all the time in the world."

"No you don't. We've got to be in Paterson first thing in the morning."

"Why's that?"

"Because Roach is coming by Sheila Love's house to get Harpo's things and take them to him."

"Did Rodney tell you that?" I was standing at the kitchen counter, deliberating between hot coffee and cold beer.

"No, that jag-off didn't tell me nothing. I got that from Sheila."

"What was she doing there?"

"Sheila works at Friendly Ice Cream. She acted real unfriendly to me until Rodney went to the bathroom. Then she sneaked over and told me about Roach going to see Harpo. He's coming by her place at ten o'clock."

I frowned as I opted for coffee. "Why would Sheila be feeling so cooperative all of a sudden?"

"I don't know, and I didn't have a chance to ask. I just know she was a whole lot more cooperative than Rodney."

"What was his angle?" I asked as I sat down beside her on the couch.

"Rodney was angling to get me into bed with him. If I do, he says he'll tell me where Harpo is." She reached into her pocket and pulled out a key. "This is to his place. He says I'm welcome anytime—front door or back."

"Are you going to take him up on it?" I was trying to make light of it, but I was seething at the idea of Rodney coming on to her.

"Are you kidding!" Harmony put the chill on me with a murderous look and slid toward the other end of the couch.

"Of course I'm kidding."

"Well, don't. I don't even like to joke about that ugly creep putting his slimy paws on me."

"I'm sorry." I held out my hand. "He didn't touch you, did he?"

"Oh no, he tried to persuade me with sweet talk and charm. Of which he's got exactly zero. Only he don't know it. He was sitting in a booth in back, acting like the place is his own private club, stuffing his face with free burgers and fries. At one point he took off his shades, trying to freak me out. He's got a bad eye too, only with his, it looks like somebody did some back-alley surgery with a switchblade." She paused while I lit her cigarette. "By the way, in case you were wondering, it was definitely Rodney doing the bad Nixon imitation at Judith's last night. He was gloating about beating you with that tire iron."

"I hope you defended my honor."

"I tried my best, but, you know, you didn't leave me a whole lot to work with."

"Hey, wait a second."

"Just kidding, sugar." She reached out and patted my hand. "I accused him of killing Judith. That really pissed him off. He said, 'That ain't my style, baby, that ain't my style.' "

"What is his style?"

She snorted. "Being a pimp with no loyalties to anybody, waiting for his big score in an ice cream parlor. He was riding me for hanging out with white guys, so I worked him pretty good about being Hartman's step-'n'-fetch. He didn't like that one bit. He admits going to Judith's to get the papers but says he doesn't have any intention of giving them to Hartman."

"Did he say what he's planning to do with them?"

"No. Except that he's going to make a lot of money off them. I told him he could sell them to the newspapers, but he just laughed. This boy's got no political conscience whatsoever. I don't think he even knows what's in those papers. I tried to explain their significance to him, but he wasn't interested. I think he's a snitch. Why else would he join the PRF?"

"For the glamour?"

"Yeah, right."

"I don't understand why the PRF exists. I told you Randall Edwards says Hartman himself is an FBI snitch."

"Yeah, I know, that's weird." She got up and walked to the counter for a coffee refill.

"There's something else weird that Randall told me. And I'm sure you're not going to like it."

"I'm pretty sure I wouldn't like Randall. What is it?"

"He told me someone else in the PRF is on the FBI payroll."

"Who's that?"

"James Brown."

"Harpo! That's ridiculous!"

"Not Harpo. James."

"What's the difference? They're the same person."

"You know that and I know that and Harpo knows that. But the G doesn't know it."

"Uh-uh. Harpo would never stoop that low."

"What if he thought it would help him recover the FBI papers?"

"Whew." Harmony took a long sip of her coffee. "I don't know, I just can't see it."

"Think about it. We're assuming Harpo came to Jersey to find the papers. If he can convince the G to let him infiltrate the PRF as James, he gets a layer of protection. Not to mention a few bucks thrown his way each month. If that's what he's been able to pull off, I think it's a brilliant move."

"I love my little brother, sugar, but I've never exactly thought of him as brilliant."

"How about ballsy?"

"Oh yeah, he's ballsy, all right. He got that from me." She managed a grin and gave me a wink with her bad eye. "So we've got Harpo, Hartman and Rodney—all informants." She shook her head, as if to shake out the confusion. "Maybe the whole thing is a front group."

"A front for what?"

"I don't know and I don't especially care. All I know is I want to find Harpo and get ahold of those documents." She stood over me and let out a long sigh that seemed to signal the end of the day. "And right now, that looks like an awfully big Christmas list."

I got up and tried to be casual about putting my arm around her. "Don't worry, sweetheart. There's still one shopping day left."

FIFTEEN

Nate was limping as he made his way to my kitchen table. I didn't notice the bruise on his face until he sat down.

"What happened to you?" I asked. "Constance didn't like her Christmas present?"

"I haven't bought her damn Christmas present yet. I've been too busy driving around the goddamn suburbs." He glanced at Harmony. "Didn't you tell him what happened?"

She shook her head. "I thought I should let you have the honors."

"Oh, thanks."

"What happened?" I asked.

"I had a little run-in with our friend Rodney last night."

"In the ice cream shop?"

"No, in the parking lot," Harmony said. "It was after I told him to shove it. He followed me outside and grabbed me by the arm, so I turned and let him have it." Harmony demonstrated how she wheeled and slugged Rodney. From that point on, her account took the form of a reenactment.

"Next thing I know, Nathan's out of the car charging at him. Nathan takes a big swing." Harmony lunged over the table. "He would've killed the asshole if he hit him."

I looked at Nate. "I take it you missed."

He nodded sadly. "Yeah, I missed."

"By a mile," Harmony added. "So then Rodney sticks out his leg, and Nathan trips and goes sprawling headfirst into the curb. He looked like one of the stunt guys I get to beat up in my movie. Some of them told me it's actually hard to look that clumsy, but Nathan, he made it look easy."

Nate scowled. "I thought you were going to let me tell it."

"Sorry, Nathan. You want some ice to put on that sprained ego?"

"Just coffee. Hot, strong and made this week, if you don't mind."

"So what did Rodney do then?"

"Ask her," Nate said. "I was eating concrete."

"That's when he gave me the key to his house. He tossed it to me and said, 'Be sure and come alone. Don't bring along any of your honky clowns.' Then he got into his car and drove away."

Nate buried his face in his hands and groaned. "Beaten up in the goddamn parking lot of an ice cream shop. What's my life coming to?"

"Don't feel bad, Nathan," Harmony said as she refilled our mugs. "It could've happened to anyone. Look what he did to Renzler." She sat down, lit a cigarette and spoke through a cloud of smoke. "This Rodney's one scary dude. Two days and he's already kicked both your asses."

Nate pointed his finger at her. "Watch out, Sister Shamus, it could be your turn today."

"He comes after me, I'll put a bullet through his brain."

"You'd be better off aiming where it might do some damage," Nate said.

"You want another shot at him today?" I asked. "We need to tail him to see what he does with those documents."

Nate shook his head. "If I don't get my tail out to buy Constance a Christmas present, I'm really going to get my ass kicked. Besides, you don't want me behind the wheel of an automobile in the suburbs. I'd probably run over a shopping mall. How about your FBI pal?"

Randall Edwards turned out to be just the ticket. He was tickled at the prospect of tailing someone again. Especially in a black Camaro rented with an assumed name.

"Are you sure this won't put you in the doghouse with your wife for Christmas?" I asked.

"What makes you think my wife's in the doghouse?"

"I meant—"

"I know what you meant, Renzler. Don't worry about it. I'm Santa Claus in this house. Without me there ain't no Christmas."

When I got off the phone, Nate was filling Harmony in on an early morning call he had received from Cynthia Moses, his art teacher friend at Beloit College.

110

"Cynthia had Judith Fairbanks as a student her first term. She remembers her as shy and quiet—almost mousy, is how she put it. Over the next year or so, she underwent a complete transformation. That's not all that unusual, especially nowadays with the availability of hallucinogens, but Cynthia said the change was really pronounced. Judith became one of the groupies for a radical political science teacher who came as a guest lecturer for a semester. You want to guess who?"

"Hartman DeWitt." Harmony and I blurted the name at the same time. Nate said she won the prize for saying it in a more pleasant voice and with more contempt.

"Cynthia says he was nuts, not like we didn't already know that. But the person who was even nuttier was his sister. The school's on a year-round schedule, and she came out to spend the summer with him. At first people thought she was his wife, but it eventually came out that she was his sister. They shared the same dorm room. And the two of them really took a shine to young Judith.

"Cynthia said they got busted, all three of them, along with half a dozen other students. Hartman's sister was ordered to leave, so Hartman resigned and Judith dropped out at the end of the semester."

"What did they get busted for?" I asked.

"Smoking dope naked in the quad in the middle of the night."

"Big deal," Harmony said. "Sounds like the school's kind of tight-ass, if you ask me."

"It wasn't the school that busted them. It was the cops. And the thing they got them on was disturbing the peace. They were singing the 'Star-Spangled Banner' with dirty lyrics, through megaphones."

"I recall reading about this," Harmony said. "Didn't they file suit, claiming violation of their right to free speech?"

111

"That's right. But they lost. They were trying to maintain that their views had been censored, but the court ruled it was an issue of volume rather than speech."

"Yeah, I definitely remember reading about this," Harmony said, "but I didn't know it was Hartman DeWitt. The ruling was they might have had a First Amendment case if they hadn't been using megaphones."

I formed a megaphone with my hands and raised my voice. "Nate, did Cynthia tell you the name of Hartman's sister?"

"Yeah. Lillian Summerfield."

"Judith's stepmother," I said.

"How do you know that?" Harmony gazed at me with an expression approaching awe.

I shrugged and answered in my best aw-shucks tone. "It's a guess. Summerfield was the other name on the mailbox at Judith's house."

"Well, it's a small world and getting smaller every day." Harmony knocked back the last of her coffee and dropped the mug in the sink.

"Which means it's getting more and more crowded," Nate said.

"Especially where you're going." I enjoyed the idea of Nate fighting the crush of shoppers in midtown while searching out that special something for his special someone. That was one weight of married life I was pleased to have off my shoulders.

On our way to Jersey, Harmony read me the newspaper accounts of Judith's murder, adding commentary as she saw fit. At my encouragement, she did the *Post* and *Daily News* before the *Times*.

Both papers ran pictures of the house, and the *Post* had a photo of Judith's distraught father and stepmother arriving at Newark airport. She was identified as Lillian Summerfield, and she matched the picture I had lifted from Judith's room. Both papers played up the Happy Rockefeller kidnapping angle in a big way. But except for the newspaper item that I had noticed on Judith's dining room table, there was nothing in the way of solid info to go on.

Because BITCH SNITCH was scrawled in blood on Judith's floor, one of the cops described the murder scene as having a "Manson-like" atmosphere. "Yeah, right," Harmony sneered. "Like you were at that one, too." Although there was no reference to Hartman, Judith's association with the PRF was mentioned. Harpo was identified only as "a radical federal fugitive, believed to be armed and dangerous."

The *Times* was predictably restrained but thorough. The story was buried near the back of the front section, but it included the photo of Harpo that had run with the clipping Harmony had brought when she came to see me. There was no mention of James Brown, but Hartman was identified as the founder and chairman of the PRF. The *Times* also reported that Judith's father, Edward, had once worked as an aide to Nelson Rockefeller.

"Hey, this guy sounds OK," Harmony said. "It says he quit working for Rockefeller after publicly criticizing the governor's handling of the Attica prison uprising."

"That probably means he was fired."

"Yeah, right. Listen to this quote from Rockefeller: 'We have heard nothing to suggest the existence of any kidnapping plot, but in these turbulent times I would not put anything, I repeat, *anything,* past any of these scurrilous radical groups looking to undermine the very fabric of our way of life.' "

"I think he means *his* way of life," I said.

That got a chuckle out of Harmony. "Yeah," she said, "inheriting millions from carpetbagging ancestors."

"Did you hear what Nelson said to the press after Happy's second mastectomy?" I asked.

"No, what's that?"

"Gentlemen, I assure you, this won't happen again."

"Did he really? Come on, you're kidding me."

If I had insisted I was serious, everything would have been fine. But the instant I owned up, Harmony let me have it with both barrels.

"Do you think that's funny, Renzler? A woman having breast cancer?"

"No, of course not."

"Then why are you laughing?"

"The joke's not about cancer. It's about politicians and how they never say anything straight."

"Is that right? Well, you could've fooled me. It's too bad more of Nathan doesn't rub off on you, that's all I got to say."

I started to respond, but she put out her hand and covered my mouth. "Please don't say anything, this is upsetting me."

I thought she was overreacting, but I didn't want to make an issue of it. I wasn't making light of breast cancer, but I understood how she might think I was—if she wasn't listening carefully or had some personal reason to be upset about the subject. So I just kept my mouth shut, even after she slid her hand away to light a cigarette.

I lit my own and thought over her suggestion that I should try to be more like Nate. He was, after all, more sensitive to these delicate matters than I was. And even if I didn't want to follow his example in the interest of being a more decent person, it was looking more and more like acting sensitive was essential to getting laid nowadays.

I thought about that for most of my cigarette while we drove in silence along Route 46. When we reached our exit, I decided to attempt an apology, a simple unequivocal "I'm sorry." But as I parted my lips, another thought flashed across my mind and a different set of words came careening out of my mouth.

"Fuck Nate!" I heard myself say.

"What?"

"Fuck Nate," I repeated. "He's the one who told me the goddamn joke to begin with!"

SIXTEEN

I considered stopping for a look at Rodney's place before going to Sheila's, but I figured Rodney wouldn't have given Harmony his house key if there was anything worth finding. Better to be sure we were on time to follow Roach. As Eddie Casanova, my high school baseball coach, used to say, "You can only hit one ball at a time, so one pitch is all you should ever be thinking about." Eddie doubled as a history teacher and taught in sports metaphors.

The blue Volkswagen I had seen at Hartman's was parked outside Sheila's when we arrived. I backed into the alley at the end of the block. From that vantage it was easy to keep an eye on Sheila's door, but it would be hard for anyone coming down the street to see us. After about ten minutes, Sheila poked her head outside. Her gaze stopped on our car for a moment, then she closed the door. A minute later, it opened again. This time Sheila stepped out with Roach. He was carrying a supermarket shopping bag.

"This doesn't strike me as kosher," I said as we watched Roach walk toward his car.

"Why not?"

"It's almost like Sheila was making sure we were here before letting him leave."

"She probably is. What's wrong with that?"

"Nothing, as long as she's doing it for our benefit. I'm not so sure she is."

"You think Roach has been waiting for us to get here?"

"Yeah. But I hope I'm wrong."

"So do I."

Roach took his sweet time taking off, and we cooled our wheels as long as we could without losing him. As we passed, Sheila acknowledged us with a nonchalant wave. I stayed three cars back as Roach cruised along Union Boulevard toward Totowa. When he reached Route 80, he turned onto the westbound ramp.

"Except for a few sections in Jersey, this is completed all the way to California," I told Harmony.

"Great. Let's just hope we're not going there."

Two hours later we crossed the Delaware, with far less fanfare than George Washington two centuries earlier and in the opposite direction.

"Damn. Where in the hell is this boy going?"

"Paul Weisberg mentioned a pot farm in Wisconsin."

"Damn." Harmony shook her head as she grabbed cigarettes off the dashboard. "Do you have any idea how far Wisconsin is?"

"Somewhere between Michigan and Montana, I hear."

"You hear right. If we drive straight through, we won't be there until tomorrow."

"That's far."

"Damn right it is. He better be going wherever the hell Harpo is, that's all I got to say."

"Hold on a second, don't get frazzled. We don't even know if he's going to Wisconsin."

"That's what's making me frazzled—we don't know where the hell it is we're going!"

116

"And we won't find out until we get there. So why not just sit back, relax, and enjoy ourselves."

Harmony's head swiveled, and she shot me an astonished gaze. "I never would've expected such a cheery attitude from you. I guess your cynicism's just a cover, huh?"

"Well, really. I've had a lot worse things to do than drive across country with a beautiful, charming, intelligent woman." I said it like I meant it, because I did. But it still felt strange.

"What a sweet thing to say, Renzler, I like that. And don't forget, you're in a beautiful car too, and it's almost Christmas. That makes the whole thing extra special."

I knew she was being sarcastic about the car, but I wasn't sure about the other part. She fiddled with the radio for the better part of an hour, getting nothing but religious and country stations, all filled with static. She settled on Tammy Wynette singing "Jingle Bells" for almost a full minute, then clicked it off. "Damn. I'm trying to find a few Christmas carols and all they've got is cracker music."

Roach pulled in at a truck stop somewhere between Bethlehem and Intercourse. I sneaked inside and got us take-out burgers on the professional side of the joint. When I returned to the car, "Papa Was a Rolling Stone" was blasting out of the dashboard. Harmony was singing along, and she knew every word.

Around ten o'clock, John J. Gilligan, the governor of Ohio, welcomed us to the Buckeye state and reminded us to buckle up. "And watch out for the fucking National Guard if you go near Kent State!" Harmony shouted at the billboard.

Near Youngstown, we hit snow flurries. Around Cleveland, it was starting to stick.

"Tell me about your eye," she said.

I gave her the *Reader's Digest* version, even though there was time for a two-parter in the *New Yorker*.

"I was playing for the Richmond Sailors, a triple-A team. I was batting against a pitcher who had a reputation for being wild and fast. He cranked one up, and his reputation preceded the ball high and inside. I'm not sure I even saw it. People told me there was a hush over the ballpark, one of those agonizing moments when people look at each other wondering if the guy's dead. Of course I wasn't aware of that. I didn't hear the applause when they carried me off on the stretcher. I was told there wasn't much. People were too worried thinking I was dead to clap."

I paused for dramatic effect and lit a cigarette. "Then I hopped off the stretcher and trotted down to first base."

"What! You didn't!"

"Uh-uh. I woke up looking at a spiderweb on the ceiling of the hospital room. The whole left side of my face was bandaged."

"Come on. That's not fair. How can you make a joke about that?"

"It happened a long time ago. Enough time passes, you can make a joke about anything."

"I don't buy that, but go on."

"The doctors said I was lucky—an inch or two over and it would have been lights out for good. I didn't feel so lucky. I went home and lived with my parents and sulked for a year."

"Then what did you do?"

"Oh, you're going to like this."

"You became a cop."

"Right. N-Y-P-D."

"And how long did you last at that?"

"A little longer than the pitcher who beaned me."

"What happened to him?"

"He got his control under control long enough to pitch two games for the Pittsburgh Pirates. His first outing, he struck out eight and walked six. The second, he pitched to five guys. He walked three and beaned two."

"Do you remember his name?"

"Of course. You don't forget the name of the guy that beaned you. I can still picture his face."

"What was his name?"

"It was . . . shit . . . I don't remember." This was the first time I couldn't recall the name of the pitcher who beaned me. "He was a beaner . . . It began with a—"

"A what?"

"I'm sorry. A Mexican. Don't get on my case for that right now, OK?" I grabbed a cigarette. "I don't believe it! I can't remember!"

She put her hand on my shoulder. "Don't worry, sugar, it'll come to you."

Harmony took over the driving around Sandusky, Ohio, and I took control of the radio dial. We made the switch while Roach relieved himself in a rest area. I took care of my business near a rotting picnic table. Harmony had the kind of kidneys you'd want for a chugalug contest at a church picnic, so she stayed in the car. When I got back, Buck Owens was belting out "Santa Looked a Lot Like Daddy." My traveling companion refrained from harmonizing.

Sometime after midnight, we made Indiana, a flat dark land with no sign of civilization except for a flush of fluorescence every thirty miles or so. Each service area was named for a famous Hoosier. We whistled by Joyce Kilmer, but we were down to forty when we passed Booth Tarkington. By the time we approached Knute Rockne, we were going slower than four horsemen in a snowdrift. We came to a stop in a sea of flashing lights, and a state trooper informed us that Route 80 was closed all the way to Chicago.

"You mean we've got to stay here, at this damn truck stop!"

"Out here we call them Oases, ma'am."

"Well, how long do you think we're going to be stuck at this Oasis, Officer?"

"If you're asking me when the snow's going to stop, I can only tell you I'm not a weatherman."

"I see. Well, we don't need one of them to tell us which way the wind is blowing, do we?"

The trooper gave her a baffled look. "No ma'am. But I can tell you what they say about Indiana weather."

"And what's that?"

"Stick around five minutes and it could change."

"Well, Merry Christmas, Officer." Harmony spoke in a cheery voice, but as we pulled away, she muttered, "That's the same crap they say about the weather everywhere, you dumb pig."

"Something tells me you're not in the Christmas spirit yet."

"Do *you* want to spend Christmas at a damn truck stop in Indiana?"

"You mean the Oasis, ma'am? If I have to be stranded in Indiana, there's no one I'd rather be stranded with."

"That's awfully sweet, Renzler. I hope you're not offended that I'd prefer to be spending Christmas in Holyoke with my mother."

"No, I understand. I'd like to be spending Christmas in Florida with my mother. Of course, I can't do that anymore."

Suddenly, I felt my eyes filling with tears. Harmony didn't say anything. She just reached out and put her hand on mine. I was silent as she pulled into the lot and parked one row behind and two spaces over from Roach. I couldn't have spoken if I wanted to, because I had a lump in my throat the size of a snowball.

From our spot in the lot, we had a clear view into the glassed-in complex. Most of the stranded motorists were laying out sleeping berths with rolled-up overcoats. The heartier ones were standing near the vending machines in the center lobby, drinking coffee and making new friends. We watched Roach go inside and set up camp on the east end of the complex. When our kidneys finally gave out, we went in together, taking turns standing lookout near the rest rooms. While I was on watch, I ducked into the canteen to get coffee. I was hungry enough to take a chance on one of the delicacies you usually find in the display case, but it was empty, and there was a hand-lettered sign near the cash register: NO MORE FOOD, SO DON'T ASK, JUST DRINKS.

Yeah, and a Merry Fucking Christmas to you, too.

We retreated to the car and tried to stay warm drinking coffee, smoking cigarettes and telling stories. Pretty soon the coffee gave out, the smoke got thick and the storytelling grew as tired as we were. There was nothing left to do except sleep, but that's not what was on our minds.

Harmony leaned across the stick shift, and I slid over to meet her, easing my shoulder into the opening between the seats to support her weight. It was a position that should have felt uncomfortable but didn't because it was supplanted by a much stronger sensation.

"Oh, sugar, I wish we were home cuddled up in bed."

"You and me both."

I lifted my head and our faces met, exploring in the dark until our lips touched, softly at first, then pressed together tightly as we steadied and found a purchase. We stayed like that for a few wonderful moments until our mouths opened and our tongues met, darting and pushing and sliding and reaching. She shifted her weight closer, and I lost my balance momentarily. I regained it by reaching out with my left hand and discovered, an instant after the fact, that I had latched onto her breast. I thought to pull my hand away, but it would have meant toppling into the back seat. She didn't pull away, or perhaps couldn't, so I did the thing that came naturally, stroking with my fingers. Regrettably, "Santa Looked a Lot Like Daddy" was still playing in my head.

She let out a murmur that I took for approval. We held that position for a long time, until her head shifted and fell, on the verge of sleep, then docked in the nook where my neck and shoulder meet.

"Merry Christmas, sugar," she said sleepily.

The next time I saw her she was asleep in a rocking chair, sitting before a Christmas tree decorated with black and white lights. There was a guy standing over her, but it wasn't me. It was my buddy Nate, dressed in boxer shorts with black Santas on them. "Baby," he yelled, "let's rock and roll!"

I woke up in an ice-cold sweat, half frozen, the other half good and pissed off. At Nate, not Harmony. Just then, by some quirk of brain chemistry, two words came to me and I blurted them out. "Carlos Barrera!" He was the guy who beaned me.

The clock had long since given up keeping time, so I tuned in the radio. It was six-thirty on Country 740 in Wheeling, West Virginia. I slipped out of the car and shivered my way into Knute Rockne's little acre of Hoosier heaven, where bleary travelers were curled up against cinder-block walls and plastic furniture. A few creatures were stirring, but most of the hundred or so folks camped on the carpet were still dreaming about what Santa would leave under their trees if they ever got home.

I went into the bathroom and marveled at the automatic urinal flushers that went into action as soon as you crossed the plane of a magical sensor. While stocking up on what passed for coffee, I overheard someone saying the trooper had said that the interstate was open again. I went outside, brushed the snow off the car windows and waited for Roach. He appeared fifteen minutes later. When Harmony woke up, we were driving past huge steel mills belching giant funnels of smoke into the air.

"Where are we?" She stretched, yawned and rubbed her eyes.

"Good morning, Merry Christmas and welcome to Gary, Indiana." I handed her a cup of cold coffee. "If it's any consolation, it wasn't good when it was hot."

"Well," she said. "It looks like our boy is heading to Chicago."

I slid a cigarette out of the pack in my pocket and flipped it end over end into the air. With perfect timing, I snared it with my lips.

"Hey, where did you learn to do that?"

The truth was I had learned it from a teammate in Richmond, a pitcher named Gerry Judge. Gerry smoked three packs a day, but his real problem was booze and broads. When he had too few or too many of either, he had a hard time finding the plate. In the game I got beaned, Gerry came on in relief and managed to find Carlos Barrera's knee. He later told me he had been aiming for his head. It took him four pitches to hit a guy who weighed 250 pounds. The benches cleared after it happened, and this time Barrera got his clock cleaned by my roommate, Eddie Reardon.

I didn't tell Harmony any of that. "I saw someone do it in a movie," I said.

A grin spread over her face, and her eyes caught what little sunlight there was reflecting off the snow. "Shit, you saw my picture. When did you do that?"

"The night before last, when you were seeing Rodney."

"Why didn't you mention it sooner?"

"I was waiting for the right moment. I guess I wanted to surprise you."

"Well, you did. So what did you think?"

I took a deep breath. "You," I said, "were wonderful."

"Yeah yeah, thanks. But the movie sucked, right?"

"I wouldn't say that."

"But it won't make anyone forget *The Maltese Falcon.*"

"No, it's not likely to do that. But I doubt it was intended to."

"You're right. It was intended to make a lot of money. Mostly for a few short fat bald white guys."

"You don't sound too pleased about the whole thing."

"Oh no, I am. I'm hoping it will get me noticed and I might get to play some serious roles. They're talking about doing a sequel if this one does well. If they do, my price is going up."

"I'd count on there being a sequel."

"Why's that? A lot of people were there?"

"Oh yeah." I didn't see any gain in mentioning that some of them might have been there for *Chained Cheerleaders.*

"How old were they?"

"Mostly about fifteen or sixteen. To tell you the truth, it made me a little uncomfortable."

"You mean because of the nudity."

"Yeah. Among kids that age, I felt kind of self-conscious being there."

"You're just older and more uptight about that stuff. I'm a lot freer, you know, being from a different generation and all. Was it all black folks?"

"Yeah, just about. And to be honest, sitting there through a movie where everybody's talking about killing whitey, that made me a little nervous, too."

"A little nervous! Ha! I'll bet you were so scared you almost peed your pants."

"It wasn't that bad," I lied. "I was just a little uneasy."

"I know the feeling, believe me. I've felt that way most of the days of my life."

I thought to challenge her on that, but once I thought about it, I thought the better of it. She took two cigarettes out of the pack, flipped them both, smooth as silk, lit them and sighed through a mountain of smoke. "Well, this is a cheery subject for Christmas morning now, ain't it?"

A few moments later, Roach changed the subject for us. A quarter mile ahead, the blue Beetle was making for an exit.

SEVENTEEN

We followed Roach east on North Avenue toward Lincoln Park. I wouldn't have known that was the direction we were going if Harmony hadn't told me. The street was eerily deserted, or perhaps cheerily, depending on what people were doing inside their apartments. We drove about sixteen blocks, until the rows of two- and three-story buildings gave way to high-rises. When we hit Clark Street, the park suddenly appeared to our left. Beyond it, in the distance, Lake Michigan was a foaming tundra.

Roach turned right on Clark and parked halfway down the block. We pulled over and watched him get out and walk straight to a corner coffee shop called The Original Mitchell's.

"What do you suppose he's doing, meeting someone?" Harmony asked.

"He could be going for the two-by-four," I said, noting the giant sign for the breakfast special on the window.

I might not have gotten his order right, but a few moments later we saw Roach take up solitary residence at a counter in back. From our distant vantage, he was about the size of a roach.

"You know, Brendan's office is only a couple blocks from

here," Harmony said. "At least it used to be. There's a pay phone over in the park. I'm going to call him."

"I doubt he'd be working on Christmas."

"You don't know this guy. He's dedicated. I'd like for you to meet him."

"A lawyer who works on Christmas, I'd like to meet him myself."

No matter how dedicated Harmony said he was, I seriously doubted she'd find her ex-boyfriend in his office. She had already called three times from New York, and he hadn't called back. But as I watched her in the rearview mirror, it appeared that she was talking to someone.

She was practically dancing in the snow on her way back to the car. "Brendan lives above his office now," she announced as she got in. "He'll be here in five minutes. And he told me he heard from Harpo."

"When?"

"I don't know. He said he'd tell me all about it when he gets here."

"I hope either Brendan's punctual or Roach is a slow eater."

"Oh, he's punctual, sugar."

I filed it away that O'Malley was punctual to go along with brilliant and handsome. That put him at least two attributes ahead of me, and the third was purely subjective.

"Jesus, you know what?" I said as I peered through the restaurant window at Roach. "I think I've been in that joint before."

"When was that?"

"Three years ago, during the Days of Rage."

"You know about the Days of Rage?" Harmony's tone indicated that her respect for me had just shot up tenfold.

The Days of Rage was a protest march that coincided with the start of the Chicago Seven conspiracy trial. It had turned into a street war between a couple of hundred hippies and a couple of thousand Chicago cops. Guess who won.

"I was here then," she said. "We didn't march, though. We split. That's when Chairman Fred called Mark Rudd a masochistic motherfucker for wanting the Panthers to be the ones to charge the cops. It happened right over there." She pointed toward the park.

It took me a moment to realize Chairman Fred was Fred Hampton. Mark Rudd, I was pretty sure, was one of the know-it-all campus radicals you used to see on the TV news all the time. Actually, it seemed to me that they only turned up when they were supposed to be taking their final exams.

"What in the hell were you doing here then?" Harmony asked.

"Working on a case. Nate was here too." I studied the restaurant sign for a moment. "Yup, I'm almost positive that's the place. My memory's a little fuzzy because I was on LSD."

"*You* took LSD?" Harmony's opinion of me was growing each time I opened my mouth.

"Actually, someone gave it to me—against my will."

"Oh, that must've been fun."

"It turned out to be okay—once I managed to escape and Nate came to rescue me. This is where I called him from."

"That Nathan, he's a prince, ain't he?"

An image of Nate taking liberties with Harmony in my morning dream flashed across my brain. "He can be," I said.

"Speaking of princes, here comes my guy!" Harmony was out the door before I saw where she was pointing.

The only guy I could see looked like he could have come out of a box in the park. He was wearing a red wool cap that had been stretched out of shape and a gray overcoat straight out of a Salvation Army depot. In a moment, Harmony moved into my field of vision and put a hug on the guy that could have stopped a bear's heart. Then she pulled away and began leading him to the car.

O'Malley was a head shorter than she was, and even in the bulky coat I could see that he had the build of a pretzel stick. The lenses of his eyeglasses were as thick as Oreo cookies, and he needed a shave worse than I did. Recalling that Harmony had told me O'Malley was handsome, I figured we must have caught him on a bad day.

They climbed into the back seat of the car. They were still holding hands, and I felt a stab of jealousy.

"Brendan O'Malley," she said, "Mark Renzler."

I twisted around to shake his hand, which she released long enough for that purpose. "I've heard a lot about you," I said.

"And I've heard a lot about you—as much as you can hear about someone in thirty seconds."

"Okay, Brendan, this creep we're following could leave any minute so we've got to make this fast. What is it you've heard from Harpo?"

"Except for a few phone conversations around the time he stole those documents—or when he *said* he stole the documents and then managed to have them stolen—nothing. Then two weeks ago, he calls and says, 'O'Malley, I'm sending you a Christmas gift that's going to make you a hero.' That was it. No 'How you doing, how've you been.' Now, I've been downstate the last few days taking depositions for a case that's a lost cause if ever I saw one, but the last I looked, today's supposed to be Christmas, and I still haven't gotten anything from your brother. Which, you understand, doesn't surprise me a bit."

"Yeah, yeah, I hear you. But this time—"

"I take it you don't trust Harpo for some reason," I said.

"Not just some reason—lots of reasons. If I were looking for one, I'd say it was after I jumped through hoops so he could turn himself in but he decided not to show. I almost got clipped for harboring a fugitive. Have *you* met Harpo?"

"I just spoke to him on the phone. Actually, he spoke to me. The entire content of our conversation was: 'Are you the honky my sister's hanging with?' "

O'Malley let out a chuckle. "Yeah, that sounds like Harpo."

"Brendan, it's different this time, it really is. I've seen one of the documents. Renzler got ahold of it."

"Really? How did you do that?"

"It's a long story, but I managed to pry it away from a guy who slugged me with a crowbar."

"Hmm, that's a story I'd like to hear sometime."

"It's the floor plan to Fred's apartment that they used during the raid. It came from the FBI."

"FBI or Chicago PD?"

"F-B-fucking-I. I swear it."

I raised my right hand. "I saw it, too."

"It came from Bill O'Neal," Harmony said. "He's the pig that snitched for the FBI."

"Yeah, I know, I've thought that for a while. There's this black judge—can you believe that? We've actually got a black judge here now—who called me up and told me. O'Neal's name came up as an informant in another case, but he put two and two together. The problem is I can't prove it."

O'Malley put his hand on Harmony's shoulder. "I've got to get hold of this floor plan. If I can get one document, I can file to get more. Just flood these cocksuckers with subpoenas. We know they're there. There's got to be thousands of FBI documents pertaining to the Panthers. Hanrahan got off, you know, but now we can go ahead with the civil suit."

"We'll get it to you as soon as we get back," I said. O'-Malley's intensity made me feel like I was partner to something more important than finding Harpo. "And the guy who hit me is running around with a whole stack of documents, maybe a hundred. We'll try to get those for you, too."

O'Malley let out another laugh. "Just how many shots with a crowbar do you think you can withstand?"

"Harpo was telling the truth all along, Brendan," Harmony said.

"Yeah, I guess so. You know, now that I think about it, he did call me one other time. It was about a year ago. That's when he told me the name of his partner when he broke into the FBI office. Patricia Hurley. She's wanted for a bombing in Madison. I thought he might be making that up, to impress me. He said he had tracked Patty to Toledo and found out her roommate had told some lefty history professor about the documents. The roommate thought the prof could help get the stuff out to the media. But instead of helping, the guy threatened to turn her in unless she gave *him* the documents."

"This was a professor in Toledo?" I asked.

"No, in Wisconsin. This was right after they broke into the office. Harpo called me was because he was trying to track down the professor. He thought I, being the only intellectual type he knew, might've heard of the guy."

"Had you?" I asked.

"No."

"Do you remember his name?"

"No, but if I heard it, I might."

"Does the name Hartman DeWitt ring—"

"Yeah, jingle bells."

I looked at Harmony. "That explains why your brother got hooked up with the PRF."

"What's the PRF?" O'Malley asked.

"People's Revolutionary Front," Harmony said.

"Oh, I've read about them. A bad lot is what I hear."

"You wouldn't believe how bad, sugar." As she started to give him some idea, I saw Roach coming out of the restaurant.

130

"Here's our boy, we've got to go."

Harmony threw her arms around O'Malley, giving him a hero's send-off and the bum's rush at the same time. "Thanks a million, Brendan," she said as she pushed him out of the car. "I'll call as soon as I can. Tonight, maybe."

"Make sure you get me that floor plan."

"You can count on it," I said.

"Merry Christmas, Brendan," she called as we pulled away.

"Yeah, right, Merry Christmas. Be sure and send me that floor plan."

"That Brendan, he doesn't stand much on ceremony. But I sure do love the guy." Harmony's voice was cracking a bit, and I glanced in the rearview mirror to see her wiping her eyes. She looked up in time to catch the reflection of my gaze. I felt a little guilty, as if I had spoiled a private moment, but she flashed me a million-dollar smile.

"Okay, James," she said. "Follow that bug."

Roach practically retraced his tire marks back to the Kennedy Expressway. We expected him to go north to Wisconsin, but he moved suddenly into the left lane to turn south. He made it through on a yellow light, but the driver of the station wagon between us skidded to a stop. As we pulled up behind it, I could see that it was filled with nuns.

I considered going around the station wagon and running the red, but one of Chicago's finest was stopped on the other side of the light. From what I had seen of Chicago cops, I didn't think one of them was likely to give us a Christmas pass. If he didn't issue a ticket, he'd probably try to shake a gift out of our tree, and that would cost just as much time.

When the light changed, I cut off the nuns and accelerated enough to put us into a mild skid. I was pretty sure we could catch Roach once we got onto the highway, but even a remote chance of losing him after staying on his tail for twenty hours was unnerving. As we reached the top of the entrance ramp,

I could see there was nothing to worry about. At least not on that score.

Roach was moving at a crawl on the shoulder of the highway, not more than a quarter of a mile away. At first I thought he was having engine trouble, but as I slowed down he sped up and merged back onto the highway. There were no cars between us now, just a few hundred yards of slippery interstate. We were close enough that I was able to see his hand come out the window.

Harmony saw it, too. "What the hell's he doing?"

"Giving us the finger."

"Oh, shit."

Just to make sure we didn't misunderstand, Roach began blinking his taillights on and off. I sped up until we were perilously close, then switched on my high beams. I wished it were night, last night as a matter of fact.

"Do you think Sheila set me up from the beginning, or did he spot us along the way?"

"I'd bet heavily on the first choice."

"What do we do now?"

"Stay on his ass and make him nervous until he stops for gas. Then clobber the piss out of him until he tells us where Harpo is."

"That sounds like a fine plan, Renzler. But if you keep driving like this, you're going to make me a whole lot more nervous than him and in a much shorter period of time. Like in about five more seconds."

She was right. And I didn't put it past the guy to test his brakes, just to play with our heads a little more. I eased off the gas and stayed close as long as I could. That took us back as far as Booth Tarkington's oasis. Roach kept going, but we had to make a pit stop. In a mileage test, bet on a new Volkswagen over an old Corvair any day.

EIGHTEEN

"Why do you think Hartman wanted us out of the way?" Harmony asked as we approached the oasis. "Was he moving Harpo? Or did Rodney tell him you stole the documents and he wanted to break into your place and get them?"

"You know, the second notion didn't even cross my mind. But Rodney did tell you he wasn't going to give the documents to Hartman, so that's a definite possibility. And sharp thinking on your part."

"Thanks. It's the cerebral side of Sister Shamus. But I hope I'm wrong. If Hartman steals that floor plan, what will I tell Brendan?"

"Don't worry about that. I left a copy with Randall."

"You gave it to an FBI guy?"

"Ex-FBI guy."

"Oh, that's right, and a black one."

"Hey, come on. Randall's the guy who agreed to spend Christmas Eve tailing Rodney."

"I was only kidding."

"You were?" We were standing right outside the ladies' room.

She smiled, kissed her hand and patted it on my forehead. "Yeah, I was, sugar. So just calm down."

I told Harmony I'd call Nate and ask him to check on my apartment while she got us some coffee.

"No, let me call Nathan. I want to wish him Merry Christmas."

"It's not a Merry Christmas call. We've got to make this fast."

"Brother, are you in a bad mood."

"You seem to be forgetting that we just got taken for a thousand-mile detour."

"And I'm having a hard time remembering the sweet guy who'd rather be stranded in Indiana with me than anyone else."

"I'm sorry, you're right, I'm just tired," I said. But weariness had little to do with it. The thing that sparked my irritability was Harmony's enthusiasm for calling Nate.

"Damn right I'm right. This wasn't a total waste. You got to meet Brendan."

I almost reminded her that Brendan had also gotten to meet me. Fortunately, I was able to swallow the thought. A comment that revealing could have made for an awkward ride home. I still wasn't sure what had happened last night, and neither of us had said a thing about it.

When we met back at the car, she said, "Nate told me to wish you MFC. What does that mean?"

"Merry Fucking Christmas."

"I should've known that."

"Did your call break the holiday cheer at his place?"

"Not at all. In fact, he sounded happy to hear from us." She lowered her voice and nodded knowingly. "I think the kids might be having a Christmas spat."

"Oh, I know all about those. It wouldn't be Christmas without one."

"Well this is their first. Seems Constance didn't like her present."

"What did he get her?"

"I don't know exactly. But he said, 'Let me give you some advice: Never buy art for your spouse.' "

"Oh, art. Yeah, that's always trouble."

I wasn't feeling optimistic about catching Roach, but I set off as fast as road conditions would permit. That was sixty miles an hour. Roach had been tooling along at fifty, so it would take us a while to catch him, if we were that lucky.

We came into sight of the blue bug somewhere near Akron. That was as close to lucky as we got. The oil light began to flicker, and I had to keep the gas pedal to the floor just to maintain speed. After a few minutes, the light came on and stayed on. We were steadily losing speed, other warning lights started to come on and soon the dashboard was lit up like, well, a proverbial Christmas tree.

"What's going on?" Harmony asked.

I shrugged. "The only thing I know about cars is how to put the key in the ignition." I steered onto the shoulder to make way for a truck bearing down on us. "One other thing I know about cars: I can tell when one is dead."

The rest of our day was a misadventure involving rube auto mechanics, taxi drivers, car rental agents and airline personnel. The Corvair was laid to rest at a Standard station in Freedom, Ohio. The proprietor gave me fifty bucks and a free lift into town in his pickup. We flew to New York from Cleveland, where a flight delay enabled us to feast on the remnants of the Christmas buffet at the Lake Effect Lounge. Harmony called her mom from there. I called Nate and learned that someone had trashed my apartment.

"There's something I should warn you about, Renzler."

"What's that?"

"Your cat."

"What about it?"

"Someone strangled it."

Fluffy was seventeen years old the last time I had counted, and I couldn't remember when that was. I had been more or less looking forward to her passing, because her accidents were proving costly on the slop-and-smell scoreboard. But this was definitely not how I wanted her to go. I had a special attachment to Fluffy, though she wasn't really my cat. She was my mother's. My sister had taken her in when Mom died, but I became Fluffy's caretaker when my brother-in-law developed a sudden allergy to cats.

"MFC, Nate," I said.

"Yeah, you said it, pal."

We got back to my place around midnight. Nate and Constance had made progress in the cleanup effort, but there was plenty left to be done, especially in the area of papers. All of my file cabinets had been emptied, and though most of them were little more than storage boxes for back issues of the *Hockey News* and *Racing Form,* there were still piles of files to sift through.

That could wait for another day. I went to the refrigerator and found a six-pack of beer with a welcome-home note in Nate's familiar scrawl. I opened a bottle and read the other greeting someone had left for us, on a pad on the kitchen table: "Merry Christmas, asshole. We'll be back."

"That tells us something," I told Harmony. "It means we had more than one houseguest."

She took a mouthful of beer and surveyed the wreckage. "It looks like they made themselves right at home."

I went to the phone, opened my wallet and pulled out the scrap of paper on which Paul Weisberg had written Hartman DeWitt's address and phone number. It took six rings to roust someone, and it wasn't the supreme commander himself.

"Is this Roach?" I guessed.

"That's right, who's this?"

"Your holiday traveling companion."

"Hah! Did you make it back okay, asshole?"

"Let me talk to your boyfriend, big guy."

"He can't come to the phone right now. And if he could, he wouldn't talk to you."

"Too bad. I've got something important to tell him."

"Anything you want to tell him, you can tell me."

"Why talk to the monkey when you can talk to the organ grinder?"

"Fuck you. How did you get this number?"

"I've got your number on a few scores, pal. And lover boy, too. Did you know Hartman is a snitch for the FBI?"

"Bullshit."

"Ask him. I'm sure he can explain. And have him call me as soon as he can. Tell him I've got the documents he's been looking for."

"What's that supposed to mean? Are you trying to bullshit me?"

"No. But if I was, it wouldn't be too hard."

"Yeah, you should talk. Driving all the way to Chicago on a wild-goose chase."

He had a point, but I wasn't about to let him keep it. "That would make you the wild goose, now, wouldn't it?"

"Fuck you."

"Do you want to take down my number or should I just call back every ten minutes?"

He opted to take down the number. When he went to get a pen, I couldn't hear any voices in the background. If Hartman was there, I thought he would have gotten on the line by now.

"Be sure to tell him I've got the documents," I said.

"What documents?"

"My, my," I said. "Hartman doesn't tell you anything, does he?" I hung up before he could respond.

Harmony was nodding her approval. "You're going to try to bluff him, aren't you? Offer to trade the documents we don't have in exchange for Harpo?"

"Yeah, that's right."

"Do you think it will work?"

"Who knows? I can't figure out why Hartman was holding

the documents to begin with. Especially if he's an FBI informant. By now you'd think he would have turned them in to the G. That would fetch him a nice fat bonus."

I fetched myself another beer, but Harmony turned down my offer of a refill. She moved to the corner and knelt down beside a shoe box that I hadn't noticed until now. I went over and stood beside her as she unwrapped a towel inside the box and uncovered Fluffy. "Poor thing," she said, stroking her head.

I could only nod as she looked up at me. But I didn't feel anything for the cat. I had her owner on my mind. For the second time in twenty-four hours I was speechless remembering my mother. I felt weak in the knees as I closed my eyes. When I opened them, I was face to face with Harmony. I felt like I had been gone for a moment. She was holding me up, letting my arms drape over her shoulders and my chest press against hers.

"Come on, sugar," she whispered softly, "we've got to get your weary bones to bed."

NINETEEN

The telephone version of "Jingle Bells" was playing when I rolled out of bed. A glance at the undisturbed covers on one side told me Harmony had spent the night on the couch. My clothes piled neatly by the dresser told me she had been instrumental in getting them off.

I could hear the shower going as I rushed for the phone. I made an early New Year's resolution to put an extension in the bedroom or a stop to the practice of answering morning calls.

"Good morning, Mr. Renzler. Did you enjoy your trip?" The creepy cordiality of Hartman DeWitt knocked most of the fog out of my head. The cigarette I lit took care of the rest.

"You sound awfully cheery. I expected you to be in mourning for your niece."

"Who?"

"Judith Fairbanks."

"Who told you she was my niece?"

"I've got lots of people telling me all sorts of things about you. For example, a friend of mine in the FBI tells me you're a paid snitch."

"Your friend is mistaken, as is the person who told you Judith was my niece. But you're right. Her death was a shock, and I'm saddened by it."

Hartman's voice was perfectly calm. He was a difficult guy to rattle, but that didn't stop me from trying.

"Someone else told me you're a pathological liar." I moved to the kitchen and poured a cup of the coffee that Harmony had made. I'm short on extensions, but I compensate with long cords.

"There are many misguided people who regard me as a threat, Mr. Renzler. I'm accustomed to their name-calling and invulnerable to it as well."

"I think that goes with the pathology, Professor."

I had a feeling that one stung him a little, because a tone of impatience crept into his voice. "It was my understanding that you called last night to inquire about some documents. Would you care to enlighten me as to what documents you might be alluding to?"

"The documents you were looking for when you ransacked my apartment and killed my cat, asshole. Does that provide enough enlightenment?"

"What? I did nothing of the sort! Mr. Renzler, I really have no idea what you're talking about."

"I'm not accusing you personally. I'm sure you wouldn't dirty your tender hands. When you want something done, you call on your monkeys."

"Mr. Renzler, I truly am mystified by your accusation. Perhaps you need a good night's sleep. And for whatever it's worth, I offer my condolences for your cat."

"Not much."

Hartman was right about me needing sleep. But that wasn't why I was getting rattled. In the kingdom of smooth operators, I was a babe in the forest compared with this guy, even if he was a certified wacko. I sometimes say I was born with a cigarette in my mouth, but Hartman must have arrived puffing on a pipe.

He let out a heavy sigh. "Would you care to elaborate on your cryptic message about documents or would you prefer to continue down this meandering path of lunacy?"

The idea of this lunatic putting that label on me had the odd effect of clearing my head. All I wanted to do was flash my cards and see if he'd nibble so I could get off the phone and drink my coffee in peace.

"You know the documents I'm talking about. FBI memos that were stolen from a resident agency in Beloit, Wisconsin."

"I believe I know the ones. What about them?"

"You want them, I've got them."

"What makes you think I want them?"

"You sent Rodney to your sister's house to get them."

"My sister's house?"

"Lillian Summerfield. You do know that she's your sister, don't you?"

"That is not why I sent Rodney to *Judith Fairbanks*'s house. In any case, how did you come to be in possession of them?"

I thought I had him leaning in his own obtuse way, but this

was where the bluff got steep. I didn't know what Rodney had told Hartman about his visit to Judith's.

"I found them under the floor in Judith's bedroom."

"I see." He paused long enough to make me entertain the notion that I might have him. "Your admission of that would make you a suspect in her murder, now, wouldn't it?"

"If somebody told the cops, it would. But I don't think you'll go to the cops."

"No, you're correct about that. I'd tell my story to the FBI. Being an informant has its privileges, you know."

The idea of Hartman reporting me to the G was disturbing, but not enough to give me pause. Not at first, at least. But when I paused to think about Jack Fogarty and Pete Wilson wanting to settle a score with me, I got a sick feeling in my gut. One phone call from Hartman and my life could get very miserable.

I went for a mouthful of coffee but all I gulped was air. Without realizing it, I had already drained my mug. Just then, Harmony appeared and took it from my hand to get a refill. I made do with a cigarette while groping for a quick-witted reply. The one I came up with hardly filled the bill.

"Do you want the memos back or not?"

"I assume you want to propose an exchange: the memos in return for Ms. Brown's brother."

"Those would be the basic terms. I'd also want a guarantee that you wouldn't go to the FBI about me, and I'd guarantee I wouldn't offer proof of your informant status to rival political groups."

"Mr. Renzler, I'm afraid you need some training in the art of negotiation. First of all, I don't need the documents. I have a set of them right here with me. Second of all, I don't believe you have them. Third, and last of all, as I already told you *and* his sister, James Brown is in isolation and perfectly safe." He barely paused to catch his breath, but I could tell that even he

141

was winded. "I believe that concludes our present conversation, but I do encourage you to maintain contact."

I got in my final words just before the click of his phone hanging up. "Fuck you, asshole."

Harmony shrugged and sent me a smile from the doorway. "I take it you struck out on your bluff."

I rubbed my bleary eyes and scratched my itchy head and nodded. "It was like Bobby Brown batting against Vida Blue."

"I've never heard of either of them. If they're not on the Red Sox, I don't know them."

It was still early and there'd already been a lot to shudder about, but this was the scariest thing I'd heard so far. "*You*—a Red Sox fan?"

She nodded, and I felt my jaw drop and my shoulders droop.

"Come on, slugger. Do you really think I care about some bourgeois plantation game?"

That sent me to the showers, from which I emerged feeling partly like a brand-new man and vaguely like my old tired self. Nate had arrived in the interim, and he and Harmony were at the table going at it, but this time the only thing spread across it was the newspapers.

"The story on the Happy Rockefeller kidnapping plot is turning out to be a bust," he told me. "You'll find it on page seven."

As I read the story, I also learned that the search for Harpo Rollins was colder than Christmas in Indiana. The nation's top crime-fighting agency had yet to figure out that Harpo had become James Brown. As for Judith Fairbanks, to counter the possible crush of curiosity seekers, her father had opted for a private funeral. That closed the door on my attending in the hope of satisfying my curiosity about her associates.

Randall Edwards called as I was finishing my first satisfying cup of coffee in three days. After an exchange of holiday pleasantries that basically amounted to me sighing with relief that the great day was over and him sighing with regret that for him it still wasn't, he filled me in on tailing Rodney.

"I get there around eleven," he said. "Around noon a guy pulls up in a red Volkswagen. I never did get a good look at the guy, because he was wearing a cap and I didn't get close enough. A white guy though, I'm pretty sure of that. Anyway, your boy Rodney comes right out, gets in the car and they drive to that giant shopping mall on Route Forty-six, the one that's supposed to be the world's largest."

"Willowbrook."

"Yeah, that's it's. By the way, I can't for the life of me figure out why they need another shopping mall out there. Looks to me like the whole damn state is nothing but a shopping mall. So anyway, I figure the boys are going shopping, right? *Wrong.* They park way out in the lot, a mile from any of the stores. It's a huge lot, there are other cars out there, because the place is mobbed. But they didn't look for a closer space. They knew right where they were going. They had to meet a couple of guys. You want to guess?"

He didn't give me time to tell him I didn't.

"Jack Fogarty and Peter Piper! I didn't believe my eyes when Fogarty rolled down his window. I was hanging back a few cars, so if they noticed me they'd think I was looking for a space. But once I saw Fogarty, I decided to pull closer. I had to make sure it was him.

"He was on the passenger side. He gets out just as I'm going by. I could see he had an envelope in his hand, so I slowed to a stop. He glances my way so I take off and circle around real quick and come back. This time I came to a full stop. Fogarty is still standing there, leaning on the door of the VW, talking to the driver, the guy in the hat. But he didn't have the envelope anymore. I rolled down my window in case I could hear what they were saying."

"Randall, that's kind of daring, getting that close."

"Nah, it was OK. I kept my elbow up to guard my face so he wouldn't get too good a look at me. When I got there, he was backing away from the door and pointing with his finger. I heard him say, 'Saturday afternoon—you be there.' And his tone was definitely not friendly. That's when he noticed me."

"Oh, shit."

"Yeah, so I call out, real quick, 'You guys leaving?' so they'll figure I'm looking for a space. Fogarty yells at me, 'No, we're not leaving.' His tone wasn't friendly to me either. I took that as my clue to move along. I didn't dare go back, which means I wasn't able to follow your boys."

"Don't worry about it," I said. "That's about the fastest and most productive tail job in history."

"Oh no. Once I tailed a guy from his house right to the bank he was robbing. Of course I had a good tip on that one—the guy's wife."

"Now *ex*-wife, I would guess."

"Yeah, about five minutes after I nabbed him."

"So it looks like Rodney is selling the papers to the G," I said. "And you're pretty sure Fogarty gave him a payoff but Rodney didn't turn over the documents."

"Yeah, I'm almost positive that's what Saturday is about. My guess would be Rodney and his partner were demanding half up front and the rest when they turn over the papers. That's how I'd do it. If you tried to pull off a straight swap with the G, you'd find yourself in a federal slammer faster than you could say 'Gay Edgar Hoover.' "

"I take it you weren't able to hear what time they were going to meet or where."

"Nope, just this afternoon. And I didn't get an ID on the owner of the car. It was too late to run the plate by DMV."

"Monday will be soon enough. I have a pretty good idea who it was anyway."

"Who's that?"

144

"A white guy named Juan."

"Sounds like there's a story there."

"My friend Harmony says the guy is probably trying to be in solidarity with people from the Third World."

"What does that mean? No, forget it, I probably don't want to know."

I asked Randall if he was up for tailing Rodney again, but he said his family commitments were so cemented that he'd end up wearing a cement overcoat if he broke them.

"I called all day yesterday so you'd know you had to take care of this. After a while, I figured you must've gone out of town."

"Yeah, I did."

"Where'd you go?"

"Chicago."

"For one day? That's ambitious."

I told Randall how little ambition had to do with it and started to gave him the twenty-five-words-or-less account. By the time I got to twenty, he was being summoned from the phone. When I hung up, I offered Harmony and Nate the chance to redeem themselves on the Rodney watch.

"What are you going to do?" she asked. It could have been my imagination, but her tone made it sound like she was going to miss me.

"Hartman said he has a set of documents. If he was lying, he would've shown more interest in my offer. But If I can boost his set, we might be able to reopen the negotiations."

"Are you going to the PRF office?" Nate asked.

I shook my head. "I think he's keeping them at his house."

"You're talking about breaking and entering," Harmony said.

"Depending on New Jersey law and what time I get there, it might be called home invasion."

TWENTY

The neighborhood Christmas lights weren't yet blazing when I arrived at Hartman DeWitt's subdivision in yet another black Chevy Camaro. This time I had gone through Avis instead of Angelo Albani. The rates were higher, but at least I had license plates.

On my first swing through, I noticed that Hartman's driveway was one Mercedes lighter than it had been during my previous surveillance. But a telltale VW was still parked there. The license plate number didn't match the bug we had crawled behind to Chicago. Nor did it match the plate of the car Rodney had been in when Randall Edwards had tailed him.

I left the subdivision and followed a street that led up behind Hartman's house. It was still a municipal park, but a few hundred acres smaller than the one I had played in as a kid. I parked midway between a pair of no-parking signs that were spaced about a quarter of a mile apart. I doubted anyone would be out ticketing at this time of year, but if a local cop was feeling conscientious, I wasn't worried about adding another ticket to my collection.

I could see through the bare trees to the subdivision about fifty yards below. With a gray coat and black pants, I hoped I wouldn't be too noticeable to anyone who might be passing the time looking out the window. I'd also had the good sense to wear sneakers, which provided decent if soggy footing in the snow.

I paused at the edge of the woods behind Hartman's house

while contemplating my final approach. Interior lights were visible on the first floor and through a ground-level basement window. I watched the first floor for about five minutes without seeing any movement. Then I made a dash for the lighted side of the basement and crouched beside a ratty shrub. It didn't offer much protection from a snoopy suburbanite, but I was counting on Hartman's neighbors being less than vigilant about guarding his property. A guy who didn't bother with Christmas lights seemed unlikely to warrant that sort of thoughtfulness.

The curtain on the window was sheer and flimsy, affording a good view into the room. It was a finished basement, as they say in real-estate parlance, carpeted and paneled with an eye more toward economy than taste. Two familiar figures were seated on the floor: Sheila Love and Third World Juan.

I figured Juan was loving every minute, because he had Sheila as I suspected he wanted her: naked and alone. He didn't have any clothes on either. They were sitting cross-legged, holding hands and gazing at a large book spread open before them. My guess was they were studying the inspirational writings of their supreme commander, but it could have been a new edition of Kahlil Gibran. Juan was puffing on a cigarette, which I didn't realize was marijuana until he passed it to Sheila.

I'm slow to catch on to that kind of stuff, but I'm quick at sizing up other situations. My read on this one was that the VW in the driveway belonged to Juan, and Hartman had ordered him and Sheila to watch his house. Where Hartman had gone and for how long was anyone's guess, but I thought he might already have been away when we had spoken on the phone. Possibly he was gone when Roach and I had swapped insults the night before.

Roach was the wild card. If Hartman needed the house guarded, he'd be the guy to do it. I figured he must've been

147

handling a more important assignment. That could entail anything from protecting Hartman to moving Harpo.

Through the window I could see Sheila and Juan graduating from hand-holding to tentative groping. Assuming they were the only ones home, I wouldn't have any trouble getting inside. I stayed pressed against the house as I moved to the back door. In my pocket I had a ring of master keys that a locksmith pal had once traded for a pair of hockey tickets. I also had a few tools for backup in case none of the keys worked. But I thought to try turning the knob first and made the pleasant discovery that the door was unlocked.

Most likely someone had been careless, but there was an outside chance I was expected. I wasn't in the mood to take chances. I entered the kitchen with my gun drawn.

Hartman's home was middle-class suburban all the way, from the ceiling tile and shag carpeting right down to the gaudy gold light fixture over the dining room table. If I looked in the kitchen cabinets, I probably would have found SpaghettiOs.

I moved into the living room, past a color TV, console stereo, matching easy chairs and sofa. Hartman even had the love seat to complete the set. As I neared the door to the basement, I heard music playing below. It was loud enough for me to learn that Papa still was a rolling stone and to believe that Sheila and Juan couldn't hear me.

I found the room I thought was looking for on the first floor. I reached that conclusion because this door was locked and the doors to the other rooms weren't. Unfortunately, it was located right above lovers' lounge. I hoped by now they were going at it like a pair of hungry mutts.

I negotiated the lock with the fourth key I tried. When I pushed the door open, I could see a phony mahogany desk, a pair of floor-to-ceiling bookcases and enough filing cabinets to hold the records of a major bank. If I had to search through all of them, it was going to be a long visit.

The floorboards creaked under the carpeting as I stepped inside, but I figured that was neutralized by all the bad vibes the Temptations were giving off. I went to the desk in the hope that Hartman kept his important papers separate from his files. Before I got there, I noticed the only unconventional piece of furniture in the house.

It was straight and sturdy, but the design was primitive. So were the materials. Instead of pine or oak, the builder had used two-by-fours. That made it look strange enough, but the cluster of wires running from the arms to a black box on the floor were what made it a conversation piece. Paul Weisberg's tale about an electric chair turned out to be true.

The bloodstains near the chair on the carpet made me think it had recently been in use. The stains were dry, but they hadn't been there long enough to lose their color. They were splattered over a square-yard area, lending a polka-dot pattern to the bland off-white. I would've given odds that the redecoration had come courtesy of Harpo Rollins.

Only one of the six desk drawers had a lock, and it took about thirty seconds to determine there was nothing of interest in five of them. The one with the lock was a file drawer. The lock was strong enough to withstand the curiosity of someone like Sheila or Juan but no match for a guy with a jeweler's screwdriver, a bobby pin and a can-do attitude. I popped the sucker in less than a minute.

The rack inside was hung with green file folders, but they were all empty. I had a sinking suspicion Hartman had recently cleaned out his files. But when I pushed the folders into a tight accordion, I saw a manila envelope lying on the bottom of the drawer.

There were about fifteen sheets of paper inside. As I flipped through them, I spotted several pages of FBI letterhead, but none having anything to do with the Black Panthers. At least not directly. The dates on most of the papers were from the first three months of 1971. About half of them consisted of two long letters from Hartman DeWitt to J. Edgar Hoover. The rest were equally long letters from the crime-fighting legend himself.

When I got through the first page of Hartman's first letter, I heard myself mutter aloud. "Holy fucking shit."

Hartman was definitely an odd bird, but he was a crafty one as well. Few people have the smarts or balls to blackmail the top law-enforcement officer in the United States. But that's what Hartman had been able to do for almost a year and a half.

The smart move for me would have been to pocket the letters and hightail it out of there. I hadn't found the papers I had come for, but in terms of utility for negotiating with Hartman, these were every bit as good. They were so good, in fact, that I couldn't stop reading them right there.

With his first letter to Hoover, Hartman had enclosed copies of the documents that Harpo and Patty Hurley had stolen from the FBI office in Beloit. He said he had two sets of them. One was being held by someone who had instructions to make them public if anything unusual happened to him. In return for not releasing the documents, Hartman demanded twenty-five hundred dollars a month.

The rest of the letters were a detailed negotiation of how the arrangement would work. Hoover agreed to Hartman's demands, but he insisted that the PRF chairman also serve as an informant and file reports on other political groups. In his response, Hartman sounded practically gleeful at the prospect of being a junior G-man. His tone reminded me of Elvis Presley getting his honorary badge from Nixon. But Hartman upped the ante to three grand a month, half to be paid in cash and half to be deposited in a bank account in Zurich. Hoover didn't flinch about the money, but in his final letter he made it clear that if the documents ever became public, Hartman would be "a very dead man."

The bottom letter was dated a week after Hoover preceded Hartman to the grave and was written by his successor, L. Patrick Gray. The new FBI director was terse in confirming that the arrangement would continue. But he also was cutting Hartman back to two grand a month. Gray said that the bureau's COINTELPRO operations were more embarrassing to Hoover than to him. He closed by expressing hope that no harm would befall Hartman, but he said he couldn't guarantee it.

The letters were so engrossing that I didn't notice the music had stopped until I was putting them back in the envelope. I felt the presence of someone behind me before I heard anything. By the time I heard something, it was too late to reach across the desk for my gun.

"Put up your hands, you honky bastard!"

I obeyed Sheila Love's command and turned very slowly. The weapon in her hand was a .44 magnum. Actually she was using two hands, which was a smart idea from her standpoint. Except for the gun and a string of braided leather beads, Sheila was still wearing nothing. If this had been a movie, like *Sister Shamus*, for instance, it could have been a sexy scene. Of course it wasn't a movie, but that didn't stop Sheila from talking like it was.

"Move one muscle and I'll blow you away!"

"Hartman would not want you to shoot someone in his house, I guarantee it."

"Shut up."

"Sheila, you know, I think he's right." Juan stepped out of the shadows to join her in the doorway. In the absence of jewelry, he was dressed lighter than she was. I noticed a bruise on his left thigh and wondered whether he had sustained it during their scrimmage. "Maybe we should try calling Rodney. He'll know what to do with him."

"Fuck Rodney. I don't need Rodney to handle this honky. I could break his arms if I wanted—just like *that.*" Sheila took one hand off the heater long enough to snap her fingers. The gun wobbled as she did so.

"You really could?"

"Sure I could. You want to see me?"

TWENTY-ONE

Greetings, brothers and sisters. Harmony Rollins here. I hope you don't think I'm horning in on Renzler's story. It's just that I noticed he's got this bad habit of leaving out details when it comes to relating somebody else's part of the story. Like the other night when Nathan and me went to that ice cream shop to meet up with Rodney. Renzler wrapped that all up in less than a page, but it took him ten times that just to tell about going to Hartman's house and sitting out front watching it while nothing happened.

Now the part of the story I'm about to tell is really important and I wanted to make sure you get the complete version instead of the one you'd get from Renzler. Please don't get me wrong. It's not like I don't appreciate all the guy's done for me, because I do, I really do. In fact I don't know where I'd be without him though it certainly wouldn't be here in New Jersey.

Anyway here goes. Nathan and me leave for Rodney's house

around eleven. I drive because Nathan won't, can't and's scared shitless by the idea. That's what's so refreshing about him. He's not into this macho trip where he's got to be in charge all the time. Unlike Renzler, who's more of a traditional male, if you know what I mean. But I'm not going to start bitching about him, because I know his heart's in the right place and the more you get to know him, the more he grows on you. Plus unlike some guys I know, you can educate him. I just don't think anyone's tried up to now.

We don't have any trouble finding Rodney's place because Renzler drew us this map which has everything exactly correct. In fact he kind of overdid it a little but that's the kind of guy he is. He assumes you know nothing. If you can get past feeling like an idiot, it's all pretty cool.

When we get there we can see Rodney standing in his living room talking on the phone as we drive past. I go around the block and park near the corner. Maybe twenty minutes later, no more than half an hour, Rodney comes strolling out to his car, carrying a brown envelope under the arm of his leather coat. He's grinning like the happiest nigger you ever saw, and when I make that observation to Nathan, he says, "Looks like a guy who's expecting to get one of two things: money or sex."

"Maybe he's planning on getting himself some of both."

"Now that would be a damn shame. An asshole that big doesn't deserve to be so lucky." I think Nathan's still sore about Rodney kicking his ass the other night.

Following somebody's not as easy as you think, if you've only seen it done in the movies. It's especially hard for me because we don't have any idea where he's going and I don't know the roads. I try to stay far enough back so he doesn't see us, but every time he takes a turn, that means I've really got to step on it. He takes four, maybe five turns in the first couple of miles, which makes it pretty tense for a while. But

153

then he gets on Route 46 going west, and that gives us a chance to relax.

When Rodney gets near the big shopping mall where he met the FBI pigs a couple of days ago, we're expecting he might turn off. The parking lot is so jammed full of people you'd think Christmas was still a few days away. Nate makes a comment to exactly that effect and I have to explain to him it's all because of people returning bourgeois shit they didn't want in the first place for other bourgeois shit they won't find a use for anyway.

Rodney goes flying right past the shopping mall, which gives me the feeling the pigs want to have their powwow in a nice secluded spot this time around. That doesn't bode well for Rodney and I wonder if the boy's smart enough to be thinking the same thing himself. Another mile or so down the highway, he gets into the right lane and pulls off at the parking lot of this big squat box of a building that looks like it's designed to be the warehouse of the future. It's shiny silver-gray with rows of narrow slits for windows that look like the coin slots in vending machines. In glossy black letters above the entrance, it says: RAMAPO WASTE, INC.—CORPORATE HEAD-QUARTERS.

"Are you thinking what I'm thinking?" I ask Nathan. "Is this place some FBI front?"

"Nope. I think it's just the shiny new lid on a garbage can company."

"In about two years, sugar, it'll look like a garbage can."

Rodney pulls into the lot and goes around the corner of the building, but it turns out he isn't going to Ramapo Waste. When we get to the far corner of the building we can see there's this little motel tucked away off a gravel road in a grove of trees behind it. It looks like there's a river snaking down behind it, and maybe the place used to be a little resort. But not anymore. Not since they built a giant garbage can in front of it.

The neon sign to the place is blocked from road view by the new building. Without the lights turned on, it's hard to read that it's called the Two Bridges Inn. Something tells me they don't bother turning on the lights anymore, but maybe it's just closed down for the winter.

I stay parked at the corner of the building while Rodney drives up the winding gravel road to the motel. There's another car parked in front, but we're too far away to tell if anybody's in it. But we don't have any doubts it belongs to those FBI jerks Fogarty and Wilson.

"I don't think we should try to drive any closer than this," Nathan says.

"I agree with you. I say we get out and walk from here."

"Too cold. And besides, we've got these." He pops open the glove compartment and pulls out a pair of binoculars.

"My, my, Renzler thought of everything, didn't he?"

Nathan shrugs. "He's a professional snoop. You don't think he'd rather walk around in the mud than sit in his car and listen to the ball game, do you?" That Nathan, he's got an answer for everything and it's always so nonchalant you want to poke him.

He hands me the binoculars and I narrate for him while watching what's going on. "I don't see anyone in the car. Rodney's going to one of the rooms. He's knocking on the door. Someone's opening it. It's one of the FBI pigs. Fogarty. He's inviting Rodney in, but Rodney's backing up and looking around. I think our boy's getting a little bit nervous, Nathan."

"I don't blame him. I'm feeling a little nervous myself."

I know what he means. Suddenly, I can feel my fingers getting sweaty. It's like we're about to watch a guy get killed, which just might happen.

155

"Any sign of the other guy—Peter Piper?" Nate asks.

"Uh-uh." I pan away from Rodney and Fogarty for a moment and look near the cars. "Oh yeah, there he is. He's crouched behind Rodney's car on the driver's side."

"Yeah, I can see him."

"He's got something in his hand."

I move back to Rodney and Fogarty. Rodney still doesn't want any part of going inside, and it looks like he's winning the discussion. "They're exchanging envelopes. Rodney's not even looking at his. He's starting to walk away, now he's stopping. Fogarty told him to wait. Fogarty's pulling the papers out of the envelope and looking at them. Now he's nodding at Rodney. Rodney's turning, shuffling sideways back to his car. He's starting to get that grin on again."

"Here comes Wilson!"

I can see Rodney's expression changing, and I have to drop the binoculars to try and get a view of the whole scene. By the time my eyes adjust to the change, Fogarty and Wilson are about to make Rodney into a sandwich. Fogarty hits him from behind, and Wilson comes at him from the front with the thing in his hand. Before you know it Rodney hits the ground, and they both start in kicking him. I go back to the binoculars and their faces come through large and clear. They're laughing. I can see that the thing in Wilson's hand is a length of pipe.

Rodney's shades are off and he's grimacing in pain and screaming at them. It's terrible to have to sit and watch any black man getting beaten by pigs, even Rodney. Wilson lifts the pipe and comes down hard on Rodney's leg. He does it again, once, twice, three times. Each time he connects, Rodney lurches about five feet. He's trying to grab for his ankle, but every time Wilson goes to hit him again, Rodney has to pull away his hands.

156

"Oh man, this is fucking brutal," I say, letting go of the binoculars.

"I hope you aren't getting any notions about trying to help him."

"No sir, I'm just hoping they don't kill him. After they're finished, I think it would be a great time to ask him where Harpo is."

"Exactly."

Wilson hits Rodney twice more, then Fogarty leans down and pulls something from Rodney's pocket. I think it's the envelope with the money. This ain't turning out to be Rodney's day after all. As they get in their car, Fogarty turns and blows Rodney a kiss. What an asshole. They're out of there in a flash, and I have to move quick to back our car far enough behind the building so they don't see us on their way out. As soon as they get on the highway, I drive back to the gravel road and up to the motel.

Rodney's still on the ground when we get there, writhing in pain and clutching at his leg. When we get out of the car, he gets a look of recognition, then relief, on his face. "Oh baby," he says, "those pigs broke my fuckin' ankle."

"Oh baby," I say back to him, "you're breakin' my fuckin' heart."

He calls me a whore and a honky fucker and a few other things so disgusting I wouldn't repeat them in polite company. I got an answer for that: I give him another kick in his ankle.

This time he doesn't scream or nothing, he just lets out a pathetic yelp.

"Do you have a little boo-boo, sugar?"

"C'mon help me, I gotta get to a hospital."

"*Help* you? Of course we'll help you. That's what friends are for. And right now we're the closest thing to friends you got. Ain't that right, Nathan?"

"That's right. But you know, for some reason, I'm not feeling particularly friendly today."

"No, neither am I."

"C'mon, help me, baby, I can't even get to my car."

"Sure I'll help you. But first you got to help us."

"What do you want?"

"Just tell me where my brother is and how to get there."

He thinks that over two seconds before giving me an answer. "DeWitt's keeping him at the farm, it's out in Wisconsin."

"Where in Wisconsin?

"I'm not sure how to get there."

"Bullshit, you've been there!" I ask Nathan if he wants a shot at him, but he says he just had his shoes shined and doesn't want to get them scuffed.

I get set to give Rodney another kick with my boot, but he begs me off before I hit him.

"All right, all right, I'll tell you exactly how to get there."

Rodney starts giving the directions so quick, I don't even consider the possibility he's making them up. He's not that smart or loyal to Hartman. But I tell him he's not being specific enough anyway and make him go back through it while Nate writes it all down. This time he adds a couple of details, like gas stations and churches where you have to make a right or left, and gives us the phone number.

When he's done, I say, "Great, let's get going, Nathan."

"Hey, c'mon! I could die out here!"

"He probably could," Nathan says. "It might take a while before the garbage-can guys smell something fishy."

"Probably not until the weather gets warm." I'm smiling big-time when I say that, and Rodney gets this petrified look on his face and starts in begging some more.

"Please! I gotta get to a doctor."

"Well, seeing how you asked so nicely. I suppose we should give the boy a lift, don't you, Nathan?"

"It's okay with me. How far do you want to take him?"

"I'd say as far as his car."

"Sounds good." Nathan leans down and starts pulling Rodney up by one of his arms.

"C'mon. How the fuck do you expect me to drive?"

"Carefully," Nathan says, "very carefully."

TWENTY-TWO

"Sheila, if you don't mind, I think I'm going to put on my clothes." Juan was holding his hands over his crotch, presumably to shield his pecker from my line of vision.

"I sure don't mind," I said.

"Shut up, asshole." Juan withdrew one hand long enough to point at me. Despite his attempt to sound threatening, his tone was a little shaky. I figured his romp with Sheila had probably created some concerns about her state of mind.

"He wasn't asking *you*." She waved at me with the gun. "Sure, go ahead," she told Juan. "But make it fast. And bring me a Coke and the rest of that reefer."

"I'll be right back."

Sheila turned her gaze on me, and I tried to answer it without pissing her off. I wasn't sure if she'd prefer me to avert my eyes or admire her physique. I tried to play it neutral by looking past her. That didn't work.

"What're *you* looking at?"

"It's hard not to look at a body as good as yours." I tried to make it sound more like a statement of fact than a compliment. I didn't know how Sheila would react if she thought I was coming on to her.

"You think I got a great body, huh?" She almost smiled, and I didn't correct her self-elevation from good to great. Then she snickered. "My body's a whole lot better than them white bitches you ball. *If* you be getting any, which I seriously doubt."

I didn't see any gain in discussing my sex life with her, so I remained silent.

"So what the hell are you doing here, anyway?"

"Looking for James."

"Well, he ain't here. Hartman told you he's in isolation."

I pointed at the electric chair. "Isolation? They've been torturing him. Can't you see the bloodstains?"

Sheila gave the floor a glance and me a shrug. "This is Hartman's private room. Nobody's supposed to be in here."

"Aren't you concerned that something may have happened to your boyfriend?"

"He ain't my boyfriend. He was balling the white bitch. And it turns out he's a snitch."

"Who told you that—Hartman? He's the snitch. It's in these letters. He had a deal with the FBI." I reached for the papers.

"Don't you fucking move!" Sheila was back to ready and aiming in an instant. I obeyed her an instant later.

Juan returned with the Coke and a stick of marijuana. It was rolled in a paper designed like an American flag.

Sheila ordered him to light it and pass it to her. She took it with her left hand and clutched the gun with her right. She took a long drag and spoke while holding her breath.

"This pig's saying Hartman's a snitch for the FBI."

"It's all right here in these papers."

"Shut up." Sheila waved the gun. Again it wobbled. That

160

didn't stop her from having another go at the joint.

Juan stepped forward to have a look.

"Leave the papers alone, don't touch them." Sheila didn't wave the gun at him, but she spoke with the authority that went with holding it.

Juan stopped halfway to the desk. I think he might have summoned the nerve to challenge her ever so slightly if the telephone hadn't interrupted their standoff.

"You answer it."

Juan marched out of the room. Sheila resumed her spread position, holding the gun with both hands. She ordered me to stand against the wall, next to the electric chair. I thought about charging her, but she covered herself well. After a few moments, she sidled to the desk. As she glanced down to read, I could see her straining to keep one eye on me and one on the letters.

"You wrote this shit," she said. "You were planting them to frame Hartman."

I didn't see any gain in refuting her, but she seemed to be demanding a denial. "I don't even know how to type." That seemed like the sort of thing she might be able to relate to. It was, judging by her response.

"So what? You could've had someone type them for you."

As I weighed the wisdom of a reply, Juan returned. "That was Roach. He was calling from Newark airport to get the address of this lawyer in Chicago he's supposed to go see. He left it on the dining room table. He sounds really pissed. Rodney was supposed to go but—"

"Shut up! Would you just shut up? We don't want *him* hearing anything."

"Sorry. I didn't think I was saying anything important."

"*Every*thing's important. How many times have you heard Hartman say that?"

Juan shrugged. "I told Roach about Renzler. I told him you had everything under control."

I found it interesting that Juan didn't consider himself a partner in my capture, but Sheila didn't seem to notice. I noticed that she didn't pass him the joint.

"Yeah, and what did he say to that?"

"He says we should tie him to a chair in the basement and wait for him to get back. I didn't tell him we were in this room. He was mad enough at Rodney already."

Sheila rolled her eyes. "I don't need Roach to tell me what to do." She paused and appeared to be thinking it over. "Here, you hold the gun on him," she said at last. "I want to try something."

"What are you going to try?"

"You'll see."

Juan looked nervous as he received the gun with two hands, but he got a grip and aimed it at me. "We've all been trained in the use of firearms. So don't try anything funny."

I wondered whether Hartman really was planning to have his troops kidnap Happy Rockefeller. But I didn't ask. All of my attention was focused on Sheila.

She stood still and stared at me, as if to size me up. She looked to the wall, then at my feet, and took one step back. She seemed to be counting the number of steps to the wall. "Right about here," she said, pressing her toe into the carpet to mark a spot about three steps from the desk.

"What's there?" Juan asked. "I don't see anything."

"You'll *see.*" She took off on "see," starting out like a shot-putter. She did a half spin and brought her leg up and around, on a line for my head. It was a deft move, smoother than I expected, and her balance was better than I would have guessed. As I braced to take the blow, I felt like a goaltender guessing where a player is going to shoot the puck. I also felt like a lech,

162

because I still had space in my brain to process the way Sheila's breasts jiggled as she made her pivot.

I expected her to fade to my right, so I moved left.

Wrong move.

Sheila's follow-through was right up there with her opening form. I took the blow full force on my nose. I felt it all the way to the top of my head and halfway down my spine. My eyes started to spit. I tasted blood, smelled it, saw it and might have even heard some of it splatter onto the wall. I felt my shoulder kiss the floor. I felt the carpet against my face. I felt relieved that Sheila wasn't wearing shoes.

With Juan holding the piece, I hadn't wanted to do anything too aggressive. I'd wanted to find out what Sheila had before giving him an impulse to pull the trigger. I'd found out good, and now that I was on the floor I wasn't about to let myself find out again. I covered my face and let out a few grunts of pain. I didn't have to do much acting to make it sound authentic.

Lying on my side, I watched Sheila advance on me through the cracks between my fingers. With my nose stinging and eyes watering, she was mostly a blur. I could make out Juan a few steps behind her, a pale fuzzy shadow with a mouth hanging open wide enough to let out a single "Wow!"

Sheila opted to come at me with another spin. As she swung around, I kicked straight out and up with my legs. I caught her dead on, right in the spot where she would have a gut ten years down the road. Five maybe, if she liked to get stoned and pig out on Friendly's ice cream.

For one sweet moment, I had Sheila doing a balancing act on the bottoms of my shoes. A moment later, she was airborne. She landed quickly, back on her heels, arms flapping out from her body, grabbing for a hold of something.

All she got was air. Juan got all of her.

She fell into him, ass first, causing him to tumble backwards to the floor. He released one hand from the gun the instant she made contact. He let go with the other the instant he hit the floor. He made a perfect seat when she landed a moment later.

The gun flipped a few feet to their right. Sheila scrambled to grab it, but I scrambled faster. I beat her to it by a step and used it to step on her hand. She managed to reach up and punch me on my lower back, but it was like being hit with a marshmallow.

I stepped off her hand and smiled. "Don't feel bad, hon. You just need a few more years of practice."

She snarled and kicked at me. I sidestepped and showed her the gun. "Try that one more time and this here piggy's going to make your foot one little piggy short."

The threat of losing a toe seemed to take the fight out of her. Or maybe it was simply the idea that she had lost. She buried her face in the carpet and started to sob.

I didn't make any effort to console her. "Get up and get your fat ass into the chair." I gave her leg a little kick to nudge her along. As she got up, I let Juan see the piece. "You strap her in."

He responded with the same obedience he had shown Sheila. She required some prodding, but it wasn't anything I couldn't handle. When Juan was done fixing the straps, I told him to sit on her lap. I ripped the wires off the handle of the chair and used them to tie him to Sheila. I finished the job by covering their mouths with masking tape from the top drawer of Hartman's desk. As I taped Sheila's mouth, she tried to take a nip out of my hand.

"Bite all you want. I just don't want the neighbors to hear you barking."

I picked up the correspondence between Hartman and J.

Edgar and left without saying good-bye. On my way through the dining room, I paused to rummage through the papers that were strewn on the table. It only took a moment to find the one I was looking for. Just as I suspected, the lawyer whose address Roach had called to get was someone I knew—a handsome, brilliant friend of Harmony's.

I called directory assistance and got Brendan O'Malley's phone number. But when I called to warn him about Roach's impending visit, there was no answer.

TWENTY-THREE

Harmony and Nate were double-parked on my couch, with grins on their faces and drinks in their hands. No matter how fast I could get my hands on one, my mood was no match for theirs.

"What happened to your face?" Harmony was on her feet as soon as I hit the kitchen.

"Sheila gave me a love tap with her foot."

"Oh Jesus." She was at the refrigerator pulling ice out of the freezer before I could get there. "We were starting to get worried about you."

"*Starting* to get worried? I've only been gone all day."

She gave me a look but didn't say anything. Until she held up an almost empty tray. "Oh shit, we're just about out of ice."

"Gosh, I wonder how that happened."

She dropped the tray on the table, moved her hands to her

hips and tried to lock eyes. It wasn't easy, because mine were focused on the tray as I tried to pry the last lonely cube from its aluminum nest.

"Are you mad at us or something?"

I didn't attempt a reply. It wouldn't have been easy, because she barely left space for one.

"I'm sorry we used all the ice. We didn't know you'd be coming home with a shiner."

"I want the ice for a goddamn drink, not for my face."

"Hey, Renz, take it easy." Nate looked startled enough to almost think about getting up.

Right about then, I managed to separate the rack from the tray. The tray slid off the table and the rack popped into the air. They landed on the floor.

I shrugged and finally looked at Harmony. I could see the underpinnings of a smirk coiling at the edges of her mouth. "You shouldn't let the ice sit out and melt and then put it back in the freezer."

She backed up as I moved to the refrigerator to get a beer. "If you had a hard time, I don't blame you for being pissed. But don't be pissed at me. It wasn't me that kicked your ass."

"It's not my ass, it's my face." I wheeled to deliver that one, but it missed her as she raced ahead to her next line.

"I was busy kicking Rodney's ass." Now the smirk was in full bloom.

"*You* kicked Rodney's ass."

"His ankle, actually. After Peter Piper broke it."

I drank half the bottle of Rheingold that I had grabbed by mistake. Some fiend had left it during a party, and I hadn't gotten around to getting rid of it. I did so now by tossing it into the trash can from a distance of about ten feet. Then I went back to the refrigerator for another. I didn't speak until I sat down.

"Now that I'd like to hear about," I said finally. As she

started to speak, I added, "*After* I call O'Malley to warn him that Roach is coming to see him." With that, I got up and walked to the phone.

"What's Roach going to see Brendan for?" Harmony was following me across the room.

"I assume to recover the COINTELPRO documents your brother sent him that never got there."

"I don't understand. How do you know Harpo sent documents to Brendan?"

"Brendan said Harpo told him he was sending a Christmas gift. I'm betting it was a set of the documents." I tossed the sheaf of papers I had found in Hartman's desk onto the table. "Here's a curious set of documents, too. Take a look at the scam Hartman pulled off on J. Edgar Hoover."

"What?" Nate lifted himself off the couch and lumbered over for a look.

Harmony seemed uncertain whether she should look at the letters, help me call Brendan or start relating the details of their encounter with Rodney. "It sounds like we've got a lot of catching up to do," she said as our hands met on the handset of the phone. "What do you say we call a truce and fill each other in on what's happened?"

"That sounds like a fine idea," Nate said.

I nodded but didn't say anything. I was still mad, and it wasn't about ice cubes or getting kicked in the chops by Sheila Love. It was the idea that Harmony and Nate were having a cozy time together while I was on my own.

"We found out where they're holding Harpo," she told me.

"You did? Where?"

"Holy fucking shit!" Nate was just finishing the first page of Hartman's first letter.

"Yeah, that's exactly what I said," I told him.

There was no further comment about me losing my temper, though the therapist my last ex-wife had talked me into see-

167

ing would have accused us of leaving "important issues unresolved." In other words, I was still mad and they knew it, but it wouldn't come up until the next time I got mad, and there definitely would be a next time. There, have an insight on me and save yourself fifty bucks.

Next time arrived sooner than I expected. I went on a little rampage when I learned they had helped Rodney to his car. By then we were packing for an impromptu trip to Wisconsin.

"Oh, that's great, you guys are brilliant," I said. "What happens when Rodney warns Hartman that we're coming? They move Harpo to another location."

"Don't worry, Rodney ain't going to call him."

"How do you know?"

"I just know, OK?"

"No, it's not OK. It's pretty dumb, as a matter of fact."

"What the hell were we supposed to do? Bring him back here? Leave him to die?"

"I rather like the second option."

"Now look who's talking like it's the movies instead of real life." She raised her finger. "I'll tell you what. Soon as we get back, I'll buy you a whole bag of ice to piss on or cry in or whatever it is you want to do. How's that?"

"And I'll replace the bourbon we drank," Nate added.

I didn't say anything. I was feeling either too stupid or too mad to muster a reply. Plus the silence was broken by a phone call.

I could have named a dozen people who might be calling at that moment, so I was prepared for just about anyone. But when I grabbed the phone, I was caught off guard by the tiny voice that answered my gruff hello.

It was a woman, on the elderly side, I guessed. She asked for Harmony Rollins in a lilting whisper that made the name sound like the sweetest phrase that had ever been spoken.

Pride of authorship can have that effect. I'm sure my mother gave the nicest possible flavor to the pronunciation of Mark Renzler, though she was at the natural disadvantage that comes with learning to speak in Jersey.

I covered the mouthpiece as I handed Harmony the phone. "It's your mom."

She shook her head and looked toward the ceiling as if to beg forgiveness. Then she started speaking in a blitz of apology. "Mama, Mama, I'm sorry. I was going to call, but I've just been so busy. I was planning on coming up tomorrow, but—" Harmony's tone changed suddenly. "You got what in the mail? How big an envelope? Yes, that's right. He used to be my boyfriend, that's right."

Harmony shot me a glance. The guilt was gone from her face, and her eyebrows were dancing in jubilation. "Mama, here's what I want you to do. Put the envelope in the bookshelf and wait for me. I'll be up as soon as I can."

I signaled her with my hand. "Tonight."

She shot me a puzzled look, then asked her mother to hold on while we conferred.

"Mama got the documents in the mail."

I nodded. "Harpo sent them to O'Malley with her return address, and it got returned to her for more postage."

"How did you know that?"

"I'm not as dumb as I look." I was giving her my best know-it-all smirk. With Sheila's footprints on my puss, I probably looked dumber than I imagined. "You should go there tonight."

"No, I want to go with you guys."

"Go get the documents."

Harmony sighed. "Mama, you want to say hello to Nathan?"

Nate took the phone and caught up with Liza Rollins while her daughter and I hashed things out. I convinced her it was important to have the documents in case we had to negotiate with Hartman for Harpo's release. She didn't like the idea, but I think she could tell I wasn't in the mood to give in.

An hour later we were at La Guardia, catching the last flights out to Boston and Chicago. As I moved to give Harmony a good-bye hug, I mumbled an apology for losing my temper. She told me to forget it, that we'd all had a long day. Suddenly, I felt overwhelmed with regret that she wasn't coming with us. I had the urge to give her a real kiss, the kind that keeps you thinking about it until you get the chance for another one, but with Nate standing there, I felt too self-conscious to go through with it. Plus, as I maneuvered into position, my mouth collided with one of her tire-size hoop earrings. I had to settle for a peck on the cheek and tried to convey my feelings through the tenacity of my embrace.

As we pulled apart, her eyes were moist.

"Everything's going to turn out OK."

She nodded. "I'm finally going home to see Mama." As she backed away, a smile spread over her face. "Tell my little brother I'm going to kick his ass for all the grief he's put us through. And you two be careful."

"She's something else, isn't she?" Nate watched admiringly until Harmony's legs disappeared down the boarding tunnel.

"You said it." As I turned to reply, he was already bounding across the terminal to our departure gate. I had to step lively to catch up with him.

"If you don't mind my saying so," he said, "that was quite a hug the two of you had. I was tempted to avert my eyes."

"Maybe next time you'll go ahead and succumb to temptation."

"I guess I kind of spoiled your moment, huh?"

"Yeah, as a matter of fact, you did."

Nate didn't answer right away, because we had to give our tickets to the attendant. Halfway down the boarding tunnel, he said, "Well, someone's got to protect the young girl from old men with indecent designs. It might as well be Uncle Nate."

That stopped me dead in my tracks. I felt my bag drop, then listened like a bystander to the response that jumped out of my mouth. "The uncle act is getting real tired."

Nate spread his arms and almost blinded me with a glare of incredulity. "What's that supposed to mean?"

"It means I think you've got indecent designs of your own."

"Designs, no. Impure *thoughts,* yes. What straight guy wouldn't? But you, I can tell, would like to act on them. I'd never lay a hand on her."

"Bullshit. You already have."

"What? When?"

We stood glowering at each other with hands on hips. To a casual observer, we probably looked like two guys about to have at it. I picked up my bag and stepped onto the plane before someone got the bright idea to call security.

"What the hell are you talking about?" Nate whispered as we started down the aisle.

I glanced over my shoulder. "Four years ago. On my kitchen table."

"Oh, Jesus."

I didn't say anything else until we got to our seats. "I walked in on you," I said. "I didn't stay for all of it."

"Well, Jeez, I'm glad to hear that." Nate shook his head. "I don't believe it."

"What don't you believe? That I saw you?"

"No, that's irrefutable. The detail about where the deed took place takes care of that. And please, spare me any further details. Whatever it looked like from your point of view, I'd rather it stay your private memory. The thing I don't believe is that you're holding it against me. I mean, I've heard of being jealous, but not retroactively. You didn't even know her then. That was ancient history."

"Ancient history? It was four years ago."

"Things were different then. It was the sixties." He was grinning going on laughing.

"Don't give me that sixties crap, Nate. I don't think this is funny."

"Come on, Renzler, she was only a kid then."

"And you weren't."

"Sure I was. I still am. I always will be." He paused, waiting for a reaction.

I didn't give him one.

"Come on, aren't you going to challenge me, say I'm a pathetic old fuck who won't let go of his youth?"

"No. I'm content just to think it."

"Harmony was a free spirit then. We'd had this flirty thing going for years. It was nothing. It just happened."

"It looks to me like you've still got the flirty thing going."

"Of course we do. It'll always be like that. Jesus Christ, I'm getting it from all sides."

"What do you mean—Constance?"

"Yeah, Constance. We're getting married in four months. Does that mean anything to you? Do you think that means anything to her? Do either of you think there's a chance it might mean something to me?"

"Oh, I see." Until then, it hadn't even dawned on me what effect Harmony's presence might be having on Nate's countdown to bliss. I had forgotten how blissless the countdown can be.

Nate shook his head. "Jesus Christ, when does this goddamn plane take off? I'm dying for a cigarette."

"So am I."

"Listen, Renzler. If you want to hop in the sack with Harmony, go right ahead. She may be willing to do it. But I don't think you could handle it."

"Why not?"

"Because you're not a hop-in-the-sack kind of guy. *You've* got to have a relationship. It's in your altar-boy genes."

"I see. Well, thanks for putting my sense of decency in such an attractive light. We can't all be brought up Unitarian, you know."

"Aw, come on, stop being so damn sensitive. This woman's twenty-six, and you're staring down the barrel at fifty."

"I'm forty-fucking-one."

"Going on sixty-five. She's much freer about her sexuality than you are, that's a fact. You don't just want to sleep with her, you're falling in love. And love, for you, is a very deep hole."

He had a definite point there. I shifted in my seat, wondering when the hell we were going to take off.

"Okay, so maybe I am falling in love with her. Maybe I just want to enjoy that."

"Fine, go ahead, enjoy it. But it won't last." As if to emphasize the point, he issued a long yawn. "You're overmatched, Renzler. She'll break your fucking heart. I'd be willing to bet on it."

I almost took that as a dare and even thought about laying down odds. But I knew he was right. I didn't stand a chance with Harmony. We'd already had whatever we were going to have in a car in Indiana. In bucket seats, no less.

Just then our copilot drawled a big Texas hello over the rinky-dink intercom. It seemed there was this little piece of trouble with some of them doodads on the control board. Not to worry, though, because a crew of mechanics was on their way. As soon as they had the problem licked, we'd be heading for Chi.

"Yeah, like fucking tomorrow," Nate groaned.

The prospect of sitting on the runway till doomsday, coupled with Nate's assessment of my prospects with Harmony, had the effect of deflating my spirit and depleting my meager energy reserve. Suddenly, I felt properly ready to sink into my annual holiday depression.

"I think it's time to get some sleep," I said.

"Not me. I'd rather stay up all night bickering like a pair of old queens." He made a show of punching his courtesy pillow and parking it between his head and the window. He was silent for a few minutes, except for his breathing, which got gradually deeper. Just when I figured he was gone, he said, "By the way, Renzler, I should probably tell you: Harmony was making inquiries along the same lines about you today."

TWENTY-FOUR

The area around O'Hare Field in the middle of a December night is just what I had imagined Reykjavík, Iceland, to look like after hearing it described by someone who'd stopped there on the way to Europe. When Nate assured me Reykjavík was far more grim, I realized he was the one who had described it to me.

It had snowed and gotten colder since Harmony and I had been in Chicago, and the suburban expanse to the north looked like a tundra. By the time we neared Beloit two hours later, with the sun yawning on the horizon, Nate said, "Now *this* reminds me of Reykjavík."

We had to wind our way through town in pursuit of a state route that had been laid out with the idea of offering visitors an opportunity to support local merchants. We probably would have obliged on behalf of several dingy taverns we passed, but they were closed. Instead we settled for take-out coffee and candy bars from the SuperAmerica, an aggressively red, white and blue gas station on the corner of Fourth Street and Liberty.

Liberty led to Route 81, which, according to Rodney's directions, grazed the back side of the PRF pot farm about fifteen miles west, near Brodhead. About ten miles into the Siberian countryside, I began wondering why I had any confidence in Rodney's directions.

"If you see enough snow this white, slush probably doesn't look so bad after a while," I said.

"Yeah, it looks so sparkling pure, I'm getting an almost irresistible urge to pull over and deflower it."

I was feeling the same urge, though not necessarily for the same reason. I found a choice spot beyond a tiny bridge that had a sign announcing that it spanned the Sugar River. We hadn't seen a soul for five miles, but within seconds after our zippers were down, we had an audience approaching in a sedan a half mile to the west. If we had been on the side of a four-laner in the suburbs of New York, I'm sure we would have just kept on pissing. But out here we felt conspicuous. We inched down the hill toward the base of the bridge to avoid being seen.

The sedan slowed down when it neared our car. We were too well hidden to provoke moral outrage from its occupants, but I caught a glimpse of them as they passed. Considering I didn't know anyone in Wisconsin, it might seem remarkable that I recognized the only other people on the road at that godforsaken hour in that godforsaken place. But it wasn't a coincidence they were there. Seeing them eased my doubts about Rodney's directions, but it also raised my anxiety. A sudden chill came over me that had nothing to do with standing in a snowdrift exposing my pecker to subzero elements.

Jack Fogarty was driving, Peter Piper was riding shotgun. We considered following them, but we were so close to Hartman's place that we decided to press on.

"How the hell do you think they were able to find the place?" Nate asked.

"It could be they've known where it was all along. Or maybe they asked Rodney the same question you and Harmony did."

A faded red barn and farmhouse came into sight about two miles farther, just past County T. Unless Rodney had put in a last-minute twist, this was our destination. We made our next possible right, on Halfway Tree Road, a diagonal that angled slightly back in the direction we had come from. Half a mile along that, we came to a gate fronting a long driveway that curled back to the farmhouse. The driveway was visible in the snow because of a few sets of tire tracks. At least one set of tracks had been made by a white Mercedes that was parked by the house. I had seen the car once before—in Hartman De-Witt's driveway.

I drove toward the house, but we didn't go all the way there. I stopped about fifty feet away after noticing a trail of footprints and red spots that led away from the house toward the barn. Tracking in the great outdoors is hardly my specialty, but I didn't need Daniel Boone to surmise that the red spots were blood.

The snow was ankle-deep near the car, but we were in it up to our knees as we neared the barn. Along the side of the barn it had drifted to shoulder depth, but we didn't need to get that close. The trail we were following led behind the building. By that point, one set of footprints widened to indicate someone had required assistance or force to go farther. The trail ended at a huge tree about twenty-five yards behind the barn. A plaque posted by the state of Wisconsin indicated that the tree marked the halfway point between the Mississippi River and Lake Michigan.

If we had stopped to read the small print under the heading, I assume we would have learned how this piece of historical trivia had been determined, but we were more interested in investigating the groans coming from the other side of the tree.

Hartman DeWitt's eyes and mouth were closed, and his face was the color of a September sky. That was enough to determine that he wasn't the one making the noise. It had to be coming from the black and blue guy lying next to him. His eyes were closed too, but his arms were wrapped tightly around his torso. I was plenty cold in my winter coat, but this guy only had on a T-shirt and jeans.

As we moved in close, Hartman's companion actually opened his eyes. "Who the fuck are you?" he whispered.

"Harpo," I said, "that ain't any way to greet someone who traveled a thousand miles to save your life. But just so you know, I'm the honky your sister's been hanging with."

"Renzler. I've been hearing about you. From this shithead." He nodded toward Hartman.

"I'm Nathan Moore, Harpo." Nate took off his coat and laid it over him. "Do you remember me?"

"Uh-uh."

"I was a friend of your mother's."

"You the fat guy that was always hanging around trying to sell your paintings?" Harpo's voice was stronger. The idea that he wasn't going to die must have revived him considerably.

Nate shot me a glance. "Charming, isn't he?"

"Harpo, can you move?" I asked.

"If I could move, you think I'd still be lying here?"

Only then did I notice the length of rope that ran from the base of the tree to Harpo's chest. I took out my keys, which have a pocket knife on the chain, and began sawing away.

"Hurry up, man, I'm fuckin' freezing."

I was already a Popsicle. If Fogarty and Wilson had left right after dumping Harpo and Hartman, that meant he had been out there at least ten minutes, not counting how long it had taken them to drag him outside and tie him up. When I was done, I tried to gingerly slide the rope out from under him. But Harpo sat up and yanked it off with frozen fingers.

"Do you think you'll be able to walk?" Nate asked.

"Uh-uh. No way. Two pigs broke my fuckin' ankles with a pipe."

"Federal pigs," I said. "Fogarty and Piper."

"Yeah, that's right. But it's Wilson, not Piper."

"His real name's Pete Wilson, but his nickname is Peter Piper."

"How d'you know that?"

"It's a long story. But you'll be pleased to hear that your sister kicked him in the nuts last week."

"Oh, Harmony. Yeah, I want to hear about that."

As Nate lifted Harpo at the knees, I grabbed him under the shoulders. I could see burn marks up and down his arms.

"Who burned you?"

"Hartman, his faggot friend Roach and this Negro named Rodney whose ass I'm going kick as soon as I'm able."

"Harmony took care of Rodney, too. On that one, she got sloppy seconds after Wilson did his ankles. Did Fogarty and Wilson kill Hartman?"

"Fuck no. He was mine. Strangled the motherfucker with my own two hands. If I had to die, he was going first."

We half carried, half dragged Harpo to the car. We must have done a good job, because he barely complained at all. At one point when Nate's knee bumped his ankle, he let out a yelp and called him a dumb motherfucker, but he apologized right away.

178

"Where's the nearest hospital?" I asked when we laid him on the back seat.

"Uh-uh." He shook his head. "I ain't going to no fuckin' hospital."

"You need medical attention, pal," Nate said.

"There's a doctor in Beloit. Alice Christie. She'll be able to help."

"Is there anything in the house you need before we go?" I said.

"Yeah, my clothes. And there's a bottle of bourbon in the kitchen. Grab that. And someone ought to go to the barn and get us some reefer."

"Sounds like you're planning on having a party."

"Yeah, why not? I haven't felt this good in a long time."

Ten minutes later we were back on the road, with Harpo huddled under a blanket, him and Nate passing a joint and all three of us sharing a pint of Old Crow. Harpo also swallowed a dozen aspirin that Nate had in a travel pack. I knew he was in pain, but except for an occasional wince, he wasn't showing it.

About halfway to Beloit, he shouted, "Ah shit, man, stop! I just remembered: I got to call a guy right away."

"Who's that?" With no public phone in sight, I didn't even bother to slow down.

"This lawyer in Chicago."

"O'Malley?"

"Yeah. How'd you know that?"

"Harpo, you wouldn't believe all the crap I've learned in the last few days. Why do you need to talk to O'Malley?"

"Because those FBI pigs are on their way to his place. They're going to beat on him until he hands over these papers I sent him. We got to save them. That's what this whole thing is about, you see, these FBI memos that—"

"Yeah, I know, COINTELPRO memos. How did Fogarty and Wilson find out O'Malley had them?"

"Hartman told them. He sang as soon as they twisted his arm."

"Who told Hartman?"

"I did." Harpo gave his confession in a whisper, but he delivered his defense at full volume. "They were torturing me, man. Every day. Cigarette butts, electric shock. I held out two weeks. I would've gone longer, but I figured O'Malley had the damn papers long enough to do something."

"When was it that you finally gave in—yesterday?"

"Yeah, I guess that's when it was. I've lost track of the days."

"I was at Hartman's yesterday when Roach called to get O'Malley's address. Hartman sent him to get the papers."

"Did you talk to O'Malley? Is he doing anything, or does he just got his finger in his ass?"

"Don't worry about the papers. They're safe—at your mother's house."

"What? How'd they get there?"

"Next time you mail something important, make sure there's enough postage on the envelope."

"Are you kidding? Shit, man. How much does it cost to mail a damn letter in this country these days?"

TWENTY-FIVE

Harpo started laughing, and in a few moments he was going full tilt. Nate asked him what was so funny.

"I'm thinking about that poor sucker O'Malley. He ain't

going to know what hit him when those pigs start rattling his chain. I should probably call him anyway, give him a little warning."

"Don't bother. We'll take care of it." My tone was not friendly. I wasn't surprised that Harpo was less concerned with O'Malley's welfare than that of the papers, but it annoyed me. And I was relieved he wouldn't be with us much longer. Before we dropped him off, I asked him some questions to fill in some of the blanks in my mind.

Harpo said he had traced Hartman to Paterson and joined the PRF under the name James Brown. Then he went to the local FBI office to offer his services as an informant. Fogarty agreed to pay him a hundred dollars a month and assigned him to find out where Hartman was keeping the stolen papers. He took that as carte blanche to search the homes of practically everyone in the PRF.

"That really floored me, man, that the FBI knew Hartman had the papers. That crazy motherfucker was blackmailing the FBI. Which takes some balls, I got to admit."

"I read Hartman's correspondence with the FBI. He said he had two copies of the documents. Is that what you were able to find out?"

"Yeah, I guess that's right. Of course, I didn't care. All I needed was one. I figured if I could prove myself to Hartman—which shouldn't be too hard considering the clowns he's got worshiping him—I could gain his trust and find out where he was keeping the papers. Then steal them and bail. But the FBI started getting impatient. They were really turning up the heat on me. Not Fogarty, but this other guy in the group who was another informant. He was like my unofficial supervisor."

"Let me guess," I said. "Paul Weisberg."

"Yeah, yeah. Man, you really figured this thing out. That's

why my sister likes you. She goes for the smart ones, no matter what they look like."

"Thanks a lot."

"Hey, I didn't mean anything by that. I just—"

I ignored Harpo and spoke to Nate. "When Randall followed Rodney to the first meeting with Fogarty and Wilson, I thought it was Juan who drove him, because the guy had a Volkswagen. But it was Weisberg. Rodney used him as his go-between."

"And presumably Weisberg got himself a cut of the payoff."

"Yeah, I would think so."

"What are you two going on about?" Harpo asked.

"It's too complicated to explain now. Tell us how you got the papers."

"Well, this ex-Panther from Chicago, Bill O'Neal, showed up to visit Rodney. It turns out they're friends. Now O'Neal is the motherfucker who helped the FBI murder Chairman Fred Hampton. It's all in the papers. That's why they're so important."

"He drew the floor plan for them."

"Yeah, that's right. Harmony told me on the phone that you got that. Anyway, O'Neal didn't recognize my face, but he knew my voice. He started saying I seemed familiar and all. I was afraid he was going to say something to Rodney and blow my cover."

"I don't think he did," I said. "I think he tipped off the FBI instead. A few days after you disappeared, two FBI agents came by Sheila Love's house looking for you—not James Brown, but Harpo."

"Is that right? Yeah, that doesn't surprise me one bit. I knew from the day I met him he was a rotten motherfucker. Anyway, when he showed up, I figured I had to make my move."

"What did you do?"

"I persuaded Hartman to invite me to his house."

"How were you able to do that?"

"How do you *think* I was able to do it?"

Harpo had a way of making you feel dumb. I wondered if he had learned the skill from his sister or if it ran in the family. The answer to my question was obvious the instant he made me think about it.

"Sex," I said.

"Yeah, that's right. Only it didn't get that far. Once I had Hartman alone, I showed him a different kind of pistol than the one he was expecting. I had him on his knees begging in no time. I should've wasted the motherfucker right then and there. Instead I just locked him in the closet."

"In retrospect, it does seem like that would have been a good idea," Nate said.

"It seemed like a good idea then. I just couldn't bring myself to do it. He was so pathetic."

"The reason Fogarty and Wilson finally moved on Hartman was because Rodney sold them the second set of the papers," I said. "It was buried under the floorboards in Judith Fairbanks's house. She was Hartman's niece, did you know that?"

"Yeah, she told me that once. She's the one who screwed everything up in the first place. Me and a friend of hers boosted the papers. Patty told Judith, then she went and told Hartman. He talked Patty into giving him the papers, then he split with them. I didn't know Judith then. I found all this out from Patty after I tracked her down in Toledo. She was afraid I was going to kill her—and don't think it didn't cross my mind. Anyway, once I got to Jersey, I thought Judith might have the papers. That's why I was trying to get close to her."

"Sheila thought you were sleeping with her."

"Is that right, did she tell you that?" In my rearview mirror, I could see that Harpo was grinning. "Well, Sheila, she's kind of an excitable girl."

"Tell me about it." I was tempted to ask Harpo what he saw in Sheila, but we had more important things to cover. "Judith was murdered. Did you know that?"

"Whoa, whoa, what?"

"She was beaten to death in her house. It was in all the papers."

"Sorry, man, I haven't exactly been keeping up with the news."

"If you were, you'd have found out the FBI has you pegged as the number-one suspect."

"Me! That's bullshit! Where did they get that?"

"Someone tipped them off. I think it was Hartman. They're not looking for James Brown. They're looking for Harpo Rollins."

"Man, I'm confused."

"Did you tell Hartman who you were?"

"I don't know. Yeah, I think I maybe did, when I made him give me the papers."

"Well, after Judith was killed, I think he tipped off the FBI about Harpo Rollins to take the heat off the PRF."

"Yeah, that's the kind of thing he'd do. When did this happen, Judith getting killed?"

"Three days before Christmas."

"When was that?"

"Five days ago."

"I think I still would've been at Hartman's house. That's where they were keeping me. Until a few days ago. Then they shot me up with something. The next thing you know, we're at the farm, just me and Hartman. I woke up when he was trying to lift me out of the trunk of his car. He had me handcuffed the whole time. I got no regrets about killing that motherfucker."

We were in Beloit now, and Harpo started to direct me to Alice Christie's house. He said he knew where he was going, but after a few wrong turns, I realized he was working on trial and error. I stopped at SuperAmerica so Nate could look her up in the phone book. While he was doing that, I asked Harpo how he got caught.

"I went to see Weisberg and told him Hartman caught me snooping around his house and I had to split. I told him that so he wouldn't suspect me of stealing the papers and the FBI wouldn't start looking for me."

"Weisberg told me you said Hartman had accused you of sedition."

"Yeah, I might've thrown that in. Hartman was into those three-dollar words. So was Weisberg. I told him lots of stuff to keep him going. I told him I suspected Rodney was Harpo Rollins. The day I left, I told him I thought Hartman was keeping the papers at Judith's. I didn't know that, but I wanted to give him something that would keep him occupied."

I nodded. "We met up with Fogarty and Wilson while they were watching her house. They were probably searching it whenever she left."

"When was that?"

"The day Harmony played the nutcracker on Wilson. The same day Judith was killed."

"This would've been about a week earlier. I asked Weisberg to swap cars. But it didn't work. I had to go to the Western Union to get the money Harmony sent me, but Rodney and Roach saw me. They took me back to Hartman's. That's when all the fun started."

He shifted in his seat and winced in pain.

"Don't worry, the fun's finally over. You're going to be OK."

He toasted me with the last of the Old Crow. "I'm feeling

185

no pain already, my man. Funny how just knowing you're going to live can do that."

"You don't think it was a coincidence that Roach and Rodney found you, do you?"

"I don't know. You tell me."

"I think Hartman called Weisberg and told him you took the papers. He knew Weisberg was an informant, and neither of them wanted the papers made public. That would've ruined both their scams. It would've gotten Hartman killed. I imagine Weisberg told him about the car swap. You didn't tell him you were going to Western Union, did you?"

"No, of course not." He paused, and for a moment I thought I might have insulted him with the question. "But shit, I guess maybe I might've told him something."

"What do you mean?"

"He said he could try and get me some money from Fogarty. I told him my sister had wired me some. I didn't mean to be giving him information, I just wanted to keep as far from Fogarty as possible." He shook his head. "Man, I fucked myself, didn't I?"

"With all the heat you had coming down on you, I think you played the whole thing pretty cool."

Nate returned to the car armed with coffee and donuts and the news that Alice Christie's place was only a few blocks away. On our way, I told Harpo about Hartman sending Rodney to Judith's house to get the papers and him dropping the floor plan memo and the crowbar on me.

"You're lucky he didn't kill you. That Rodney is one sick boy. If you ask me, he's the motherfucker that probably killed Judith. And I'll bet that ain't the only thing he did to her, if you know what I mean."

I told him I did, but I didn't bother telling him I thought he was wrong. I had my own idea about who killed Judith, and I was damn sure it wasn't Rodney.

TWENTY-SIX

Alice Christie, MD, ran a clinic out of an old Victorian house in a neighborhood seedier than I expected to find in small-town America. But Beloit was more a city than a town, industrial rather than agricultural. Her clientele was all black, judging by the handful of people waiting in her living room.

She was about forty, tall and thin, and her hair was knotted in tiny braids with plastic tips on the ends. She wore an African-style robe instead of a medical smock. She gave off a sense of warmth, but her facial expression was a mile from a smile. When I told her why I was there, she simply nodded and told me to pull the car around back and leave Harpo in the basement.

"Don't tell anyone you brought him here. No one. Do you understand?"

I said she had my word, but I had a feeling she didn't think that was worth all that much. When I told her I thought Harpo's ankles were broken and he would need X rays, she shrugged. "I've handled worse than broken ankles, Mr. Renzler, I assure you."

There were no tearful farewells when we left Harpo on a cot in the basement. The closest he came to thanking us was when he shook my hand and said, "Renzler, I'm going to tell my sister you're all right for a white boy."

I thought we'd be imposing if I asked to use the phone, so I didn't call Brendan O'Malley until we hit a Clark station on the edge of town. I was still unable to get through, but this time there was a change in phone status: I got a busy signal. My gut told me someone had taken the phone off the hook.

The highway had appeared icy in spots on our way north, but in the light of cold day I could see that the pavement was as dry as a martini the way my father taught me to make one. I kept the speedometer on eighty except when we came to toll booths, and we were in sight of O'Hare in an hour. That still left plenty of time for Roach and Fogarty and Wilson to inflict some damage on Brendan O'Malley, assuming he'd had the misfortune of making their acquaintance.

I got off on North Avenue, as Harmony and I had done on Christmas morning. When we got into familiar territory, I began scouting for a pedestrian who looked capable of giving decent directions. Before seeing any such creature, we happened upon Wells Street, where O'Malley's place was located.

The block was in need of spiffing up, and there were signs that developers had already started. But not in the droopy two-story building that served as Brendan O'Malley's home and office. I parked by a hydrant, leaving it to Hertz to fix any ticket we might get. I had the only gun, so we pulled the tire iron out of the trunk for Nate.

A three-step brick stoop led to the entrance on the right side of the building. The door was unlocked, and we stepped into a tiny anteroom with a pair of wood-and-glass doors. One faced left and led to the office; the other faced straight ahead to a flight of stairs. Each door had a security plate straddling the frame, designed so visitors had to be buzzed in. Above O'-Malley's name on the buzzer panel was a red bumper sticker with a clenched black fist and a brief statement: POWER TO THE PEOPLE.

Getting inside the door to the stairs required no power at all. I didn't bother to check whether it was unlocked or if the lock was broken. I was more focused on the voices coming from upstairs. I was able to distinguish three of them. Two had

188

Jersey accents. They were saying things like, "Start talking, asshole, or we'll burn your fucking face off." The third voice didn't betray any regional identity, but it was only repeating phrases in monosyllables: "No, no, no; God, no; please no."

The stairway led to a landing, then veered sharply left, a ninety-degree angle before half a century of sag, warp and tilt had set in. We crept that far and peered around the corner. There were five steps to the top, where another windowed door fronted a sparsely furnished living room. We couldn't see anyone through the glass. The voices were coming from the rear of the apartment, to our right.

The top step was deeper and wider than the rest, giving way to extra space on either side of the doorway. To the right was a shallow closet where O'Malley kept two ratty coats, three ratty flannel shirts, a ratty umbrella and a half-gallon can of rat poison. To the left was a crawl space holding a few boxes and two ratty pairs of work boots. The nooks looked to be more a result of bad craftsmanship than good design, but I knew they were going to prove useful to us.

Nate and I conferred in whispers while O'Malley was letting out another series of moans. The plan we came up with called for Nate to crouch in the crawl space and me to stand in the closet. When I'd had enough of a whiff of O'Malley's topcoat to know it hadn't seen a dry cleaner since leaving the Salvation Army, Nate busted the glass door with the tire iron and shouted, "You suck, O'Malley, you commie pinko faggot!"

The racket of shattering glass gave way to instant silence. After a long pause in which I could visualize Fogarty and Wilson scratching their heads and trading befuddled looks, one of them muttered, "What the fuck?" To which the other replied, "Pete, go take a look and see what's going on."

Just as Wilson's footsteps became audible, he called out, "FBI. Come out with your hands up."

189

I took that to mean he was holding a gun. Needless to say we didn't follow his orders.

A moment later, I heard the crunch of glass beneath Wilson's feet. He stopped at the doorway, and I saw his right arm from the shoulder down to the pipe gripped in his hand. Nate could have nailed him then, but he waited, counting on Wilson to be curious enough to move into the stairwell. He was.

With the glass knocked out of the door, Wilson could have stepped right through it. But he used the knob, reflecting the superior breeding that separates an FBI special agent from your basic PD slob. To do so, he had to use his left hand. As the frame swung toward me, I had my gun trained on his head, two feet away tops as he took a tentative step down.

That was the last step he negotiated with one of his feet. Nate swung the crowbar dead on, pulverizing the sucker's wrist. The blow knocked him off balance, and his left hand was too busy grabbing for his injured right to reach out and steady himself. Plus he had the added inconvenience of me ramming him with my shoulder. It happened so fast he didn't have time to cuss. The only sound that came out of his mouth was a drawn-out "whoa." That formed a nice bass line to the melodic chime of the falling pipe, which preceded him down the stairs.

Wilson cleared the landing without slowing down for the turn. The wall helped considerably with the change in direction. He went into it headfirst and low, then resumed his descent with the precision and grace of a broken Slinky. I dashed after him while Nate turtled back into his nook. Wilson stopped at the third step, but I helped him down the rest with a kick that dented his face.

Upstairs I could hear footsteps coming fast and Fogarty's voice. "Pete, are you okay?"

I showed Wilson my gun and said, "One word and you're dead, cocksucker." But his mouth was too occupied sucking

190

in air to present any threat of uttering speech.

I imagine Fogarty came through the door with less caution than Wilson, because after the initial crash and grunt from above, he tumbled all the way to the bottom of the stairs without assistance from me. His gun preceded him by about six steps. I snared it off a bad hop before he crash-landed on his partner.

Our only concern at that point was being spotted by a passerby. But with threats of mayhem, we were able to coerce them up the stairs rather quickly.

Brendan O'Malley was handcuffed to a chair in the kitchen. His legs were within inches of a hot radiator. He was naked save for a pair of boxer shorts. There were burns on his chest and legs. His face was bruised and bloodied, his eyes red and swollen. When he saw me, his expression twisted into what would have to pass for a smile until his face healed.

"Sorry about the fucking mess you've been dragged into, Brendan. Are you all right?"

"Better than I was five minutes ago, worse than I was the last time I saw you."

I introduced O'Malley to Nate while Fogarty went into his pockets for the keys to the cuffs. We had him propped against the stove next to Wilson. They were quite docile with Fogarty's gun aimed at them. I was holding it in the hand that didn't have a cigarette in it.

There was one other person in the room. O'Malley told us he had arrived late the night before and was responsible for much of the work that had been done on Brendan's face. But Roach's own face was now showing plenty of wear and tear. He was lying under the table, hands and feet bound behind his back with duct tape. His mouth was shut tight with a strip of the tape. As Nate peeled it off, I greeted him with a nice big "Hiya, asshole."

He glowered but didn't speak. I'm sure he was relieved to

be getting rescued, no matter who was doing it.

O'Malley tried to get out of his chair, but his legs wobbled and he had to sit back down. "Oh, man. These guys have been torturing me, demanding those documents that Harpo stole. I kept telling them I don't have them, but . . ."

He began to sob, and Nate stroked his shoulder. "It's OK, pal," he said. "The worst is over."

"Ah, ain't that sweet," Wilson said.

"And ain't that a dumb thing for someone in your position to say." As Nate took a step toward him, Wilson covered his head with his arms. Nate kicked him in the ribs, and the arms jerked back to his side as he groaned. Nate flashed me the grin I've come to know and love through the years. "Damn, this is fun. I've been wanting to beat the crap out of an FBI agent since before I even saw Efrem Zimbalist Junior."

"Enjoy it while you can," Fogarty said, "because you're not going to get away with this."

"Oh no? Who's going to stop us—L. Patrick Gray?" Nate laughed at his own crack longer than was warranted, then turned to O'Malley. "Brendan, you want a couple of shots at these cocksuckers?"

O'Malley deliberated a few moments before shaking his head. "Once I start, I don't think I'd be able to stop."

Nate wheeled and delivered a soccer-style kick to Fogarty's gut. "Yeah, I know exactly what you mean."

I told O'Malley about Harpo's problem with insufficient postage.

"Jesus, Harpo." He shook his head in exasperation. "I'd like to kill him, you know that."

"These two law-enforcement professionals came very close to doing it for you. Harpo's in a lot worse shape than you are." I crouched down and spoke to Roach. "They also murdered your boss."

"You fucks! You lousy fucks!" Roach's body twitched as

he yelled. He tried to roll himself at Piper, but the legs of the table blocked his advance.

"We didn't murder anybody," Fogarty said.

"No. You just broke the guy's ankles and left him to die in the snow. Which he did."

"Where is he?" Roach fought back sobs as he looked up at me.

"On the farm, behind the big tree."

O'Malley looked baffled, but he didn't ask to be filled in as he got up. "I'm going to see if I can manage to put on some clothes. The phone's behind the refrigerator if you want to call the cops."

"No sir. Brendan, I've got no intention of doing that. How long do you think they'd hold two FBI guys?"

"You're right. What am I thinking?" He shook his head. "Well, what are we going to do with them?"

"Cuff them, for starters." Nate motioned for Fogarty to turn around. "Hands behind your back, Jack."

"I suggest appointing a guardian." I looked at Roach. "How would you like to take over the care and feeding of two federal pigs?"

"I'd like it just fine." With his swollen face and wet cheeks, Roach had the look of a pouting kid who'd finally gotten his way.

"Him?" Wilson pointed at Roach with his good hand. "He'll kill us! And you know it."

I was almost certain Wilson was right. Considering the extent of my involvement in abusing two feds, I feared that pushing them off the earth was the only way to get myself out of an ungodly mess. It had been a long long while since I had played the role of judge and executioner. The last time had been when I avenged the murder of Larry Sturgis. Larry was the guy who got me off the cops and into the private-investigations racket. That was on August 21, 1956, the last and only time I shot and killed someone. It happened in a stairwell on Valentine Avenue in the Bronx. The guy's name was Sal Riccio—at least that's what he was calling himself that night. Sixteen years later, I still dream about it on bad nights. On real bad nights, the dream flip-flops and Riccio is about to shoot me. My ex-wife Katie O'Leary told me the dream was my subconscious telling me that if I hadn't killed Riccio, he would have killed me. That made some sense, but it would have made more if Riccio had been carrying a gun.

This time, with Roach doing the dirty work, I was serving only as judge, not executioner. Still, I knew I'd think about it for a long while and dream about it even longer. But I figured if I was in the position of signing a death warrant, it might as well be for someone who had left three people for dead and screwed up Randall Edwards's life.

"I doubt he'll kill you," I told Wilson. "Though he might break your ankles and leave you in a snowdrift. Which would be fine with me. You know why?"

Neither of them attempted to guess, but I paused to allow them time to do so. "Because you sick pricks killed my mother's cat."

It took half an hour to make the arrangements. We located Fogarty and Wilson's rental Oldsmobile and moved it to the alley behind the building. We had to use every inch of the spacious cargo area to stuff them into the trunk. With their hands cuffed and mouths taped, they weren't able to put up much resistance.

Roach hobbled to the car and got behind the wheel.

"Whatever you do," I said, "make sure you do it way the hell out in the country."

He nodded. "I know just the spot." He pulled the gear shift down to drive but paused before taking off. "Renzler? Before Hartman died, did he say anything about me?"

I lied, and I don't know why. "Yeah. He said he loved you."

"Thank you," he said softly, pushing his hand through the crack in the window.

I didn't feel like shaking it, but I did anyway. This time I knew exactly why I was doing what I was doing. I would have given odds that Roach was going to kill himself.

O'Malley didn't want to go for medical help until two o'-clock, when a friend of his came on duty in the emergency room at Northwestern Hospital. By then we had all spoken to Harmony, three guys to whom she felt deeply in debt, two of whom had been rewarded long in advance. She told me she was leaving for New York in an hour. When we met back at my place that evening, I had a feeling I'd finally get my turn to collect.

TWENTY-SEVEN

I suppose it may seem like I'm butting into Renzler's story again and I guess that's exactly what I'm doing, but it's really important for people to know what's in the FBI memos my brother stole and I just don't think Renzler has the patience to explain it all. I hope I don't appear ungrateful because he's really a beautiful human being in his own way. It's just that he has this attitude like no one should be surprised that our government is a bunch of crooks who'll stop at nothing to get what they want.

Anyway I'll try and make it quick.

It's so wonderful to see Mama again after all this time, I'm overjoyed as a matter of fact. But we're not done hugging five minutes before I get myself a look inside the mysterious envelope that got sent back to her.

There really isn't much of a mystery, since I know before opening it that it contains the FBI memos. But I'm dying to get a look at them, and they turn out to be even more incredible than I expected. There's no note to Brendan, which is just like Harpo not even to say hello. But considering how much pressure he was under, it could be he just didn't have the time.

Once I start reading, it's easy to see why the FBI is so desperate to keep the memos from being made public. Some of them are written by J. Edgar Hoover himself, and most of them are stamped "Confidential" or "Do Not Remove" and have a heading that says "Counterintelligence Program—Racial Matters" or sometimes just "COINTELPRO."

One thing that's clear from reading the memos: Hoover was truly deranged and a total racist. In 1967 he started this top-secret counterintelligence program, ordering FBI offices around the country to do whatever it takes to disrupt black political groups and prevent the rise of a black messiah. He calls Martin Luther King a "burrhead" and approves plans to spread rumors that Stokely Carmichael is a CIA agent and tell Eldridge Cleaver's wife he's having affairs with teenage girls.

In another memo Hoover orders agents to submit ideas for "crippling" the Black Panther Party. The tactics they come up with include infiltrating local chapters and trying to provoke them to commit crimes, writing phony leaflets and anonymous letters, spreading rumors that people are paid snitches to make everyone paranoid, wiretapping people's phones, breaking into houses and leaning on the local police to arrest people who haven't done anything wrong so that all the money they raise for their programs will get wasted paying for bail bonds and legal fees. In most of the memos they're out to get the Panthers, but they've also been using some of the same tactics to harass groups like the Puerto Rican Independence movement, SDS, the United Farm Workers and the Socialist Workers Party.

The thing that scared Hoover the most about the Panthers was the success of their free-breakfast programs. There's a memo from an FBI agent in San Francisco saying the program there is supported by moderate blacks and whites, and Hoover sent the guy a blistering response saying that's exactly the point and that's why he should be thinking of ways to destroy it.

The memos that interest me the most are the ones from Chicago. In January 1969, almost a year before Fred Hampton was murdered, the head of the Chicago FBI, Marlin Johnson, composed an anonymous handwritten note and sent it to Jeff Fort, this badass leader of the Blackstone Rangers, a street gang that was having a turf battle with the Panthers. Here's what the note said:

> Brother Jeff—
>
> I've spent some time with some Panther friends on the West Side lately and I know what's been going on. The brothers that run the Panthers blame you for blocking their thing and *there's supposed to be a hit out for you.* I'm not a Panther, or a Ranger, just black. From what I see these Panthers are out for themselves not black people. I think you ought to know what their up to. I know what I'd do if I was you. You might hear from me again.
>
> —A black brother you don't know.

In the memo Johnson sent Hoover to get his approval, he says he hopes it will provoke Fort to kill Fred. So it turns out the FBI was trying to get a gang leader to murder Fred long before they decided to help the Chicago police do the job. And

197

the most amazing part is, this dude Johnson says they were thinking about sending the same sort of note to Fred, but they decided it wouldn't work because the Panthers aren't as violent as the Rangers. Which is a fact. So it's okay with the FBI if Jeff Fort and the Blackstone Rangers peddle drugs to black kids, as long as they can stop the Panthers from feeding them breakfast!

The more I keep reading, the more upset and angry I get. I practically jump down Mama's throat when she comes to my room to call me to breakfast. I want to cry or scream or kill someone, but I manage to compose myself and have a pleasant morning with her. I keep assuring her Harpo will be fine even though I have no way of knowing what's happening out in Wisconsin, which has also got me real worried.

I finish reading the stuff after breakfast. I see the floor plan again, plus there are memos in which the Chicago FBI takes credit for having Fred killed and arranges to give Bill O'Neal a three-hundred-dollar bonus for his help. Three hundred stinking dollars! When I think about O'Neal, it just makes me more furious. He's one of the ones who spread rumors that Harpo was the snitch and he even went to Mrs. Hampton's house in Maywood to ask if he could be a pallbearer at Fred's funeral, which he was. I heard he left Chicago around the same time I did, but if I ever see him again I know I'd kill him in a second.

Around noon I get a phone call that puts me in a better mood. It's Renzler and Nathan and Brendan calling to tell me what's been happening out there. Hearing that Harpo is alive and being able to tell Mama that for sure is a huge relief. Plus after staying up all night reading about how vicious people can be, it's a trip to be reminded how lucky I am to know three guys that wonderful who are willing to do so much for me. That's what we've got to do: Expose the bad people but make sure we cherish the good ones. It's what the struggle is all about.

I'm totally exhausted, and what I should do is take a nap, but I'm too wired to sleep and I decide my place is back in New York to get things moving with the memos. It just about breaks my heart to tell Mama I'm leaving so soon, and I can tell she's disappointed, but I promise to come back in a couple of days, and by then I'll have more news about Harpo.

After dropping off my rental car at Logan Airport, I'm clutching the envelope with the documents like it's solid gold. To be on the safe side, I'd like to make copies and send a set to Brendan right away, but I couldn't find a Xerox machine anywhere in Holyoke, and now I can't find one at the airport. I feel apprehensive only having the one set, but I know I'll be able to make copies once I get to New York.

Luckily this isn't the flight on which I die in a crash. I've got to search all over La Guardia to do it, but I finally find a Xerox machine that only breaks down a few times, and I manage to make a set of fuzzy copies that will have to do for now. I keep the original set under my arm and stuff the new one into my purse. Once that's done I feel a whole lot better.

Things have been so topsy-turvy lately that when I get to Renzler's building I almost feel like I'm returning home, even though if my own apartment was as sloppy as his, I'd probably set fire to the place. When I get off the elevator, I notice right away that the hallway is dark, but I don't think anything of it except that the bulb must've burned out and it'll probably take the super three months to replace it.

The door to Renzler's apartment is just to the right of the stairs, but I'm so focused on trying to get the key in the lock that I don't notice the guy sitting on them. In fact I think I probably smell him before I see him and by then it's already too late. I can hear him move, and it's only a second or two later when I feel this terrific pain in my side where he pokes me with one of his crutches.

I've got the door unlocked and pushed slightly open, but I'm knocked a couple of steps away from it when he hits me. My eyes have adjusted to the light enough so I can see him coming towards me, but mostly what I see is the doorknob just out of reach, like in a dream where you're paralyzed and you can't get your body to move at all. I kind of lunge for it, but he whacks me again, and this time he gets me in the back, knocking me forward into the door.

It gives and I go sprawling inside, I think maybe he tripped me too because I feel a stab of pain in my shin as I go down. I'm flat out on my belly but I roll right over on my back and try to kick the door closed. All I get is air though, because I'm still close to the doorway and the door is wide open and I've got Rodney standing over me. He yanks the door closed, slamming it on my leg, which gets caught against the frame, and he holds it there. That's the first time I'm aware of hearing anything, which is me letting out a scream of pain and then him laughing.

He pushes the door open again and I can move my leg away, but now I'm really in trouble. I can see him lifting one of his crutches up, and I brace for more pain because I know he's going to hit me with it, only I don't know where.

My stomach, he jams it into my stomach, and now I can't get a breath. He may be hurting bad from the beating he took, but he's still got plenty of strength left. I can tell that because he jams the crutch between my legs and pushes me across the floor like he's playing shuffleboard.

Rodney needs his crutches to move, which gives me time to roll back over to my hands and knees and try to crawl away. But the next thing I know I feel one of the crutches come down on my spine and I'm down on my stomach with my face pressed against this throw rug of Renzler's that's covered with cat hair.

He flops down on top of me, planting his knees into the back of my thighs and pushing out so my legs are spread like a frog. Then he leans forward so his weight is on my back and slides his hands underneath me and starts feeling me up. That's the worst, absolutely the worst.

He puts his head down next to mine so we're cheek to cheek, and I want to choke from the overpowering smell of his cheap cologne. Now it's even worse, and he whispers in my ear. "Baby, if you say a fuckin' word or try and get away, I'm going to slice these luscious tits right off, you understand?"

All I can manage to say is "uh-huh," and that's barely audible, so I nod my head as hard as I can. While I'm doing that, he slides his hands back out. Then I hear a loud click, the unmistakable, terrifying click of a switchblade.

As he's getting off me, he slides the blade from my neck all the way down my back. It doesn't hurt, it just tingles. I don't think he's cut me, but the idea that he could and would scares the living daylights out of me. I'm not about to try anything unless I'm sure it will work. Right now, it looks like my best strategy is to hope like hell Renzler and Nathan get back real quick.

I wait until Rodney's completely off me and standing up before I turn over and look at him. I'm aching all over when I get to a sitting position, and I feel a chill on my back that makes me realize he sliced my blouse open. When I take stock of things I see that my wardrobe ain't holding up well at all. I've lost the heel to my right boot, I'm missing half the buttons on my blouse and it's torn in three places. But my blue jeans are hanging in there.

Rodney's got his shades off, and he's leaning against the wall grinning. "So where's your honky boyfriends?" he asks.

I tell him they'll be back in a little while, it could be any minute.

"That's nice. I got some plans for them." He holds up his knife to give me an idea of what he's got in mind, then suddenly asks, "What you got in the envelope?"

I don't answer, because he's already limping over to take a look. I don't even remember dropping it, but it's on the floor near the door, right next to the other things I don't remember dropping: my coat and purse.

"Oh, some more of these things," he says as he's sliding out the memos. "Baby, you're really making my day."

He orders me to get the phone and bring it to him. That's when I find out how hard it is to walk. But it's even harder for him. When he sees that the base of the phone won't reach, he recites a number in New Jersey for me to dial and has me bring him the handset. He tells me to stand right next to him and all the while he's on the phone, he's grinning and staring inside my blouse. The guy makes me totally sick to my stomach. I think about Renzler criticizing Nathan and me for not leaving him to die. You want to know something? He was right.

"Yo, it's me," Rodney says when somebody answers. "Guess what. I got some more of those FBI papers." There's a long pause, and then he looks at the documents and says, "Yeah, they look like the same ones to me." After that there's an even longer pause, and he stops grinning for a few moments. "Oh, no, this time *you* can deliver them. And I want all the money up front or there's no deal." The guy must be objecting, because Rodney says, "That's your fuckin' problem, boy. You want these papers, you pay for them tonight. Yeah, tonight. My place. Half an hour. If I ain't there, wait for me."

Rodney hands me the phone to hang up and says, "C'mon, baby, get your coat on, we gotta go."

"I thought you wanted to wait for my honky boyfriends."

"Change of plans, baby, change of plans." He pushes me

202

towards the door and shows me his knife. The blade's like six inches long. "Try and get away and I'll give you a new Virginia."

I can't tell if he's making a joke or if he really thinks that's what it's called. But I got more important things to think about. If I'm not there when Renzler and Nathan get back, I'm sure I'll never see them again. Rodney is going to kill me. And that's not what worries me. It's what he's thinking about doing to me beforehand that's scary.

I feel so embarrassed playing a detective in the movies who gets to kick everybody's ass but being a pushover when it comes to a real life-and-death situation. But in my movie there's this scene where I get captured and leave a message for a friend by writing in lipstick on my bathroom mirror. I don't have any original ideas, but in Hollywood they say you don't need to be original to be successful, in fact it helps not to be.

"Before we go, sugar, I've got to use the little girls' room."

"Bitch, are you asking me or telling me?"

"Asking you, of course. Come on, Rodney, please. I've been holding it since I got in the cab at the airport."

"You got one minute. Move."

I thank him. It burns me to do that, but I figure if I play the docile girl, he might let his guard down. I decide not to take my purse in with me. If I do that, he'll want to look in it, and then he'll see the papers. I had some of my other lipstick in the medicine cabinet, but I can't remember if I packed it up when I went to see Mama.

It's still there. Finally something's going right. I flush in case he's listening for me to pee, which I suspect he probably is just for the fun of it. I keep the message short and simple: RODNEY'S HOUSE.

When I come out he asks if I feel better now. Can you believe this guy?

"Much," I say. And I thank him again.

As I start out the door ahead of him, he says, "Hold on. Aren't you going to bring your purse?" He bends over and picks it up. As he hands it to me, he shakes his head. "I never known a woman who went anywhere without her purse."

I thank him and smile. "Sugar," I say, "I ain't just any woman."

Unfortunately, that doesn't distract him the way I want it to. He grabs the purse back from me and says, "I better have a look in here first."

My heart sinks down to my ankles. So much for taking the time to copy the damn documents.

TWENTY-EIGHT

The smell was the first thing that told me something was wrong. At first I thought it might be poor Fluffy going moldy in her shoebox, then I realized it was men's cologne. I couldn't identify the brand, but I recognized it as the sissy juice of choice among the guys who hang out at the Orange Julius.

Nate was able to identify it by wearer. "Fucking Rodney's been here."

The instant he said that, I could associate the smell with being clubbed with a crowbar. As my nose fended off the assault, I detected a far more pleasant fragrance beneath it, a fragrance that triggered an even more unpleasant thought.

"Harmony's been here, too."

We yelled and searched the apartment but couldn't find any sign of her. Until I got around to relieving myself, as I had vowed to do the instant I got home when we had been stuck in traffic on the Triboro an hour earlier. There was a note on my bathroom mirror: RODNEY'S HOUSE.

Nate had the presence of mind to grab all the beer in the fridge while I put mine to finding the house key Rodney had given to Harmony. She had hung it on the nail by the door where I, in theory, hang mine.

Having the key was one of those small blessings that you don't take time to be thankful for. Like not having returned the rental car before we had split for the airport the night before. Then there was the matter of guns. Nate had Jack Fogarty's, I had Peter Piper's. I had a feeling that might turn out to be a big blessing.

We were going on thirty-six hours without sleep, but I was wide awake as we ran the gauntlet up Riverside Drive to the bridge. I hadn't blown so many red lights since Petey Peterson's dad was my third-base coach in Little League. Big Pete was obsessed with playing the percentages like they do in the big leagues, so he hadn't noticed that nine out of ten eleven-year-old catchers drop the ball when you run into them.

I had the speedometer up to ninety within thirty seconds after we paid the toll at the bridge. We were sucking down beers and cigarettes, barely saying a word. We both knew what the other was thinking.

From West Seventy-second Street to Paterson in twenty minutes must have been some kind of record. But as I parked around the corner from Rodney's, I only felt like it had been twenty minutes too long.

There were no lights on outside, and the place looked dark inside as well. But when we got to the front steps, we could see that behind the sheet Rodney used as a curtain, the living room was dimly lit.

"Candles," Nate said.

I said I could barely hear him above the music blaring from inside.

"It's the O'Jays. The guy deserves to die for that alone."

Maybe so, but the O'Jays were our ticket inside. As I turned the tumbler with the key, I was certain Rodney couldn't hear me.

Being uncertain which room he and Harmony were in, we decided to enter from front and back. I handed Nate the key. "On the count of twenty-five I'm going in. One, two . . ."

As he wheeled away, he said, "I'll be in on twenty-six."

While my palm got sweaty on the doorknob, I considered changing plans. Every number I counted represented another moment for Harmony to be in danger. But if I went in without backup, I might be putting her in more danger.

On twenty, I pushed the door open. If it creaked, I was sure Rodney couldn't hear it. I sure didn't.

My vision adjustment was instantaneous. I had already been standing in darkness, and the room I was looking into had candles on the floor. It was through a doorway to my left. Straight ahead was a separate doorway that probably led down a long hall. I didn't notice because I wasn't looking far in that direction. I saw as far as I needed to see—to the light-switch panel.

The room was bigger than I expected. Not wide, but long. The candles were at the far end, four of them, maybe fifteen steps away. That's where Harmony was, too.

It's remarkable how quickly your eyes and brain can put a scene together. I doubt it took two seconds for mine to take the whole thing in. Of course, I had already taken in a similar scene at the Capitol Theater a few days earlier.

In the movie, the scene lasted all of half a minute. But it was thirty uncomfortable seconds, which is probably why it had made a strong impression. I knew right away that it had made an impression on Rodney, too. Otherwise, he wouldn't be trying to reenact it.

The more remarkable thing about the brain is that it can entertain other thoughts while getting bombarded with visual messages. I was conscious that Nate would be plowing in the back door any moment. And I had still had space left over to register my dislike for the O'Jays.

Harmony was flat on her back, on a bed on the floor. She was naked from her jeans up, and her jeans were down to her knees. I knew her hands and feet were tied to the bed frame, but I can't say I actually saw the cords on her wrists or her ankles. I was too intent on locating Rodney.

I spotted him down along the right wall, the same one I was stationed near. Harmony's eyes darting to her left clued me to look in that direction. Rodney's hand was raised, and something was dangling from it.

In the movie the guy used a belt, but I figured Rodney was just sick enough to have a real whip or a chain. I could already detect another difference in his adaptation. In the movie, the guy was wearing clothes.

There was probably enough light to shoot the cocksucker right away, but I decided to play it safe. The extra moment it took to flick on the light gave Rodney a chance to bring the strap down on Harmony's stomach one more time. I could see her wince as she took the blow, but my vision was focused on Rodney. It was my first look at him without his shades. His mouth hung open as he whirled to see why the room was suddenly so bright. The hand with the strap went up to his eyes to block the light. His left hand was working a balancing act on a crutch.

In that condition, the guy was easy pickings. I had made up my mind I was going to kill him and I knew I could do the job with my hands. That seemed like the smart choice—no risk of his neighbors hearing a gunshot. But it also might prove useful to kill him with an FBI gun. I chose the second option, but not for any strategic purpose. I simply wanted the guy dead, and right-this-instant didn't seem soon enough.

As I took aim at Rodney's chest, Nate suddenly loomed up behind him. That forced me to hesitate and readjust my angle. By that time Rodney had crumpled to the floor.

With the stereo blasting, I could barely hear the gunfire. So much for alarming the neighbors. I counted three shots as Nate advanced, scowling as he fired. Later, he would tell me it had been four.

I started across the room to free Harmony, but Nate was already kneeling beside her. I turned my attention to cleaning up our mess.

"I'm going to turn off the light," I warned them. Before doing so, I looked Rodney over long enough to be sure he was dead. One of the bullets had gone into the back of his skull. That alone should have made bingo.

After flipping the switch, I stood over Rodney and fired twice into his back. Nate and Harmony looked startled as I turned to face them. "We're going to make this look like a Fogarty-Wilson execution," I explained. "Nate, be sure to bring the gun." I didn't know where we'd toss it, but I'd be able to think more clearly once we were out of the house.

I moved to the foot of the bed and helped Nate finish loosening the electrical cords from Harmony's boots. There were a dozen strap marks on her stomach, but she was all smiles as we lifted her to a standing position for a three-way hug.

"I'd make a great ad for a waterbed, don't you think?"

I assumed she was speaking for my benefit, since Nate hadn't seen *Sister Shamus*. In the movie, she makes the comment about her attacker, after turning the tables and suffocating him with a pillowcase and leaving him sprawled on the bed.

"I love you," I said. "I love both of you." Then I backed away from my lines and gave her my coat.

"We've got to get the documents," Harmony said.

"Where did he put them?"

"He sold them to a guy. A weird little guy with blue eyes and—"

"Paul Weisberg."

"Yeah, that must be him. Rodney called him P.W. He left about an hour ago."

That told me where my next stop was going to be.

"He gave him an envelope with the money. Rodney was pissed, because it wasn't as much as he wanted. But the guy promised to bring the rest tomorrow." She pointed to the front of the room. "Rodney put it under the cushion of the sofa."

I steered them toward the front door, taking a wide path around Rodney to avoid leaving footprints in his blood. I went to the sofa, pulled up the cushions and found two envelopes. I figured one of them was the first payment Rodney had received from Fogarty. As I stuffed the envelopes into my pocket, it dawned on me that I was unofficially on the government payroll. Maybe I'd use it to pay my taxes.

When I got to the doorway, where Nate and Harmony were waiting, I wiped the light-switch panel with my handkerchief. We were out of there five minutes after Nate had started shooting.

TWENTY-NINE

"Are you okay?" Nate and I asked in unison as soon as we got back to the car.

"Yeah, I'm fine." Harmony closed her eyes and nodded as

I started the engine and drove off. "I'm sore and I'm angry and I ache all over and I'm totally embarrassed, but I'm fine."

"Did he . . . ?" Nate worked up the nerve to raise the question before I did, but he lost it in midsentence.

"No. He didn't. He wanted to, but he couldn't get hard." She half smiled as she shook her head. "Ain't that something. The big bad pimp stud can't get it up. Of course, he blamed it on me. He said I wasn't being cooperative. That's why he started with the belt. He said he had to get me in the right frame of mind. The hardest part was having to listen to his crazy jive and forcing myself not to respond for fear it would only make him crazier. But Nathan, you gave him my response. I appreciate that. I really do."

"I've never shot anyone before. I've never killed anyone. I've always wondered what it would feel like. You know what? I don't feel anything. I thought it would really shake me up. But it didn't. It's done, he deserved it, and that's it."

"You'll think about it, believe me," I said.

"Yeah, I suppose you're right."

"Nathan, let me tell you something: If you hadn't've shot him, I would've. And I wouldn't have given it a second thought. Not a one."

After the ordeal Rodney had put her through, I wasn't about to challenge Harmony on that point. I wasn't about to challenge her on anything.

"So, do you know how to get to this P.W. creep's house?" she asked me.

"Yeah. But I think we should get you to a hospital first."

"Hell no. I got beat up worse than this at the convention, and I didn't go to the hospital then. I went to jail. All I need's a cup of coffee and a good night's sleep." I could feel her shoot me a glance. "And I could use a good back rub."

"She was looking your way, Renzler. I guess that means I've got to take a number."

210

"Nathan, what you've got to do is get yourself home. Otherwise Constance is going to start looking for someone else to rub her back."

"We're practically married. We don't do that kind of stuff anymore."

We took care of our coffee needs with another stop at one of North Jersey's fine diners. On our way to Paul Weisberg's house in Ridgewood, Harmony recounted the secret details of COINTELPRO depravity that she had discovered while reading the stolen FBI memos. Despite what I had seen of Fogarty and Wilson, the skeptic in me was still inclined to think she was exaggerating. But I didn't offer a peep of doubt. I wouldn't dare do that until I had a chance to read the memos myself.

Weisberg's house was dark when we pulled up. There was no sign of his Volkswagen, but the white Impala with PRF plates was still parked on the street.

As Harmony started to get out, I told her to wait. "I'm going to the door alone. If you see me go inside, you guys can come knock."

"What if he's got a gun?"

"Mine's bigger," I told her. "Don't worry. This guy I know I can handle."

I took precautions just the same. I darted to the porch, rang the bell, then got down low. If Weisberg came to the door with a heater, I could blow his pecker off before he saw me.

He didn't answer the bell for round one. I rang three more times before returning to the car.

I'd be lying if I said I wanted to do anything but go home, climb into bed and rub Harmony anywhere she wanted until the new year. But I knew my stomach would be in knots until I had tied up all the loose ends I could.

"I'm going to wait," I said. "You guys should go home."

"Uh-uh. We're not going anywhere without you."

"That's right," Nate said. "We're sticking it out."

"Believe me, I can handle Weisberg. We don't need three. In fact, that's too many. The thing we have to worry about is being noticed by a cop, and that's more likely to happen with three people. Especially if one of them's black."

Harmony and Nate exchanged glances. "How are you planning to get the documents?" she asked.

"Grab him by the collar and tell him to hand them over. If I'm feeling generous, I might offer to return some of the dough he dropped on Rodney. Of course, if he's carrying them under his arm, I might just knock him on the head and grab them."

"How are you going to get home?"

"I'll take the Impala. I assume your brother wants his car back."

"Damn. That's Harpo's car right in front of us?"

I nodded.

"If you knock Weisberg on the head, how are you going to get the keys?"

"Harmony, come on. If that happens, I'll take Weisberg's car." I took her hand. "Don't worry. I'll get back home."

If truth be told, I was a bit disappointed that was all it took to convince them. They were gone in five minutes.

I parked my weary bones in Harpo's backseat and tried to sort things out. I couldn't remember a time when I'd been left with so many bodies to bury. Fogarty, Wilson, Hartman, Rodney. Probably Roach. There could be six if I included Judith, but I already had that one figured out. Plus I had an FBI-issue gun in each pocket.

Weisberg didn't leave me much time to think things through. But it was enough. Drawing inspiration from the memos Harmony had described, I formulated a few COIN-TELPRO tactics of my own. It would be a fairly sloppy cleanup effort, but the situation was awfully messy to start with.

212

As Weisberg pulled up behind me, I released the door handle so I could pop out in a second. He made things easier by coming around the front of his car. That saved me about a dozen steps. But his cooperation ended there. I expected him to be carrying the documents. Unless they were stashed in his Dunkin' Donuts bag, he wasn't.

He was ten feet away from me when he got to the lawn, less than that when I hopped out of the car.

"I hope you got enough donuts for me."

I thought my greeting might startle Weisberg into dropping one of the items in his hands. But he was still holding coffee in his right and the donut bag in his left. The only thing that dropped was his mouth.

"Remember me, Paul?" I took another step closer.

He nodded. "Yeah, you're the investigator who came around last week. Sorry, I forget your name."

I was almost certain that was a lie, but there was nothing to be lost by playing along. "Spenser," I said.

"What are you doing here? Did you find James?"

I ignored the second question. "I'm here to retrieve some papers, Paul. Do you see the gun?" I lifted it from my coat pocket to catch his attention. When his coffee dropped, I was sure I had it.

He nodded. "Yeah, sure, I see it. But I don't know anything about any papers, I swear."

"I think we should go inside and talk."

"Yeah, sure, of course." Weisberg picked up his cup and started for the house. I followed two yards behind him, moving closer as he mounted the steps. I was right over his shoulder, holding the storm door open with mine, when he unlocked the main door. He picked that moment to hurl the coffee.

With gravity and leverage in my favor, I had no trouble blocking it with my left hand and knocking it right back in his puss. Both of his hands shot up to cover his face, and he whined with pain. The folks at Dunkin' Donuts make their coffee hot. That's why I like it, though my loyalties lie with Chock Full O' Nuts.

I helped him into the house by planting my foot on his ass and pushing. Since he entered on his stomach, I took the liberty of flipping the light switch. The living room was decorated in a blending of styles that might be described as Mom and Dad Meet Grateful Dead. I assumed that Weisberg's parents had died and the house was something they had left him to be grateful for.

"Nice place you've got here," I said, resting my foot on a rattan table that had a wine-bottle-turned-candle-holder on it.

Weisberg tried to scowl as he got to his feet, but fear was the predominating expression on his face.

"Okay, where are the fucking papers, Paul?"

"I don't know what you're talking about."

I gave him a kick in the shins that crumpled him. "Don't bullshit me. I know you're an FBI stooge, I know you helped Rodney sell the first set of memos to Fogarty, and I know you got the second set from Rodney tonight. So start talking and save your legs."

He pulled his hands away from his shins, planted them on the floor and pushed himself to a kneeling position. "I don't have them."

I lifted my foot for another kick.

"I swear, I don't have them. I already unloaded them."

"What do you mean you *unloaded* them?"

"I sent them to the bureau, to Washington."

"Bullshit." I gave him another kick. I was afraid he might be telling the truth. If he was, I figured he deserved a kick anyway.

"Cut it out, man! Please! I already sent them, I swear I did."

214

"That doesn't make any sense. Why would you send them to Washington? Why didn't you go through Fogarty?"

"Are you kidding? After what he and Wilson did to Rodney?"

"You only got the papers tonight. How could you have sent them already?"

"There's an all-night post office in Passaic. I just got back from there."

"Oh, shit. Tell me you're lying, Weisberg, please."

He shook his head. His voice was barely above a whisper. "No, I'm not. I'm telling the truth, I really am."

I kicked him again. "You asshole! Why the hell did you do that?"

"Hey, cut it out, please!" He waited to make sure I wasn't going to hit him. "For the money. I did it for the money."

"What money? *You* had to pay Rodney."

"Yeah, I know, I did. I had to give him my cut of what Fogarty paid him the first time. And then some. But they promised me a huge bonus. It's all going to work out OK."

If I wasn't so disgusted, I would have been amused that Weisberg seemed to think I was concerned he might lose money. "They *promised* you? You're a fool, Weisberg."

"No, it's all set. I talked directly to Sullivan about it."

I didn't bother asking who Sullivan was. "You sent them both sets?"

"What do you mean, *both* sets? There were only two to start with. Rodney got both of them. The first time he gave them—"

"Yeah, yeah, I know all about it. In other words, you didn't bother looking inside the envelope he gave you."

"I didn't have time. It was . . . You mean there was another copy of the papers in there?"

I didn't even bother to nod.

"Shit," he said, "I could've . . ."

"You're a fool, Weisberg. They're not going to pay you a goddamn cent."

"How do you know?"

I didn't answer the question. I just stared at the poster of Janis Joplin above the La-Z Boy and wondered what the hell I was going to do. There were no papers to be carried home, no victory to be savored. The best I could hope for was to cut our losses. Imagine going to a racetrack where there was no betting permitted or playing poker just for the fun of it.

Only this was much worse. It wasn't a game.

THIRTY

I gazed down at Weisberg, who was gazing up at me with his mouth hanging open, like a dog waiting to be told if he should sit up or roll over. If the guy was half as dumb as he looked, at least I had my patsy.

"You did just great, Paul. You fetched the documents, you're not going to get a bone *and* you're going to have Fogarty and Wilson biting at your ass for going over their heads."

He nodded. "Yeah, I know, I was worried about that. But as soon as I get the money, I'm out of here. Sullivan promised me ten grand."

"Forget Sullivan. He's a liar." I shook my head. "I could've put you in touch with someone who would've gone twenty."

"You're kidding. I don't get it. I thought you were trying to find James."

I let out an impatient sigh. "Hurry up. I'll give you five minutes to pack."

"Where are we going?"

"Not we, pal—*you*. I'll drop you at the airport."

"No way. I'm not leaving now."

"Fine. You can take the bus for all I care. I was just offering to do you a favor."

"What the hell are you talking about?"

"Weisberg, believe me, if you had the brains to figure out how big a pile of shit you stepped in, you'd be begging me for a ride."

"You're crazy. What shit am I in?"

"Killing Rodney. That sounds plenty deep to me."

"I didn't kill Rodney!"

I shrugged. "One of his neighbors heard the shots and saw your car leaving the place. She got down most of your plate number and gave it to the cops."

"Hold on! I didn't even know Rodney was dead. He had some chick there with him."

I was relieved to hear him put it that way. At least he didn't know who Harmony was.

"The neighbor didn't say anything about any chick. She just saw your car. That's why I figured you wouldn't want to drive yourself. The cops will be out looking."

While waiting for that to sink in, I started to empty the bullets from Fogarty and Wilson's guns. I shot him a warning glance. "I've got another one of these things. So don't get any ideas about trying something cute."

"No, of course not." He rubbed his face. "I don't know what the fuck's going on."

"Well, I guess you're not taking me up on my offer. Just give me the keys to James's car and I'll be on my way. He said he wants it back."

"So you found him. Is he okay?"

"He's fine."

"Well, that's good."

"Not for you, it isn't. When he found out you ratted him out to Hartman, he said he's going to come rip off your head and shit down your neck. That's a direct quote." I watched as Weisberg gulped. "That's probably just talk. I don't think he'll actually do anything. Unless you give me trouble about taking the car."

"No, no, man, that's okay. The keys are in the kitchen."

He turned, and I followed him past a battered couch that was covered with an Indian print sheet. There was some bounce in his step, probably resulting from relief that he was about to get rid of the gun-wielding wacko with the sharp feet. But I still thought he'd end up accepting a lift. I preferred it that way, but it wouldn't be a tragedy if he didn't.

I laid the guns down on the kitchen table while he searched in a drawer for the keys. "Have you got a towel?" I asked.

"What do you need a towel for?"

I held out my hand. "Just give me a goddamn towel, Paul."

He rolled his eyes before tossing me a dish towel, then watched as I wiped the guns. "What're you doing?"

I held out my hand. "The car keys."

As soon as he handed them over, a wave of regret washed over his face. "Wait. If you take James's car, what am I going to drive? I can't use mine."

"Yeah, that's a problem." I shrugged. "I'll leave you these in case you have to shoot it out."

"You're crazy. I don't need any guns. Get them out of here." He moved to the table and pushed them toward me.

I shook my head. "You can't possibly expect *me* to get rid of the guns *you* used to murder Rodney."

"What!" Weisberg looked at his hands as if they were covered with shit. "You asshole, you're trying to frame me!"

I smiled. "And it's going to work. You know, Paul, I think Elvis would make a better FBI agent than you." I braced, expecting he might charge me in a fit of rage, but he just buried his face in his hands. The depressed types can be harder to deal with.

I could have left then, but I preferred having him as far away as possible for an extended period. "I'll give you five minutes," I said.

He lifted his head. "I need more time than that. I need a day."

"A day! Dream on. I want to be out of here before the cops come knocking with a search warrant."

"They couldn't get a search warrant that fast." The sudden certainty in Weisberg's tone indicated he had considered going to law school.

"Maybe they'll come in shooting, like the Chicago cops did at Fred Hampton's place."

I couldn't tell from Weisberg's reaction whether he knew who Fred Hampton was. It could be that he hadn't been curious enough to read the memos, which was a scary thought. Or maybe he had read them but the name didn't blip on his radar, which was even scarier. Of course, right then, Weisberg had good reason to be thinking only of himself.

He looked at the table. "What about the guns?"

"Don't worry, I can get rid of them."

"Why should I trust you?"

I glanced around the room. "Who else did you have in mind?"

"Oh man, oh shit."

"Four minutes," I said. "We'll dump the guns on the way to the airport."

He turned quickly, and I picked up the guns with the towel and followed him.

"Fuck, I don't have any money," he muttered.

I thought about the envelopes in my pocket. "I can lend you some."

"Fuck you. I've got credit cards."

"Uh-uh. You'd be better off using cash." I pulled out the envelopes and cradled them in my left hand. "Take your pick. One of them already has your fingerprints on it."

"Who the hell are you?" he asked.

We drove the first leg of the trip in silence. I had the bundle of guns in my lap, and I think Weisberg had a lump in his throat from leaving the old homestead.

I took Route 17 to Route 3 to the turnpike. I slowed down and pulled to the shoulder when the road was surrounded by the grassy swamp near Secaucus known as the Meadowlands. New Jersey's sleaziest pols and greediest developers were said to be at work on a fantastic plan to build a sports stadium near there. For now, it was still the Garden State's favorite cut-rate cemetery.

I tossed the bundle onto Weisberg's lap. "Roll down your window and throw them as far out as you can. After you throw them, don't look back."

He nodded and followed my directions. Once the guns were disposed of, he seemed to relax. He started asking me questions, but I only responded when I saw some benefit in doing so.

I told him I didn't kill Rodney and he would be much safer not knowing who did. I told him Rodney's murder was just the tip of the iceberg and the whole thing was much bigger than he could imagine. "Once you saw those documents, you became a marked man. Just like Rodney."

"Who the fuck are you?"

"You'll never know, and you're better off not knowing." I paused, not sure if I could get out my next line with a straight face. "Paul, I'm CIA."

"Bullshit."

Despite the instant dismissal, I thought Weisberg might be gullible enough to believe me once he had a chance to think

220

things over. But it really didn't matter. All I hoped for was that if he did end up talking to the cops or the FBI, he'd at least mention the possibility of the CIA being involved. That would make him appear to be more of a crackpot than he was.

"Fine, don't believe me," I said.

I didn't utter another word until we reached the spaghetti ramp leading into Newark Airport. "Do you want domestic— or international?"

"Very funny," he said.

Five minutes later, I left him standing outside the new international terminal.

I got back to my apartment around midnight and made the disappointing discovery that Harmony wasn't there. It was actually something of a relief, because I dreaded having to tell her I hadn't been able to recover the documents. But my stronger reaction was alarm.

I dialed up Nate right away. Constance answered on the fifth ring. Her hello turned into a yawn and stayed that way for five seconds.

"I know it's late, Constance, but I have to check: Is Harmony over there with you guys?" Just as I finished asking the question, I noticed a note from Nate on the table.

"Yes, she fell asleep on the couch. Nate went over to your place and left you a note. Didn't you find it?"

"Yeah, I'm sorry, I did find it. Just now."

"If you found the note, why are you calling?"

"You're right, Constance, good question." Now I was the one yawning.

"I hope all this nonsense is finally over, Renzler. It's Christmas and I've barely had a chance to see my fiancé."

"I know, Constance, I know." I spoke in the most conciliatory tone I could muster, but I wasn't able to apologize. I merely assured her that the nonsense was indeed finally over.

But as I dropped onto my cold lonely bed—colder and lonelier than usual due to my shattered expectation that I would find it warm and full of Harmony—I closed my eyes and managed a rueful smile: For my pal, Nate, the nonsense was just beginning.

THIRTY-ONE

One of my deepest secrets is that beneath my outward appearance of indifference, I am in fact a very conscientious person. So I was not at all surprised to find myself sitting bolt upright in bed when even the hands on my Utica Club clock were still asleep. My inner timekeeper was telling me it would not be a personal foul to call Randall Edwards at this hour.

Randall assured me he still had a copy of the floor plan memo and even humored me by checking to make sure. He wanted to hear everything I had learned about COINTELPRO, but he and his wife were presently engaged in some mad plotting of their own: dissuading his in-laws from staying a day longer so they could all ring in the New Year in Times Square.

"I plan to spend the night at the cheapest place I know to get drunk in New York," he said.

"Where's that?"

"My house."

He invited me to join him, but I said I had plans of my own. Which was true. I was expecting to have a real actual New Year's Eve date.

"Tell me what you hear," I said. "There's a ninety-nine-percent chance your pal Fogarty and Wilson are dead."

"I heard *that*. And I want to hear more. Soon."

We agreed that the next morning would not be out of the question.

"One more thing," I said. "Who's Sullivan?"

"Bill Sullivan? He was one of Hoover's top hacks. He's been there almost from the beginning. I heard they're moving him out, but he's still behind the altar. What does he have to do with this?"

I told him that in addition to being the author of some anonymous dirty-tricks letters, Mr. Sullivan was about to receive just such a note from me.

"I don't know his title. Just send it to him in D.C. and mark it personal and confidential. He'll get it."

After the surge of relief that came from making sure we still had the floor plan memo, I couldn't lose enough energy to go back to bed. I went to the can, the coffeepot and the typewriter in that order. Three hours and twenty crumpled sheets of paper later, my minor masterpiece was finished:

> Mr. Sullivan:
> We may be on different sides but there is at least one thing we have in common—hatred of traitors. Roach Zimmer is responsible for the deaths of several people, including two SA's and fugitive Harpo Rollins. They had help from disloyal members of the PRF. If I were you, I'd start searching for the murder weapons in the Meadowlands.

It would have been finished sooner if Harmony hadn't arrived and decided to help. By the time we were done, I was glad we weren't collaborating on a screenplay. I'm sure she felt the same way.

I had to convince her the note should be vague so Sullivan would have lots of ground to cover. And I gave in reluctantly on her idea of saying Harpo was dead. I thought that might put him under suspicion of writing the note. But her contributions did help. For example, it was her suggestion to change "if I *was* you" in the last sentence to "if I *were* you," to add a tone of formality that might make Sullivan think Hartman was the author. "After all," she said, "they might not find Hartman's body."

The letter went right into the mail, a brisk stroll down Broadway to the Ansonia postal station. On our way back, Harmony broke the news that momentarily broke my heart. With things under control, she had decided to return to her mother's right away.

"I was thinking it would be real nice to spend New Year's Eve with you," she said.

"Just us? Or Nate and Constance, too?"

"I suppose we've got to include them."

I found the resignation in her voice most encouraging. "We'll take them to the cheapest place I know to get drunk in New York."

"Where's that?" she asked.

"My place."

"Good idea. Constance will want to be home in time to watch the ball drop on TV."

She persuaded me to let her take a cab to the airport so I could get some rest. She didn't go so far as to say I'd need my strength for New Year's Eve, but I figured I had earned the right to pretend that was what she meant.

I wasn't feeling very restful. I had tied up the loose ends as well as I could, but I was still ankle-deep in muck. I was assuming that Fogarty and Wilson hadn't gotten around to writing their monthly reports and, if they had, that my name wasn't in them. I figured they wouldn't have revealed their embarrassing encounter outside Judith Fairbanks's house, and I didn't think they would report breaking into my apartment and killing my cat. The FBI was supposedly cleaning up its act after Hoover's exit. At the very least, I figured that meant they were no longer boasting of their lawbreaking in print. Of course, I couldn't be sure about any of this, but I wasn't about to burglarize an FBI office to find out.

If all my assumptions proved correct, the G would have only the word of Paul Weisberg to go on, and it would probably take a long time to find him. I now wished I'd had the presence of mind to offer him some tips on changing his identity, but my head was spinning pretty fast when I dropped him off. For the rest of my life I'd have to live with the nagging worry that the feds could come knocking on my door any moment. That feeling would diminish over time, but I knew it would never completely go away.

There were only a couple of knots left to tie, and they didn't really affect me. Before driving to Jersey one last time, I called Friendly Ice Cream to find out when Sheila Love was scheduled to work. Since I didn't regard Sheila as a candidate for perfect attendance, I called back to confirm she was there. This time Sheila answered the phone.

I took off right away, carrying the framed photograph of Hartman DeWitt and Lillian Summerfield that I had taken from Judith Fairbanks's house. I also brought Sheila's address book.

Sheila had two booths to cover when I strolled in. One was an all-American family of four—mom, dad, big sister, little brother. They probably had a dog waiting for them in a station wagon outside. The other booth was a high school foursome—three pimply boys and a girl with frizzy hair. I assumed from their red eyes and loud giggles that they had toked up on pot before coming in for ice cream.

I took a counter seat in back, across from the teens and right where Sheila had to pass to get behind the counter. While she was taking the family order, her expression changed from indifference to hatred, and I knew she had caught sight of me.

"James says hello," I said as she walked by. She ignored me, but she had to station herself a few feet away to pour the family's sodas. To her back, I said, "And he wanted me to tell you that he *wasn't* fucking Judith Fairbanks."

"You told him I said that?" She wheeled to face me, and I caught of gust of Coke.

"Which means," I said, "that it was a really dumb idea for you to kill her."

She put down the glasses and moved in close. "You don't know what you're talking about. *Pig.*"

"Sure I do. You thought the white chick was stealing your man so you went to her house and beat her with a crowbar. And you were so mad at James that you left his name on a matchbook. From this lovely establishment." I spread my arms to take in the splendor of Friendly's.

"You can't prove that."

"You're right, I can't." I pulled the envelope with the picture of Hartman and his sister from my pocket. "By the way, James wanted me to give you this." I tilted the envelope down until the picture slid out facedown on the counter.

Sheila took it with both hands, studied it a moment, then put it down and glowered. "What is this?"

I smiled as I picked up the picture by the corner, noting it was the bottom-right so I could wipe off my fingerprints later. "Now I can prove it."

She hissed in a whisper that carried all the way to mom and dad. "Get the fuck out of here, or I'll—"

"What? Call the pigs?"

She sighed heavily, turned and picked up her tray of sodas.

"One more thing." I tossed her address book onto the counter. "Thanks for letting me borrow this."

Sheila glanced, stopped, glanced again, then dropped the Cokes. She cussed at me just loud enough and long enough to make mom and dad decide to leave. I didn't wait to hold the door for them. In the back the teens were quadrupled over in laughter.

It took half an hour to drive to Ho-Ho-Kus. Once again, I parked near a driveway filled with cars and hoofed it to Lillian Summerfield's house. This time I went to the front door.

I pried open the mailbox with one hand and dropped the picture out of the envelope with my other. It landed with a clunk, and I thought the glass might have cracked. That was just fine with me.

I stopped at the first diner I came to. After ordering a cheeseburger, I went to the phone and dropped a couple of nickels on Ma Bell and a dime on Sheila Love.

I asked the voice that answered if she was Lillian and got a tentative-sounding yes. "Go to your mailbox," I said. "You'll find a picture with the fingerprints of Judith's murderer on it."

"Who is this?"

I ignored the question. "Tell the police you found the picture somewhere in Judith's room where they haven't looked. The woman who killed her is named Sheila Love."

"Who the hell is this?"

I didn't answer that one either. I just gave her one more thing to think about before hanging up. "Your brother is dead. The FBI killed him."

I drove home with a full stomach, a feeling I had done all I could do and a certainty I had done all I was going to do. Then I rested up for the New Year.

Constance had already booked a party for Nate and herself, so I only had to cook for two. I decided to make the only menu I ever make, the only one I know how to make—lasagna, with steamed artichokes for appetizers. Plus, of course, drinks, drinks and more drinks.

Around five o'clock, I answered the buzzer and heard Harmony's voice fuzzed out from five floors below. I told her to come right up, but she insisted that I come down. She said she had a surprise for me.

There were two surprises, actually, though the second one was more like a shock. I found her standing by the curb next to a small white car. We hugged for a moment, then she backed away and held out a set of keys.

"What're they for?"

She made a sweeping gesture toward the car. "It's a thank-you gift. They call it the Pinto. You're going to love it."

I felt my jaw drop. No one had ever bought me a car before. Of course I had only owned two in my life. But no one had ever given me such an extravagant present.

"It's white—that's a problem, isn't it? That's the only color they had."

"No, no. There's no problem. It's terrific. I'm just flabbergasted. I don't know how to thank you."

"I know a way." She stepped toward me, placed her hands on my shoulders and delivered the second surprise. "You can drive me to the airport."

"The airport?"

"Yeah, I've got to go to Kennedy."

"When? You mean, like now?"

She nodded. "My agent called me at Mama's. They've decided to do a sequel."

"Tonight? But I made dinner."

"I know, I'm sorry. I hope you didn't go to too much trouble. I couldn't bring myself to tell you over the phone. I've got to be in the Philippines tomorrow."

"The Philippines?"

"Yeah, it's crazy. The director's already shooting another movie there, and they finished early. But he's got the cast and crew for two more weeks, so they're going to start filming right away."

"Congratulations." I tried to sound sincere, but my tone was halfhearted at best.

"Thank you." It might have been my imagination, but her tone seemed lacking in enthusiasm too.

"Don't you at least have time to come up for a drink?"

She looked at her watch. "My plane leaves in an hour and a half. How long does it take to get to Kennedy?"

"From here? In my new car?" I shrugged. "Half an hour." That was at least a thirty-minute lie.

As we went inside, I figured I was the only guy in the history of New York who hoped his new car would get towed away before he got a chance to drive it.

"So," I asked, as I heavy-handed Old Grand-Dad into my most delicate glassware, "what's the name of the movie?"

"They haven't decided yet. It's a toss-up between *Sister Shamus in Macon County* and *Sister Shamus in Algiers.*" She held up her hand. "Don't ask."

I didn't. I was focused on the more pressing concern of persuading her to stick around. But I wasn't merely persuading. I was pleading.

"Please can't you stay for dinner? I've got the table all set for us."

She gazed over the spread of what passed for my fancy dishes, then sized me up with a movie-queen smile. "You know, I've always had a soft spot for this table. Didn't there used to be a tablecloth on it?"

Afterword

In 1968, FBI director J. Edgar Hoover publicly proclaimed that the greatest threat to national security was the Black Panther Party, a curious band of militant black men in berets who'd taken up arms in Oakland, California, for the avowed purpose of resisting police brutality. Secretly, Hoover had already directed FBI field offices to infiltrate and disrupt the group, which at the height of its short-lived existence had half as many members—five thousand—as the FBI had agents. In the late sixties, one in fifteen Panthers was a paid FBI informant. With approval from their supervisors, many of these informants acted as provocateurs, encouraging their associates to commit crimes and participating in crimes themselves.

The FBI campaign to destroy the Black Panthers was part of a top-secret counterintelligence program that was conducted during the sixties and seventies and was designed to discredit and disrupt the civil rights movement and the political left. Dubbed COINTELPRO by the FBI, the campaign included a wide range of dubious and illegal activities carried out by agents and paid informants, from wiretapping and media manipulation to burglary and murder.

As indicated in the novel, the existence of COINTELPRO first became public after the 1971 break-in at the FBI resident office in Media, Pennsylvania, though it was not yet known by that acronym. There was no subsequent burglary at an FBI office in Wisconsin; this is a fictitious event that serves as a plot vehicle for the novel. However, all FBI documents mentioned in the novel, including the floorplan to Fred Hampton's apartment and the FBI "hit" memo to gang leader Jeff Fort, are real; their existence did not become known until 1974, two years after the time period of the book. *Left for Dead* is essentially a manipulation of time, not facts.

The information relating to the killing of Fred Hampton and Mark Clark and the December 4, 1969, pre-dawn raid by Chicago police is also true. For example, the police were permitted to carry their own weapons and went armed with shotguns, semiautomatics and a submachine gun. They did have a floor plan drawn by the FBI with help from an informant named William O'Neal (who also very likely planted the two illegal weapons that police were allegedly seeking during the raid). The survivors all were charged with attempted murder, even though ballistics reports showed that only one of almost a hundred rounds fired could have come from a Panther gun. (The charges were dropped after a deal was struck between local and federal authorities that kept the FBI's role secret.) Cook County State's Attorney Ed Hanrahan did announce that Hampton had fired at the police, even though he had been drugged with barbiturates (very likely by O'Neal) and was killed while asleep. An FBI memo did term the raid a "success," and O'Neal was paid a bonus for his work.

No FBI agents or Chicago police were convicted of wrongdoing in the raid on Fred Hampton's apartment. During four official investigative proceedings, the FBI's role remained secret. It did not become known until five years later, during the discovery phase of a civil suit filed by raid survivors and relatives of Fred Hampton and Mark Clark. During what was then the longest civil suit in history, an inadvertent slip by an FBI witness led to the discovery that the FBI and Justice Department had withheld thousands of pages of COINTELPRO documents from the plaintiffs. The suit was not settled until 1983.

In 1990, informant William O'Neal committed suicide by running onto the Eisenhower Expressway in Chicago. In 1993, the building at 2337 West Monroe was razed by the city of Chicago.